Spilled Blood

Clay Warrior Stories

J. Clifton Slater

Books by J. Clifton Slater

Clay Warrior Stories

Clay Legionary

Spilled Blood

Bloody Water (Fall 2017)

Galactic Council Realm

On Station

On Duty

On Guard

I'd like to thank my editor Hollis Jones for her work in correcting my rambling sentences and overly flowery prose. Also, I am grateful to Denise Scherschel for her help in structuring the book. Her amazing illustrated book <u>Zippy McZoomerman Gears Up</u> is a must read for children with disabilities.

I also own a debt of gratitude to T.R. Harris, author of <u>The Human Chronicles Saga,</u> and Tom Keller, author of <u>Vegas Fae Stories,</u> for coffee, advice and guidance.

J. Clifton Slater

E-Mail: GalacticCouncilRealm@gmail.com

Twitter: @GalacticCRealm

FB: facebook.com/Galactic Council Realm

Spilled Blood takes place in 266 B.C. when Rome was a Republic and before the Imperial Roman Empire conquered the world. While I have attempted to stay true to the era, I am not an historian. If you are a true aficionado of the times, I apologize in advance.

Forget your car, your television, your computer and smart phone; journey back to when making clay bricks and steel were the height of technology.

Clay is the fundamental nature or character of a person, according to the Merriam-Webster dictionary.

As with molded clay fired at 930 degrees Fahrenheit, a man, when subjected to the correct stress, is also transformed. From a pliable and malleable state, he develops mental and physical durability. While earthen clay becomes ceramic, a man becomes resilient.

Warrior is a person engaged in a struggle or conflict, according to the Merriam-Webster dictionary.

In the 3rd century BC, simply surviving day-to-day was a struggle. Adding to the hard life were ambitious men who craved power. While most people avoided engaging the anarchists, tribal chiefs, and king-makers, the Legions marched towards the conflict. Guarding the border between chaos and civilization were the Republic's warriors; the Legionaries.

Clay Warrior Stories are novels inspired by the soldiers of ancient Rome.

Thank you,

J. Clifton Slater

Spilled Blood

Act 1

Chapter 1 - The Voyage and the Conflict

They say you can tell a lot about a man by his choice of friends and by his enemies. Alerio Sisera's childhood friends were far away and out of touch in the western province. His Legionary friends were in the eastern region of the Republic and just as unreachable.

As for enemies, there were two. One enemy was a sect of assassins in the east. As long as Alerio stayed off their shores, he was safe.

A caveat, if he needed their help, he was considered an Ally of the Golden Valley and carried a symbol as identification.

The other enemy was a Republic wide crime syndicate going by the name of Cruor, or Spilled Blood.

Alerio heard the price on his head was seven Republic golds. Anyone to bring him in, alive or dead, could collect the bounty. If one went by coin count alone, the Cruor were a top-notch enemy.

There were also two other ways to know a man. The first, his chosen profession. As a Lance Corporal in the Republic's Legion, Alerio's record was short but bloody. According to the Legion classification, his specialty was gladius instructor and he was good at it.

Which leads to the last way to know a man. His experiences.

You could read certain skills on a man's body. A blacksmith by the burn marks from hot embers flying while he pounded molten metal. A Lute player by the thick callouses on his fingertips. An archer by the buildup of tissue on the inside of his left forearm from assault by the bow's string. For a swordsman like Alerio Sisera, the tales were told by the scars on his body.

Each scar was a permanent reminder of past sword fights.

The crescent shaped scar on the left top of his head was from an assassin's dagger. On his right deltoid were two parallel scars from a single gladius thrust. Corporal Daedalus of the Capital City Guard installed the scars during a sword competition.

An assassin inflected the thin scar tracing the back of his upper left arm during a secret trial. And finally, two thin scars, one on the underside of his left forearm, and another on top of his right arm, were both courtesy of a dead Rebel Captain.

You'd think that with all the scars and marks on Alerio that he had been part of this great earth for years. You'd be wrong. For even though Alerio was a man, he was a young one. Today he witnessed his seventeenth birthday. All of his scars had been earned before he reached the age of majority.

Of course there were no friends to celebrate his birthday; conversely there were Legion Marines wishing him anything except congratulations.

Chapter 2 - Put Your Coin Where Your Mouth Is

"Come on, one more time," a Legionary Marine challenged.

"Put up your coin," suggested Alerio as he swung the two gladii to keep his shoulders loose. "And, line up."

The eight seagoing Legionaries were sweating. Not from the weather, the air was pleasant. And not necessarily from the competition, they were fit enough to fight all day long. Their perspiration was a direct result of their squad's rapidly draining coin purse.

An hour ago, the squad had been running sword drills when a Legionary passenger climbed to the training deck. Legionaries worked out daily to keep their skills sharp and it wasn't unusual for a military transit to join in the drills. What was unusual was the duel gladii rig strapped to the young man's back.

"See that," the Century's Corporal shouted while pointing out the double sword harness. "A rooster. You can't use two gladii effectively at one time. The only reason to carry two swords is if you're prone to dropping one and need to carry a spare."

The eight-man squad and their Lance Corporal laughed. Every Legionary knew to drop a gladius was to bring down hades on their head from an NCO.

"Or, the man totting two gladii is a showoff which is more dangerous for a unit's integrity," the Corporal continued as he warmed to the subject. "Strutting around like a rooster gets people killed. Which are you, Legionary? An incompetent or a rooster?"

Alerio Sisera's armor and single gladius rested back in the eastern Legion's quartermaster tents. All that identified him as a Legionary were the hobnailed boots and the hilts jutting from the scabbards of the duel harness.

"Lance Corporal Sisera," Alerio replied. "And the answer is neither."

"Where are you headed, Lance Corporal?" the NCO inquired. He was a little shocked by the rank based on the age of the Legionary.

"The southern Legion," answered Alerio.

Scattered laughter ran through the squad. The southern Legion occupied a thin line of Republic real estate across the Messina straits from territory controlled by the Sons of Mars, a band of mercenaries. The Legion guarded the merchants sailing through the straits. Actually, they spent most of the time fishing out drowning citizens after storms shipwrecked their vessels. Or, the ships were captured by pirates from Messina or pirates from Illyrian, or the navy of the Qart Hadasht Empire. Rowing and fighting on water was not seen as honorable. Land warfare, the might of the heavy infantry, was the backbone of the Republic.

While the eastern Legion chased Rebels, and full Legions in the west and north fought barbarians, the southern Legion played lifeguard and watched for pirates. Due to the lack of action, it provided little chance for learning battlefield tactics or getting promoted. The southern Legion was considered the cūlus of the Republic and one of the least desirable postings.

"I guess that answers the question," the Corporal stated upon hearing the young Legionary was going to the southern Legion. "A screw-up based on your next duty station."

Another round of chuckles ran through the squad.

"I am a gladius instructor," Alerio announced trying to defend himself, his equipment, and his next assignment. Then he got angry and with spite in his voice added, "And based on the underwhelming display of swordsmanship I just witnessed, something your squad is badly in need of."

As a Legionary sword instructor, Alerio would happily spend the remainder of the sea voyage teaching. After all, being an instructor was the reason he had two gladii permanently issued to him. But his temper had gotten the better of him so the exchange was getting heated.

The Corporal had gotten laughs when he voiced his judgement. And, his ego was reluctant to let the Legionary's announcement go unchallenged. Besides, the boy had insulted the swordsmanship of his squad. Nevertheless, he extended an olive branch.

The Corporal offered, "The reason you carry two gladii is to have one for a student and one for yourself."

He was trying to untangle the confrontation with the cocky, young Legionary and save face in the process. The question was a way for both of them to back away from the conflict. But the Lance Corporal dashed the reasoning aside.

"No, Treasurer." Alerio bragged, "The reason I carry two gladii is, in certain situations, I fight with two swords."

The Corporal of a Century shoulders a lot of responsibility. Broadly, one of them was treasurer and keeper of the unit's coin. Funeral funds, pay for the individual Legionary, accounting for any moneys collected in taxes or fines for the Republic, plus he kept the Century's logs. In addition to managing the funds, a Corporal was instrumental in selecting Lance Corporals for the squads and elevating specialist for extra pay. The position's secretarial duties were so encompassing, they usually kept a Corporal out of a squad's daily training activities.

Today, the Sergeant and his Centurion were meeting with the ship's Captain. After finishing the log early, the Corporal had wandered to the training deck to observe. For some reason, he decided to be a mentula and poke fun at the transit Legionary with the ridiculous duel rig.

The Corporal bristled at the stance taken by the young Legionary's pronouncement. Using two gladii went against his experience, judgement, and standard military edict.

"I've a Republic silver that says you can't fight with two gladii," the Corporal challenged while holding up a shiny coin. It flashed in the morning light and the squad smiled at the bet.

Now it was Alerio's turn to try and defuse the situation. He realized, after revealing he could fight with two swords, the missed opportunity offered by the Corporal's question. His admission had stomped on the peaceful resolution as if he had marched over a barbarian on a battlefield.

"I'm at a disadvantage," admitted Alerio. "I haven't any armor. Although, I'll be glad to run your squad through some drills."

"Lance Corporal strip," the Corporal ordered his squad leader. "Give your armor to Lance Corporal Sisera. I imagine, you'll have it back shortly."

As Alerio slipped on the borrowed armor, he dropped a silver coin on the deck a couple of feet from the Corporal's Republic silver. The unarmored Squad Leader carried over a collection from his squad and used it to bury their NCO's coin.

Word went out and off-duty ship's crew, officers, and Legionaries strolled up and dropped more coin. Some next to Alerio's silver, while others placed coins on the stack with the Corporal's. It went on like that for as long as it took Alerio to strap the duel rig over the borrowed armor.

Once the duel rig was strapped on, Alerio reached over his shoulders and drew both gladii. As they came fee, he twirled both before launching them into the air. The swords crossed high over his head and he effortlessly snagged both as they tumbled towards the deck. He finished the demonstration by running mirrored sword drills as he paced across the drill deck. He finished and turned to face the squad.

"Squad, standby," Alerio shouted.

The Corporal and the squad leader were shocked the young Legionary would issue an order to their squad. Before they could object and regain control, Alerio continued.

"Two files," Alerio commended in a loud, no nonsense weapons instructor voice. In addition to the vocal instruction, he directed them with both gladii. Once the squad was formed up in two lines, he ordered, "Draw!"

The squad members were stacked four to a side and stood facing the young Legionary. At the order to draw, the training deck echoed with clicks as the steel gladii separated from their leather sheaths followed by a swoosh as each blade sliced the air. Quiet settled on the squad as eight gladii hovered in the guard position.

The NCOs expected to see a sword fight. Instead, the young instructor walked down one file and adjusted some Legionaries feet and the sword's position of others. He worked down one side, turned around, and adjusted the other file. Once back at the head of the two files, he began to speak.

"In a shield wall, you'll have enemies coming at you from the left and the right," Alerio explained. "In this drill, you'll be the enemy. Advance on me two at a time. I'll treat you as you treat me. Fight hard and I'll fight hard. Come soft and I'll hold you on the line until your arm falls off from exhaustion. Go for blood, and I'll put you in the infirmary. Clear?"

"Yes, instructor," the squad shouted back.

The Corporal shifted his eyes longingly to the stacks of coin. Along with the squad leader, they were already saying goodbye to their bets.

"First two, advance," Alerio growled. "Fight!"

On Alerio's left, the Legionary was massive. He opened the assault with an attempt to smash through Alerio's blade. After the big Legionary's blade was knocked to the side, he received a hard smash to his shoulder. Alerio's blow drove the thick Legionary off balance. He stumbled and ended up sprawled out on the deck.

"See me later for further instructions," Lance Corporal Sisera said out of the side of his mouth.

Now the Legionary on Alerio's right was a better than average swordsman. His only fault was his obvious dependence on the man that was just felled, who should have created an opening for a strike. The Legionary lunged in after the brute was discarded. Alerio slapped the man's blade upward. On the down swing, he tapped the Legionary in the helmet with the flat of the blade. The man reeled away.

"In a shield wall, one strike, no matter how hard, will not end the fight," Alerio explained. "Also, fight your own fight. Depend on the men to your left and your right to hold the line. But, your fight is with the man in front of you. Next two. Step up. Fight!"

The second set and the third set went smoothly for Alerio. He countered and instructed without even being touched by a gladius tip. It was the fourth set of Legionaries where it got interesting.

The two Legionaries in the rear of the files had a chance to watch Alerio, strategize, and put together a plan. From what they'd seen, the Lance Corporal used basic blocks and strikes. He didn't seem to be very mobile.

Alerio ordered, "Next two. Step up. Fight!"

The two rushed forward while chopping down powerfully with their gladii. It was a tactic reminiscent of the barbarians in the western region. As a young boy, Alerio had spent harvest times with a veteran Sergeant and Centurion. Among their many lessons was a discussion concerning this form of attack. They also drilled him on the best defense.

Two swords swung from overhead and driven by powerful shoulders were impossible to block without a shield. So, the best defense in this case was to not stand under the falling blades. At the last thump of a heartbeat, when the Legionaries' blades were committed to the killing arc, Alerio tucked his gladii under his arms, bent his knees, and dove between the men.

He rolled, came up on his feet, and pivoted around. The two Legionaries were also turning, but they were a heartbeat behind the instructor. They each received a slap from the flat of Alerio's gladii to the sides of their knees.

"The problem with a rash attack is you lose unit cohesion," Alerio explained to the squad. The two Legionaries who attempted the duel smash lay behind him holding their knees and groaning. He pointed at the men laying on the deck while continuing, "It's always advisable to use blade control in a coordinated attack. Any questions?"

"Come on, one more time," a Legionary Marine challenged.

"Put up your coin," suggested Alerio Sisera as he swung the two gladii to keep his shoulders loose. "And, line up."

Chapter 3 - A Proper Position

There was one thing feared above all else by Legionaries, smart barbarians, and experienced savages. It was the bellow and wrath of an enraged Sergeant of the Legion.

"What in the blue cōleī, merda covered, Goddess forsaken hades," yelled the Century's Sergeant as he bounded onto the practice deck. "Is going on here?"

Everyone froze, including the naval personnel. The Sergeant eyed the two injured Legionaries, the stacks of coins, the Corporal, and his out of uniform Lance Corporal. Then, he looked over the six standing members of the squad, and the Lance Corporal with two gladii gripped in his fists that stood facing them.

"Who are you?" the Sergeant inquired with all the emotional feelings of a clay brick.

"Lance Corporal Sisera," Alerio reported. "Gladius instructor."

Everyone waited for Sergeant Chlotharius to explode. His language wasn't near as legendary as his temper or the punishments he issued for infractions of his rules. And gambling on fighting competitions, on his ship while at sea, was at the top of his no-no list.

"Gladius instructor?" the Sergeant repeated. Then he tested the young Legionary's pronouncement. "Your evaluation?"

"Some sloppy gladius work," Alerio stated. "But the biggest issue is unit cohesion during attacks. Nothing proper drilling and instructions can't fix."

The Sergeant stared at the young Legionary for a long time. Finally, he broke eye contact and strolled to the two piles of coin.

"Which one is yours, weapons instructor?" he asked.

"The smallest," Alerio responded.

"Did you tell them you were an instructor before they placed the bets?" the Sergeant asked.

"Yes, Sergeant," Alerio replied.

"Take your winnings," the NCO stated. "You are my gladius instructor for the rest of the cruise. Squad, get below and get your heavy shields and report back to the instructor. Corporal, a word, in my cabin."

The Sergeant waited for the squad members to climb down before he led a dejected Corporal off the training deck.

For the final nine days of the cruise, Alerio drilled all the shipboard Legionaries. From unit tactics with heavy infantry shields to individual gladius drills, he had them sharp and moving in unison by the time the ship entered the mouth of the Tiber river.

Alerio had just finished with the last squad on the last day of the cruise. The NCO climbed to the training deck and watched the final maneuvers. When the squad was dismissed, the Sergeant waved the instructor over to the rail.

"Good work, Lance Corporal Sisera," Sergeant Chlotharius said. "I could use a full-time gladius instructor. Interested in the position?"

"For reasons I can't go into," Alerio replied while pointing towards the docks and the city rising above them. "I'm better off in the southern Legion rather than here."

Sergeant Chlotharius had been in the Legion for fifteen years. Over the years, he'd seen Legionaries get into a wide variety of troubles. For him, Sisera was just another in the long line.

"If you get stuck in the city for a while, I'd like to buy you a mug of vino," offered the Sergeant.

"I'm not sure how long," confessed Alerio. "It'll depend on when the ship for the southern region sails."

"If you're here long and need a place to stay, there's an inn that welcomes Legionaries," Chlotharius said. "Nice enough place but the proprietor is a bit eccentric. Interested?"

"Yes, Sergeant Chlotharius," Alerio said. "I don't know a soul in the city."

"Get directions to the Chronicles Humanum Inn," the NCO instructed. "When you get there ask for Thomasious Harricus. He's the owner. Tell him Sergeant Chlotharius sent you."

Chapter 4 - The Capital City

Alerio walked down the ramp onto the dock. In his workmen's woolen trousers and long sleeve shirt, he resembled every other worker on the dock. No one paid him any attention.

He located the Legion transfer building and reported to a Lance Corporal.

"Get a decent military tunic," the NCO suggested as he read the transfer orders. "Southern Legion? Alright. Your ship isn't due in for another week. That's the earliest we expect it in port. But, depending on the weather, it could be later. Give it a week, then check in here for updates every few days."

"Can you give me directions to the Chronicles Humanum Inn?" Alerio asked.

"Go north six blocks," the NCO directed. "Turn right and cross over the boulevard. When you reach the intersection at the city's defensive wall, you'll see a Candle Maker's compound. Turn left. You'll find the inn on your right. It's about twenty-five blocks. Most people rent a carriage for their luggage."

"This is my luggage," Alerio said holding up a large hemp rope bag. "I can handle it. Thank you, Lance Corporal."

"Enjoy the city, Sisera," the NCO said then advised. "Stay out of trouble. For the slightest infraction, the City Guard takes too much pleasure in arresting and fining Legion transfers."

"I'm not planning on getting into anything except a hot meal," replied Alerio. "And, a bed that doesn't rock and swing with each wave."

Alerio left the building and stepped onto the road heading north. The dockyard was busy.

Loaded carts with grain, unworked metals or raw ores rolled towards the city. While wagons filled with finished goods arrived for shipment from craftsmen compounds. He dodged between the wagons and carts as he left the harbor area.

Six blocks to the north, the road ended at a line of well-spaced trees in an open grassy area. The lush landscape occupied about two square blocks. On a hill, in the center of the space, stood a rectangular building constructed of white marble. Four tall columns, also of white granite, held up a roof that was impossibly high. As a farm lad from the western region and more recently, a Legionary from the east, he had never been this close to such an amazing manmade wonder.

"It's the Temple of Portunus," a man in an expensive toga said. "Portunus is the protector of harbors, livestock and keys. You've come from direction of the harbor. You might consider giving a few coins to Portunus as a display of gratitude for a safe arrival."

Alerio possessed a full purse thanks to winning a sword competition before shipping off to the eastern Legion. During his time there, he hadn't spent much coin. After glancing down at his rough woolen clothing and back at the man's richly embroidered toga, he declined.

"Maybe later, Priest," Alerio said as he turned to his right and walked away.

"Blessings of Portunus on you, my son," the man announced loudly. Then under his breath mumbled, "Cheap farm hick."

Alerio came to a doublewide avenue. Horses, carts, and carriages traveled rapidly in both directions. Judging the flow of traffic, he picked an opening and jogged across the road. Half way across, he looked north and stopped. Seven blocks away, the avenues wrapped around a fountain.

A marble sculpture of rearing horses rose from the center of the fountain. Water arched up from the sides and fell majestically into a pool. The streams splashed down just shy of the mighty hooves of the horses. Alerio stood mesmerized in the middle of the boulevard.

"Get out of the road," a man on horseback yelled. "Do you want to get yourself killed?"

Alerio spun his head around but the rider was already far down the boulevard. Something cracked over his head. Looking up, he watched as a whip finished cracking and withdrew. A man in a carriage shook the handle of the whip at him.

"Get out of the road, slave," the man ordered.

Figuring he could get a better and safer look at the fountain later, Alerio picked a spot and sprinted between traffic to the far side of the road. Between the temple, the fountain, and the rapid movement of so many people, the former farm lad was in awe.

The astonishment of walking through a cosmopolitan city clouded his mind and he didn't remember to count blocks. Eventually, he smelled a Candle Maker's shop. Over a low brick wall surrounding a compound, aromatic smoke drifted upward. The pleasant aromas of the seasonings used in the candle making process brought him back to the present.

Looming in front of him was the Capital City's defensive wall. Thirty feet of stacked three-foot-long clay bricks rose skyward just fifteen feet from the intersection. As directed, he turned left.

The clay bricks of the Candle Maker's compound wrapped around the façade of the shop. Courses of brick gave a solid appearance to the lower half of the building. Above the brick the building material changed to wood. Topping off the structure was a gently sloping roof of interlocking red clay shingles.

Two other shops occupied the same block as the Candle Shop. He strolled by an Apothecary and a Cloth Seller, both were built in the same style and design as the Candle Shop. On the other side of the road, the imposing city wall angled away from the road. Where the wall edged away, it left an open space. Someone had corralled off the area. Horses in the corral chewed hay and followed him with their eyes as he strolled up the street.

Chapter 5 - The Chronicles Humanum Inn

The fencing ended at a ten-foot-high clay brick wall. The wall ended at the corner of an unusual building. The front porch and center of the building faced the intersection of the next street. Alerio stopped and gazed at the unusual building.

Where the wall met the building, the layers of clay brick continued around encasing the ground floor. Then, the bricks stepped up ten more feet creating columns bracketing the second floor. Above the brick, wooden construction rose in tiers to form another two stories. Four divided balconies were observable on each floor of the building. The inn resembled a giant four-step staircase.

Alerio strolled by the Cloth Seller shop and out onto the intersecting street. Turning to his right, he read the sign hanging over the porch.

"The Chronicles Humanum Inn," he whispered as he took the four steps up to the clay pavers of the porch.

15

Inside, a large room with tables and chairs occupied the front of the ground floor. Two Legion Cavalry Officers sat at a table on one side of the room. They had clay mugs in their hands. A large pitcher of wine sat on the table.

A counter top of white marble ran along the rear of the room. Behind the marble, stacked barrels of wine covered most of the wall. On the other end of the room, where the wall and the wine castes ended, was a double door. In the center of the room, behind the wall and the countertop sat an alcove.

Alerio walked to the marble counter and peered into the recess. In the back of the wide workspace was a long hallway. He could see light pouring into the hallway from the back of the inn. None of the light reached a man sitting at a desk in the workspace. By lantern light, the man was scribbling frantically on a scroll that dangled all the way to the floor.

The man didn't acknowledge Alerio so the Lance Corporal coughed into his hand.

"Deliveries around back," the man said sharply without looking up.

"I was told, I could get a room here," Alerio insisted.

"All booked up," the man said absentmindedly as he continued to fill in the scroll with tight, exact letters.

From one end of the great room, a voice rose. Seconds later, it climbed several more octaves. Alerio glanced around. One of the cavalrymen was standing bent over and screaming into the face of the other Officer.

"You talk about her like that again and I'll carve your guts out," he screamed.

A scraping noise from the alcove drew Alerio's attention. The proprietor's chair flew back and the man took two steps before vaulting the marble counter. He raced to get between the cavalrymen.

"Gentlemen. No fighting in the Chronicles Humanum Inn," he said softly.

He continued to speak in almost a whisper as he rested a hand on the standing Officer's chest. The Officer cocked on ear in an attempt to hear the innkeeper's voice and forgot to be mad. The men moved away from the table.

Gentle persuasion was a good way to handle an angry drunk. Pressure from light hand contact and softly spoken words allowed the man to defused the situation.

A tiny movement by the other Officer caught Alerio's attention. The sitting cavalryman pulled a four-inch knife from his riding boot. It was a tool everyone who worked with harnesses carried. The edge was honed razor sharp so it could shave rough spots from leather harnesses. In addition, it was needle pointed for punching holes in the leather for buckle adjustments.

The knife was also the perfect weapon for stabbing a man in the back. The Officer stood unsteadily and took a step towards the unsuspecting proprietor.

Alerio dropped his hemp rope bag, sprinted over, and faced the armed cavalryman.

"Sir. Is everything alright?" he asked.

For a second nothing happened, until the cavalryman stabbed at Alerio's chest with the wicked weapon. The knife hand was halfway to its target when Alerio raised the heel of his left hand and redirected it off to the side.

The cavalryman adjusted and tried to realign the blade. Alerio's hand remained in contact, and using pressure on the man's wrist, forced the knife downward.

Suddenly, the cavalry Officer punched out with his left fist. Its momentum was redirected by the palm of Alerio's right hand. The punching fist ended up harmlessly near the knife hand at the cavalryman's crotch.

Both the Officer's arms rose in an attempt to dislodge Alerio's hands. It didn't work. Alerio controlled the wrists so the arms circled outward and traveled up and over the Officer's head. This further infuriated the intoxicated man. He bent his elbows and pulled his hands downward. Alerio's hands followed them down and when the Officer's hands were chest high, Alerio pushed hard.

The Officer's hands, one still holding the sharp knife, ended up pinned against his chest by Alerio. Stepping back while trying to shake free, the back of the cavalry Officer's knees connected with the chair. The man, caught by surprise, collapsed into the seat.

Alerio snatched the knife from his hand.

At the sound of racing feet, the innkeeper had turned his head. He watched as the delivery boy, in the bleached out workmen's clothing, almost effortlessly evaded the knife. When the lad disarmed the cavalryman, without once assaulting the Legion Officer, he became curious.

"What's that?" he asked.

Smiling and holding up the knife, Alerio announced, "A leather tool."

"No lad, the fighting style?" the innkeeper asked.

"It's called sticky hands," explained Alerio. "A Legion Scout taught it to me when were stationed together in the eastern Legion."

"Hold on a second," the innkeeper said. Then he yelled in the direction of the alcove, "Erebus. I need a little assistance."

Four heartbeats later, the double doors on the other end of the great room swung open. A huge northern barbarian rushed in and moved quickly to the innkeeper.

Unlike the rest of him, his face was clean-shaven and his long blond hair was clean. A whiff of stable odors drifted off the man. The dirty clothes and the dried mud on his sandals explained the smells.

"You called?" asked the barbarian.

"Yes, Erebus." The innkeeper explained. "These two gentlemen have just checked out. Please be sure their belongings and their bodies are on their horses when you let them out of the gate."

Erebus spun on one of the Cavalry Officers and delivered a powerful fist to the side of the man's head. Before the unconscious man reached the tile floor, the barbarian hit the second Officer. He also fell. With a limp body under each arm, Erebus trudged towards the double doors.

"Aren't you concerned that you'll get in trouble for hitting Legion Officers?" Alerio inquired as the barbarian and his cargo disappeared through the doorway.

"No, they are too full of vino to remember who or what hit them," the innkeeper explained. "Now lad. You claim to be a Legionary?"

"Lance Corporal Sisera, formerly of the eastern Legion," Alerio stated. "I'm in transit to the southern Legion."

"A bit young to be a Lance Corporal," observed the innkeeper. "So where is your luggage?"

"Luggage?" asked Alerio as he walked over and picked up the rope bag. "This is all the luggage I have."

He lifted out the duel gladii rig, a saddlebag, and a pouch of personal items, two types of leather grease, and another set of workman's clothing.

"These are all my worldly goods," Alerio explained. "So, I wouldn't be needing a large room."

The innkeeper stared at the young man and the duel sword rig. Shaking his head as if he'd made a decision, he said, "The name's Thomasious Harricus, proprietor of the Chronicles Humanum Inn and scourge of the upper class. And for a young Lance Corporal who saved my life, I have a room available."

"You're Master Harricus," exclaimed Alerio. "Sergeant Chlotharius sends his regards. He may stop by in a few days to have a drink."

"And how do you know good Sergeant Chlotharius?" asked Thomasious.

"I was his weapons instructor on the passage around from the east," explained Alerio.

"A weapons instructor, and you are how old?" an astonished Thomasious asked. "And where are your armor, your hip sheath, and your uniforms?"

"I'm seventeen-years-old. And yes, I am a gladius instructor," confirmed Alerio. "As for uniforms? I've never purchased any. There was no need for formal wear in the Raider Century."

"You were a Raider?" Thomasious asked as his jaw dropped.

"Yes, sir," Alerio replied. "If that room is available, I'd like to freshen up and get a nap."

"Of course Lance Corporal Sisera," Thomasious said. "Let me show you to your accommodations."

Chapter 6 - Scourge of the Upper Class

Alerio stretched and for a second braced for the next roll of the ship. When it didn't come, he opened his eyes.

The room was fifteen feet long and ten feet wide. Plenty of room for the spacious feather bed where he lay. Other furniture included a nightstand, a writing table with a chair, and two wide dressers. Wide enough for a Legionary's armor, which he didn't own. And uniforms, which he also didn't own.

He rolled over and blinked in the afternoon sunlight pouring in through the slats in the window. From his third floor room, he had an unobstructed view of the north side of the Temple of Portunus. Even partially blocked and ten blocks away, the temple was impressive. It glowed in the backdrop of the sun's golden rays and for a moment he regretted not leaving an offering for the god.

Reluctantly, he crawled out of the comfortable bed. There was no reason to rush other than the growling of his empty stomach. Once he dressed in the woolen workman's trousers and shirt, strapped on his hob nailed boots, and hid the Golden Valley dagger and his coin purses under the shirt, he left the room.

Alerio peered over the marble counter top and watched the innkeeper, Thomasious Harricus. Two street urchins were standing on either side of the man. The lads were speaking in hushed tones and Harricus was nodding and writing furiously on a scroll. Three others were standing in the doorway at the end of the long hallway. They were eating bread and sipping from wide clay bowls.

"Excellent lads," Harricus announced as he dipped the quill in a mug of water to clear the nub of ink. "Go eat."

"You have a good heart," Alerio said when the innkeeper looked his way. "My mother always said charity brings blessings from Empanda."

"No, Alerio. I'm not helping the needy," Harricus admitted. "I'm feeding my employees. Those lads are my ears around the villas of the wealthy and politically connected. You'd be surprised what maids and gardeners hear and see. And best of all, they gossip about the dirtiest and juiciest items when they're outside the villas. My lads listen and report the stories to me."

He held up a scroll and waved it in the air.

"I turn the scandals and secrets into stories," Harricus said proudly. "Wealthy ladies pay handsomely for the tales."

"Don't they recognize their situation in the stories?" asked Alerio.

"Although I change the names, they almost certainly know some of the tales are about them." Harricus admitted. "But, that only adds to the value because they assume the rest of the stories are about other people in their social circles. They play parlor games of who is who in the stories."

A young man came in the backdoor and strolled to the rear of the alcove.

"Master Harricus. Good day, sir," the man said in greeting. He was slim and seemed nervous. His ink stained fingers twitched as he spoke, "Is it ready? Or, do I have time for a bowl of the cook's soup?"

Harricus laughed and laid the scroll on the corner of his desk.

"The Clay Ear may have a few details to add. I'll go upstairs to his room and check with him," Harricus said. "In the meantime, go have a bowl. When you're finished, the scroll will be right here."

The man bobbed his head, "Thank you, Master Harricus." He spun around and retreated down the hallway.

"One of the scribes I hire to copy the Clay Ear's scroll," Thomasious explained. "In turn, the scribes hire people to sell the copied scrolls at wealthy villas. No one knows who the Clay Ear is or where he gets his information. Are you hungry?"

Alerio took a seat at the table where directed. Soon large bowls of soup arrived, along with a loaf of freshly baked bread, two plates of cheese, and a pitcher of watered wine.

"My father and grandfather spent time in the Legion," the innkeeper explained as he popped a slice of cheese in his mouth. "They encouraged me to go in a different direction. Both said the same thing. Picking up a shield and a gladius changes you. Picking up the parchment and the quill changes your world."

"And selling salacious stories changes the world, how?" Alerio inquired as he dunked a chunk of bread in the soup.

"Oh the Clay Ear enjoys tweaking the aristocracy with the stories," Harricus replied. "It makes good coin but isn't socially significant. However, the chain-scroll I was working on when you arrived does."

"What's a chain-scroll?" Alerio asked. "In the village near my father's farm, we have scrolls for studying. But, none of them were referred to as chain-scrolls."

"It's a city invention," Thomasious explained. "When a chain-scroll is brought to me, I read the entries written by previous possessors of the scroll. Then, I add my own words of about one hundred and sixty letters before having a courier deliver the chain-scroll to another person. That person adds their words and sends it to another person. One chain-scroll gets entries from about thirty people before the end of the parchment."

"How is that socially significant?" asked Alerio as he shoved the empty bowl away. "It sounds like nothing more than gossip to me."

"The power of an idea, spread city wide, has influence," Harricus said. "As the Clay Ear, I insert my political opinions in the chain-scrolls. You see, having weak and absent Consuls and a powerful Senate isn't an efficient form of government. I'd like to see the Republic become more balanced."

"Master Harricus. You're speaking treason," Alerio stated in horror. "How can you trust me not to turn you into the City Guard? Why tell me these things?"

"Because, young Lance Corporal Sisera, you are just passing through and don't know the political players of the Capital," Harricus explained. "Plus, they're not my ideas. Rather, the reclusive Clay Ear writes them. To answer your other question of why you, it's simple. I needed to brag and you're handy."

"Don't tell me anymore," begged Alerio as he stood. "I wouldn't repeat any of this. No one would believe me anyway. However, please, no more of the Clay Ear's politics. I'm going for a stroll around the city to see the sights and to forget what you said."

"If you walk around dressed like a slave or a day worker," Harricus observed. "The City Guard will stop you if you wander into the better neighborhoods. Go see Zacchaeus, the Cloth Seller, about proper clothing. Afterwards, go to the Historia Fae and ask Tomas Kellerian about Legionary armor. He'll give you a good rate on better fitting equipment compared to anyone else."

Act 2

Chapter 7 - Fashion of the Day

Alerio took the steps down from the inn's porch, angled across the intersection, and pushed open the door to the Cloth Seller's Shop.

"Master Zacchaeus. I am in need of acceptable clothing," Alerio exclaimed. He stepped into the interior of the shop and set his rope bag beside the door.

An old man shuffled over, took the end of Alerio's shirtsleeve, and rubbed the material between his thumb and forefinger.

"Indeed you are young sir," Zacchaeus said. "Fresh off a boat, I'd guess. Unless the salt is from dragging your sleeves over salted hams."

"I just arrived from the eastern Legion," Alerio explained. "I'm in need of civilian clothing as well as a uniform."

"Ah, a Legion Tribune, I assume," the Cloth Seller stated as he turned and walked towards a pile of different colored cloth. He stood with an outstretched hand drifting over neat rolls of rich material as if trying to decide on one.

Tribunes were politically appointed Legionary Officers. Mostly they acted as administrators for the General and his staff. Young men from important families used the Legion experience later in life to further their political ambitions. A few remained and made the military a career.

"No, sir. I'm a simple Lance Corporal of the Legion," corrected Alerio.

Zacchaeus' arm dropped, and without any sign of disappointment, the old man moved to a different pile where he selected several rolls of cloth.

"Come with me young man," he ordered as he walked through a door in the rear of the storefront.

Alerio followed and was surprised by the change in lighting. While the front of the shop had been muted, in the rear work area, it resembled midday. Polished metal ovals reflected the sun's rays into every corner. Long tables topped with smooth marble had cloth sections spread over their tops. One person was cutting shapes from the material. Two others sewed the shapes together to form tunics, togas, dresses, and other garments. The last craftsman sat stitching decorative trim on the finished apparel.

"Step over here to the stool," directed Zacchaeus pointing to a lighted area in front of a mirrored surface. "And take off your shirt."

There was a knee-high stool with footprints from previous use a yard from the mirror. Not knowing any difference, Alerio stepped up on the stool. From the height, he looked down on the top of the shop owner's head. Laughter rippled through the work area.

"No. The stool is for me," Zacchaeus explained.

Alerio stepped down and the old man took his place. Even with the added height of the stool, Zacchaeus was a head shorter than the Legionary.

Alerio yanked the loose shirt over his head and let it fall to the floor. Whether it was the sight of the scars on such a young man, or the long scabbard of the dagger strapped to the small of his back, he didn't know, but the workers went silent.

A piece of olive colored cloth was draped over Alerio's shoulders. The old man began marking the material with a small piece of chalk.

"Olive color is the military fashion of the day," Zacchaeus explained as he gathered a fold of cloth around Alerio's thick biceps. "Seems the veterans returning from the northern campaigns brought back an appreciation of the forest hues."

While the tailor worked, the craftsman sewing the decorative trim held up a length of finally woven material. Bronze wire had been woven through the latticework creating bright lines in the light brown trim. The old man nodded his approval.

"We'll sew on the Lance Corporal band around your right sleeve in bronze," Zacchaeus explained. "It's reasonably priced and looks excellent against the green of the tunic. Other than the rank, are there any medals or unit designations we should include?"

"No medals. But, I am a gladius instructor," Alerio said. "And, I was with the Legion Raiders in the east."

Zacchaeus shot an inquisitive glance at the trim craftsman. The man searched through some boxes for a few moments before pulling out a thin metal tab stamped with a gladius. From another box, he pulled out a silk band painted with a scene of the sun rising over cresting waves.

The sound of the front door opening and boots walking on the flooring reached them.

"Please excuse me for a minute," Zacchaeus said as he stepped down from the stool.

He handed the marked cloth to a cutter before hobbling to the door.

Alerio looked at the cutter and asked, "How long will it take you to make the uniform?"

"It'll be a couple of days, sir," the man said as he flattened the cloth and began connecting the tailor's marks with curved lines.

Raised voices from the front of the shop carried to the work area.

"Next week old man," an angry male voice exclaimed. "You'll have all of our money. Or we'll come back and trash this place."

The heated words directed at the old man raised Alerio's curiosity. He stepped away from the stool and walked to the doorway. Two men with their faces only a couple of inches from Zacchaeus' were glaring, and poking the old man in his frail chest. Each finger jab hurt as Alerio could see by the look on the tailor's face.

"Is there a problem?" Alerio asked from the doorway.

"Mind your own business," one of the men ordered. He was thick bodied around the torso but his legs were thin and his knees knobby.

"No problem, sir," Zacchaeus stammered looking around at the Legionary. "Please, wait in the back. I'll be with you in a second."

"Yes, like he said," the other man mimicked the old tailor. "Please, wait in the back."

The second man was leaner with sloping shoulders and long arms. Both men were about the same height as Alerio.

Chapter 8 - Making Friends with the Local Crew

"We will be back next week," the first man warned. "You better have all of our money."

"You want protection," the second man sneered. "You've got to pay for it."

Alerio watched as Zacchaeus slumped in defeat as the men turned. They were almost at the front door when the man with the sloping shoulders reached out and grabbed the handle of the hemp rope bag.

"We'll just take this as a penalty for you shorting us," he stated as he picked up the bag.

"That doesn't belong to you," Alerio advised the man while striding across the room to confront him.

"It does now," knobby knees announced.

"Let's try this again," Alerio said with a smile. "Please put the bag down, and take your tiny, shriveled mentula out of the shop. Or?"

"Or?" demanded sloping shoulders as his face turned red. "Or what?"

The other man didn't say anything. Instead, he pulled an iron knife from his hip.

"Let's go," he said to his companion while pointing the knife at Alerio. "And bring the bag."

Alerio's most prized possessions, in fact his only possessions, were the duel gladii harness and the two gladii. The rig and swords rested in the bottom of the rope bag. Now the bag was about to be walked out of the door.

It's one thing to face two men when your weapon is drawn and you know they will attack. It becomes a different issue when one might bolt through the door with your property.

"Ah, I'm really sorry about distributing you," Alerio apologized. He hung his head as if ashamed while shuffling he feet as if embarrassed by his behavior.

The shuffling seemed innocent, except the movements carried him closer to the men. Guessing the lad was truly frightened of the knife and, out of fear, couldn't make eye contact, the man with the bag reached for the door handle.

"If I might ask a question?" Alerio inquired shyly still shuffling and moving forward.

"What lad? Hurry up, we've got rounds to make," the man holding his bag demanded.

He was half turned with one hand on the handle of the shop's door. His upper body twisted around to glare at the Alerio. In his annoyance, the man failed to notice the scars, or the fact the lad wasn't looking at him. Instead, Alerio was staring directly into the eyes of the man holding the knife.

"Don't you want the coin purses?" Alerio asked while tapping the money pouches suspended from his belt.

When the knifeman's eyes dropped to ogle the coin purses, Alerio kicked the man near the door. The bottom of his hob nailed boot caught the man high on the back of his shoulder. From the force of the kick, the man's torso twisted forward and his chest was driven into the shop's front door. His head rocked back before whipping forward. The man dropped the rope bag as his face smashed into the solid wood door.

Alerio didn't wait to observe the blood pouring from the broken nose or watch the man stagger from the shock of being bounced off the thick wood.

The long, curved Golden Valley dagger came out of its sheath. Alerio brought it around backhanded. The blade traced a line on the knifeman's hand. Blood drops began forming before the man knew he was injured.

"Gods! Your hand! Look at your hand," Alerio screamed as if surprised.

The cut man looked from where his compatriot was attempting to collect himself from the floor, over to the lad who suddenly held a long, gleaming blade. It took his mind a minute to catch up and focus on what Alerio exclaimed.

When flickers of pain started to flame out from his hand, the man's body went into self-preservation mode and he followed directions. He looked down at the thin line and the blood drops dripping onto the floor.

Alerio cocked his left arm and delivered a roundhouse punch to the side of the knifeman's head. The man crumpled to the tiles.

At the doorway, the man with the sloped shoulders recovered and reached for his own knife. Alerio lunged towards him. At the last second, he raised a knee. The knee caught the man's fingers between the hard bone of the knee and the harder iron of the knife's hilt. Two fingers broke. Alerio brought the butt end of the Golden Valley dagger down on the crown of the man's head. The thief crumbled to the tiles.

"That went well," exclaimed Alerio as he walked over and picked up his rope bag.

"Oh, good Eris," cried Zacchaeus while holding a palm to his forehead. "You've brought strife, discord, and rivalry down on my shop."

"You picked the correct Goddess," commented Alerio. "I couldn't let them take my bag. Sorry, if I've caused you trouble."

"They'll be back tonight," Zacchaeus wailed. "The last time I didn't pay, they destroyed a quarter of my stock. After this, I don't know what they'll do."

Alerio felt for the old craftsman. After observing him wringing his hands and moaning for a full minute, Alerio asked, "When will they come back? Sounds funny, doesn't it, as they're laying here and haven't left yet?"

"They'll come by tonight," explained Zacchaeus. "With friends. I dare not interfere or they'll kill me and my staff."

"It just so happens, my social calendar is clear for tonight," Alerio said. "Seeing as I started this, I'll guard your property overnight. If you want me to."

"I don't know what you can do against an entire gang," Zacchaeus said sadly. "But maybe they'll run when challenged by a Legionary. Yes, I accept your offer."

"Alright, but I'll need a few things from you," Alerio said. "Some clothes to change into after I remove these guys. Plus, a dark cloak and a full wineskin."

Chapter 9 - A delaying Tactic

Alerio put the wineskin strap over his shoulder and hoisted the first thug onto his shoulder. Outside, he turned left and crossed the street. He appeared to be a simple workman hauling a thick rug. He toted the unconscious body to the far side of the Wine Merchant's rear wall and rolled the body out of the carpet. A liberal dose of wine over the body completed the first phase of his plan.

As he walked back to the Cloth Seller's Shop, Thomasious stepped onto the porch of the Chronicles Humanum Inn. The innkeeper studied the Legionary. When Alerio exited the cloth shop with another rug wrapped body slung over his shoulder, Thomasious cocked his head in puzzlement.

Alerio waved with his free hand and smiled as he angled across the street in front of the inn. Thomasious waved back but didn't relax his face. Zacchaeus poked his head out of the door of the Cloth Sellers Shop and glanced up and down the street before disappearing back into the shop. Thomasious, seeing the merchant was alright, relaxed.

The second thug was dumped beside the first in the alleyway behind the Wine Merchant's wall. Then, Alerio reached down and pulled off their woolen pants before dousing them both with vino from the wineskin. As a final act, he rolled both men so they faced each other. After placing their arms so they were hugging, he smashed their foreheads together.

Hopefully, the compromising position and the smell of wine would cause confusion when they spoke with their friends. Alerio needed them to attack the Cloth Seller after dark. Not come storming in while it was still light and he wasn't prepared. He tossed their trousers into an empty barrel as he walked back to retrieve his rope bag.

A few minutes later, Thomasious watched as Zacchaeus stepped out of his shop and held the door for the young Legionary. They exchanged words before the Lance Corporal turned the corner and walked up the street. He was dressed in an ill-fitting gray tunic and carried the rope bag in one hand.

Zacchaeus noticed the innkeeper and raised a hand in greeting. Thomasious returned the wave and both merchants turned and went back inside their respective businesses.

Chapter 10 - Historia Fae, Armorer to the Gods

Four blocks later, Alerio came alongside the wall to the armorer's compound. He followed it to the intersecting street. Turning left, he noticed the same clay brick wall continued for the full length of the building's face. An iron reinforced wooden door was the only break in the steady courses of brick.

He wrapped his fingers around the heavy iron knocker and pounded it three times. A small slit in an iron band opened.

"What do you want lad?" a voice, connected to one brown eye peering through the opening, asked.

"I need a good set of armor," Alerio stated.

"So do half the Legions," the voice replied.

"But I need it tonight," insisted Alerio.

"What's your rush lad?" the voice teased. "You can die anytime. No need to fight over a lass or hurt pride. Wait for tomorrow and cool off."

Alerio realized the man mistook him for a hot headed city youth.

"I am Lance Corporal Alerio Sisera, formally of the eastern Legion," Alerio said. "Gladius instructor and Legion Raider. If it would keep for the night, I'd gladly let you get back to squatting over your chamber pot. However, my need is more urgent than your need to get the bug out of your cūlus."

"Well, you speak like a Legionary," the voice replied. "Where's your uniform?"

"I just arrived by ship and Zacchaeus says my clothing wouldn't be ready for another day," Alerio confessed. "While at the Cloth Seller's, I roughed up a couple of thugs. Now, I have a commitment to guard the shop in case the crew breaks in for revenge."

35

"Good story," the voice said as the opening slid closed.

For a heartbeat, Alerio thought he'd been dismissed. A screeching sound emitted from behind the door followed by metal scraping against metal. The door swung open. After the tortured metal of the locking mechanism, the heavy door's iron hinges were surprisingly quiet.

"Come in Lance Corporal Sisera," said a large man with wide shoulders.

He held out a scarred hand directing the Legionary to enter a second door. There was a gap of eighteen inches between the outer wall and the actual building. The Historia Fae was a villa surrounded by a defensive wall not simply a merchant's shop.

When Alerio stepped into the actual shop, he understood why. Sets of armor were mounted on display stands. One had gold inlays rippling over a sculptured, silver torso plate and along the shoulder guards. Another torso plate was silver with scrolled gold decorations. The two sets of armor alone were worth a small fortune.

"Pretty aren't they?" the Armorer said walking up to stand beside Alerio. "I wouldn't fight in them. On the other hand, for a General or a Senator who wants to make an impression during a parade, they fill the need. I'm Tomas Kellerian."

"Armorer to the Gods," Alerio exclaimed. "I read the sign outside. Do you really make magical armor with metal and leather from the land of Fae?"

"Haven't had any gods come in looking for armor, yet," Tomas admitted. "And the only magical property of my armor is you walk away from the battle. If stopping an enemy's sword isn't supernatural enough for you, you've never been in a sword fight."

"There is a bit of magic when you walk away from a sword fight," Alerio agreed.

He turned from the outlandish armor and found himself staring at an odd set of armor. It didn't have a solid torso plate. Instead, it had hundreds of small overlapping plates. Even the shoulder rigs had the tiny plates.

"It's fish scale armor," Tomas explained. "Lighter, more flexible, and the hand size plates deflect sword points."

"What about a slash or a smash?" Alerio asked.

"The armor spreads the energy of the strike over multiple plates," Tomas replied as he demonstrated with the edge of his hand. "Unlike a large plate which dents and rattles the fighter with every strike."

"I bet it's expensive," guessed Alerio.

"Not a pricy as the display armor," Tomas offered. "But yes, the tooling of the plates and linking them is time consuming. So, compared to ordinary metal armor the fish scale armor is expensive. Now, what can I do for you?"

"I need two things," Alerio reported. "Number one is a leather set for this evening. I don't expect it'll sustain much damage, but I don't know how many thugs I'll be facing."

"Come with me," directed Tomas. They left the display area and entered a storage room. Tomas pulled out a stick marked with evenly spaced lines and held it across Alerio's shoulders. Then, he strolled down a row of armor. He selected a set and carried it to a workbench.

"This should fit," he exclaimed as he unstrapped the five pieces. The shoulder rigs fit nicely on Alerio's broad shoulders. When Tomas held the torso pieces in place, there was a gap between the front and rear.

He went back and pulled down a second larger set. The front and back touched on the sides and even after a deep breath, they fit Alerio nicely. Then Tomas wrapped the short armored skirt around the Lance Corporal's hips. It was too long.

The correct armored skirt for Alerio' narrow hips came from a third and much small set of armor.

"You do need a custom set," Tomas observed as he checked the straps. "You said two reasons?"

"The second reason I'm here," Alerio explained. He reached down, lifted the rope bag, and set it on the workbench.

"I need a custom set of armor Master Kellerian," stated Alerio as he pulled the duel sword rig from the bag. "One that contours to accept this."

"Interesting cut and riveting," exclaimed Tomas as he examined the duel rig. "Basic Legion construction. How does it fit?"

"It shifts a little in a sword fight," explained Alerio. "But overall, it's a good harness."

"What do you do with the second gladius?" asked Tomas.

"Sometimes, I fight with both," admitted Alerio.

"Let's get you out of the armor so I can do the proper measurements," Tomas said as he started to unstrap the armor. "You'll leave the rig and the gladii. I'm going to make some changes in your duel rig and need the swords for balance. If we're going to do this, I want to do it properly."

"Everything you say sounds great," Alerio said. "Except, I need a gladius for tonight."

"I may have an old one around here somewhere," Tomas said with a smile.

Chapter 11 - Chronicles Humanum Inn

The inn was busy when Alerio returned with the heavy and over stuffed rope bag. Guests in the city for business had completed their day's activities. Now, they looked forward to some entertainment at the inn. Or, they were having drinks before going out to attend dinner parties with important people.

Alerio was also going out to meet people. However, it wouldn't be a dinner party and the people were on a far lower social scale.

"Good evening Lance Corporal," Thomasious said from behind the marble counter. "I hear you've had a busy day."

"Are things usually like this in the Capital?" inquired Alerio.

"Not usually. I understand you have a late night coming up," Thomasious proclaimed. "Go rest and I'll have dinner brought up to your room. Also, I'll have Erebus leave the side gate unlocked so you can go and come as you please. I can't have an armed and armored Legionary tramping through my dining hall where my guests are trying to enjoy some music."

"Much appreciated Master Harricus," Alerio said as he dodged through the great room lugging the bag filled with armor.

Chapter 12 - Night Watch on the Wall

The sun had set but the moon had yet to rise. Alerio sat on the back wall of the Cloth Seller's compound. Happy crowd noises drifted across the intersection from the Chronicles Humanum Inn. Every so often the music rose above the human chatter and he heard the melody drifting on the breeze. Alerio envied the revelers.

Then the crowd banter lowered and he could make out a few words of a man talking up a song. When the balladeer started, the audience joined him in the singing.

"O' There was a city Lass.
Under a rancher's spell she fell.
And he made pretty promises.
That made her spoiled heart swell."

"I'm a happy city lass.
Fine wines and the dancing, I'll miss.
But I will go with you sir.
Ah, the singing and balls, I'll miss."

"Fear not my princess bride.
The rancher offered the chance.
There's nothing in the city.
That's missing on a ranch."

"O' Wine, there's plenty O' wine.
When it's time to tap the keg.
Dancing, there's plenty O' dancing.
When it's time to stomp the grapes.
Singing, there's plenty O' singing.
When it's time to bale the hay.
And, balls, there's plenty O' balls.
When it's time to nurture the bulls."

"O' There was a city lass.
Under a rancher's spell she fell.
And he made pretty promises.
That made her spoiled heart swell."

"I'm a happy city lass.
Fine wines and the dancing, I'll miss.
But I will go with you sir.
Ah, the singing and balls, I'll miss."

"Fear not my princess bride.
The rancher offered the chance.
There's nothing in the city.
That's missing on a ranch."

O'...

Alerio was listening and tapping his foot in the air. As the next verse started, a dark shape slipped over the wall. Three more followed it into the Cloth Seller's compound. They came over directly across from where the Legionary sat wrapped in the dark cloak.

The song faded as Alerio dropped into the yard. Ten silent paces later, he dropped the cloak and drew the gladius. He could hear the trespassers whispering as they decided who should go first.

If these were the best criminals the city had to offer, the state of crime in the Capital was in a sad state. At least the Rebel criminals in the east had leadership.

There are two ways to initiate contact with an enemy in the dark. One was to wait and pick them off one at a time. The other was to attack directly, create chaos, and slaughter them as they scattered. Alerio wasn't subtle by nature.

"Attack! attack!" he yelled as he ran at the four men.

In the dark he could just make out shapes. For the last hour he had kept his eyes closed except when looking along the dark wall. From the way the criminals tripped and fell in the lowlight, he knew they had been staring at the lanterns hanging on the inn.

"Wine, there's plenty O' wine. When it's time to tap the keg," Alerio sang as he tripped a criminal by thrusting the blade between his legs. Then he tapped the thug on the head as he fell.

41

"*Dancing, there's plenty O' dancing. When it's time to stomp the grapes,*" another fell when the singing Alerio slapped the flat of his blade into the man's lower back. He kicked the man's head as he ran by.

"*Singing, there's plenty O' singing. When it's time to bale the hay,*" blurted out the Legionary as he kneed another thug who was hiding at the base of the wall.

"*And, balls, there's plenty O' balls. When it's time to nurture the bulls,*" sang the Legionary as he placed the tip of a gladius at the throat of one thug who charged at him with a knife.

He removed the tip long enough to spin the man around and get a grip on his collar. Alerio pushed the man towards another who lay moaning.

"Grab his feet and drag him," Alerio instructed. He twisted the collar until he felt resistance and the man's breath was cut.

He guided the chocking man as he pulled the unconscious thug. A few feet away they came upon the third criminal.

"Lie down beside them," he ordered while releasing the collar and pushing the man to the ground.

Alerio backed up to where the fourth man lay prone and unmoving. Kneeling down, he whispered to the prone figure, "I'm going to run my gladius through your heart."

The man rolled over and began to crawl over to join the other three thugs. Once they were together, Alerio, by the tip of his gladius, urged the four to sit back to back. He unwound a length of rope from his waist and used it to encircle the men.

"Now, I know you have knives. One of you tried to stick me," Alerio rasped out as if speaking were a chore. "So, here's my problem. I can stand here and guard you all night. I'll be really

42

tired in the morning. And, I really wanted to go sightseeing but having to watch you would ruin my plans."

He slapped his chest with the gladius. The metal against the leather resembled the snap of a giant whip. In the dark, it could have been anything, and the four criminals shook from the violence of the sound.

"To save me the bother, I'm going to murder all four of you," Alerio stated. "So, I can go and get some sleep. Whose throat should I cut first?"

"No, please, wait," two of them begged.

"If I let you live, I've got to get something in return," advised Alerio. "Let's say...who is the head of your crew and where can I find him?"

"Don't say a word. You know...," one warned. The rest of his speech was cut off when the gladius bounced off the side of his head.

"Sorry for the interruption," Alerio said. "Now, as you were saying?"

"Vivianus. Vivianus is the leader of the Fireguard Brigade," one blurted out.

"And if I wanted to have a talk with this Vivianus," Alerio asked. "Where would I find him?"

"Why, in Fireguard District," the man said as if it were obvious.

"Let's be specific. Where in the Fireguard District?" Alerio asked then he yawned loudly. "I'm getting sleepy and you know what that means."

"The south end," the man blurted out. "He moves from pub to pub. No one knows his schedule."

"One more question. Is there another crew coming tonight?" he asked.

"No. We're it," the talkative one said. "I swear."

"Very good and thank you lads," Alerio said. In quick session, he knocked each of them out.

It took a long time and a lot of energy to hoist each limp body to the top of the wall. Once they were lined up, Alerio climbed up and walked the wall to the first one.

His early training dedicated he put each of them to death to prevent them from coming after him. Except, this was the Capital City and he didn't want to move four dead bodies away from the Cloth Seller's Shop. He settled with giving each a temporary limp. Figuring it would be easier to spot them when he went hunting for their leader, Alerio swung the flat of his blade and broke the bones on the top of the first man's right foot. Then, he kicked the man over the wall.

Four broken feet later, he climbed down. Sticking to the shadows, Alerio reached the corner of the Cloth Seller's shop. After looking both ways, he dashed across the street to the rear of the Wine Merchant's compound.

Taking an alleyway, Alerio emerged on the far side of the street. Now, he was close to the side gate of the Chronicles Humanum Inn.

Chapter 13 - A Little Jog and a Reminder

The Capital City had awakened long before Alerio stirred. He dressed in the workman's clothing, took the borrowed gladius, and went down to the inn's courtyard.

Erebus, strolling from the stables, noticed the Legionary lunging and slashing the air with a gladius. The stableman changed course and ducked into a side building. Shortly, he reappeared. In his hand was a wooden gladius.

"We keep this for visiting Legionaries," the big barbarian stated as he offered the training sword to Alerio. "There's a training post behind the cook shed."

The courtyard behind the inn had stables, a couple of storage buildings, a small bathhouse, and a cooking shed. Behind the cook shed, Alerio located a sandy area with a striking post buried in the center of the pit.

A steady rhythm of wood striking wood filled the courtyard. It sounded as if two or even three men were using the training post. In fact, it was only Alerio smoothly switching the wooden gladius from hand to hand as he ran the drills.

After the drills, Alerio stripped off the sweat soaked shirt and laid it over the post. He jogged out the side gate and ran up the street and away from the inn. Along the side of the Cloth Seller's wall, he slowed. There were no signs of the four Fireguard Brigade thugs.

He continued his run passed the Historia Fae, circled the Temple of Portunus grounds, and headed south toward the harbor. At the first row of warehouses, he angled left and trotted away from the low buildings.

Running parallel to the harbor, he could see the merchant ships tied to piers and others anchored on the far side of the river. Among the ships were a couple of Republic navy patrol boats. He reached another warehouse area and trotted onto the street between the buildings. At the end of the last building, he slid to a stop.

A compound wall sat a block and a half from the end of the warehouse. There was no sign to identify the use of the villa behind the wall. Alerio searched and located a simple bee insignia etched lightly on the column beside the closed gate.

Alerio recognized the symbol and knew instantly this was a trading house for luxury goods. They shipped and traded fine wines, teas, and other exotic and expensive products. One of the products they offered was honey from the Golden Valley. Another product offered by the trading house was murder by assassin from the Dulce Pugno.

Alerio reached back and touched the dagger hanging from his belt at the small of his back. The curved knife with the yellow band around the black hilt identified him as an Ally of the Golden Valley. As an Ally, the trading house was bound to offer information, sanctuary and medical assistance to any Ally. Additionally, it protected him from assassination by the Sweet Fist. They wouldn't take a contract on him. Conversely, they wouldn't kill for him, unless he took out a contract and paid to have a victim eliminated. He didn't have the coin or the desire to hire an assassin.

Alerio picked up his pace. He continued the run, passed the rear of the Candle Maker's compound and almost reached the city's defensive wall. Turning left at the intersection, he headed back in the direction of the Chronicles Humanum Inn.

Chapter 14 - Fireguard District

After a soak in the bathhouse and dressing in the ill-fitting tunic, Alerio entered the great room in search of a meal. He crossed to the alcove and peered over the white marble counter.

"Late night?" he teased the innkeeper.

Thomasious sat with his forehead resting in his hands. The way he sat, it appeared as if the man had consumed a large quantity of vino and was hungover. Upon hearing the voice, the innkeeper raised his head to reveal surprisingly clear eyes.

"No Sisera, I'm bothered by a report I've received," Thomasious explained. "Sometimes gossip and politics collide. But you don't want to hear about politics. If I feed you a meal, will you give me your opinion on the gossip?"

"Master Harricus, if you feed me, I'll gladly listen to the tale of how your grandfather met your grandmother," Alerio replied.

"That's actually a good story," Thomasious said as he stood and pointed to a table. "But I'll save it for another time. Right now, have a seat, and I'll get us some food. Is braised lamb alright?"

"Sounds delicious," replied Alerio as he pulled out a chair and sat down.

Thomasious emerged from the double doors followed by a serving girl. She placed platters of lamb and roasted vegetables on the table while the innkeeper took a chair. After she left, they ate quietly for a while.

"Two Senators got into a heated argument last night," Thomasious announced.

"I thought this wasn't political?" Alerio said between bites.

"The second part isn't," explained Thomasious. "They were at a party in a mutual friend's villa. The Senators are usually at odds politically so a disagreement between them wasn't unusual. Before they were asked to leave the party and continue the discussion in a side room, a few things were said. One politician said he wouldn't support laws from absentee Consuls. Seems that two weeks ago, Consul Julius Libo took command of the eastern Legion and went to chase Rebels. Since then, he's been communicating his desires to the Senate via courier. Consul

47

Marcus Regulus is off touring the Legions on the northern frontier."

"The Consuls' words are the rule of the land," Alerio said. "The Senate's job is to implement the Consuls' orders."

"Exactly, except, the Senate has a lot of leeway as to how the orders are carried out," explained Thomasious. "That's the cause of most arguments in the Senate. Last night, Senators Faunus suggested the orders weren't logical or good for the Republic. He went so far as to question if Consul Julius Libo was indeed the author of the orders."

"Treasonous. Why is it every time we talk, it comes to treason?" asked Alerio.

"You're in the Capital City," Thomasious stated. "Most conversations in the city could be mistaken for treason. Now, as I was saying. Senator Faunus questioned the absent Consul's messages and that started the argument. The rest of the conversation between them is lost behind closed doors."

"So, what juicy story can the Clay Ear create from the argument?" asked Alerio.

"Nothing from the fight," Thomasious admitted. "However, from the brutal murder of Senator Faunus, who challenged the authenticity of the Consul's messages, and his wife, and their bodyguards, the Clay Ear might have fodder for a story."

"How many bodyguards?" Alerio asked in horror. "We're they trained? Or, drunk?"

"They were former Legionaries," Thomasious said. "According to my sources, the guards ate lightly and sipped watered wine while waiting for the party to end."

Alerio remained silent for a long time before asking, "How old was the Senator? Fat, out of shape, sickly?"

"Senator Faunus was elected two years ago when he returned from four years as a Tribune with the northern Legion," explained Thomasious. "The bodyguards were from his Legion unit. What are you thinking? A robbery gone wrong?"

"The rule of assault and defense," Alerio replied remembering the lessons from his father's former Sergeant and Centurion. "It takes three assaulters to dislodge one defender. In order to defeat the four bodyguards and the Senator, the attack would require at least fifteen trained men. Ten to twelve experienced fighters if they could get in close before the assault started. Unless the Senator was carrying bags of gold to a dinner party making it worthwhile for a hoard of highwaymen, the murder was an assassination."

"The Senator's jewelry even the ropes and staff of his office were found on his body. So, the death isn't gossip," complained Thomasious. "It's political."

"What will the Clay Ear do? Put it in the gossip scroll?" asked Alerio while pushing away his empty platter. "Or, note it in a chain scroll?"

"I'm not sure," admitted Thomasious. "Use it as a footnote in a party story, and hit it hard in a couple of chain scrolls most likely."

"Oh, while we're talking," Alerio said. "Tell me about the Fireguard District."

"If you haven't noticed, the city walls aren't complete," Thomasious lectured. "There are two places yet to be fortified. One is at the northern end of the city and the other at the center eastern edge. Rather than brick walls, those sectors have earthen ramparts. The Senate restricted all building construction along the earthen bulwarks to wooden structures."

"Because they want to save the clay bricks for the wall?" ventured Alerio. "Instead of using them to build homes and businesses?"

"No. They have plenty of clay and sand. It's the expense of completing the wall that's holding up progress," explained Thomasious. "The buildings in the Firebreak District to the north and the Fireguard District to the east are built to burn. In case an army attacks the city, the buildings will be set on fire to prevent the enemy from coming over the earthen walls."

"What about the people living and working in those districts?" asked Alerio. "What will happen to them when their homes and businesses are burning?"

"It's why no self-respecting citizen will live in the Firebreak or the Fireguard Districts," explained Thomasious. "Life in the Districts is cheap and temporary. Although the city hasn't been attacked for years, there's still a threat from the far western tribes. But the Consuls and the Senate aren't in any rush to finish the wall."

"One more question Master Harricus," Alerio inquired. "What do you know about the Fireguard Brigade? Specifically, where can I find their leader, Vivianus?"

"They're a nasty gang of shakedown artists," Thomasious explained. "Outside the Fireguard District they mostly run a protection racket. As you witnessed at the Cloth Seller's Shop, they target honest merchants without the means to protect themselves. As far as Vivianus, he holds meetings with his Lieutenants in various pubs. I've heard he picks a different one for each meeting."

"Any chance, the Clay Ear could find out which pub Vivianus will use and when he'll hold the next meeting?" asked Alerio.

"Let me check with the old sage," offered Thomasious.

"Thank you Master Harricus," Alerio said as he stood and turned for the door. "I'm going to try on my new clothes. Afterward, I'm going sightseeing. Oh, and would you ask Erebus to leave the side gate open tonight?"

"More sightseeing?" guessed Thomasious.

"In a way," Alerio replied as he reached the front door. "In a way."

Chapter 15 - New Clothes, Same Old Attitude

"Zacchaeus, the uniform fits great," exclaimed Alerio. He was standing in front of a polished metal plate and admiring the Lance Corporal stripe, the gladius symbol of a weapons instructor, and the Raider ribbon with the rising sun on his shoulder. The green tunic was loose in the shoulders and flowed along his sides without being too tight.

"Now try on the civilian tunics," suggested the old tailor.

The front door opened and closed quickly. Zacchaeus handed the other tunics to Alerio and left to check on the front of his shop. As Alerio slid one of the new tunics over his head, Zacchaeus walked in holding a piece of folded parchment. He walked directly to Alerio and handed over the paper.

'Three days to send me payment and the name of your mercenary,' the badly formed letters spelled out, 'or we burn your building, Vivianus.'

"That's interesting," said Alerio as he handed back the parchment.

"Interesting? Just interesting is all you can say," stammered the tailor. "They're going to burn my business. And they want to know your name."

"This tunic is a little tight through the chest," was all Alerio said.

The tailor reached up and pinched the fabric between his fingers and thumb. After marking the stretched material with the chalk, he let go and slouched.

"We'll talk tomorrow," Alerio assured the old man as he pulled off one and slipped the other tunic over his head. "And by then, maybe we'll have an answer for the Fireguard Brigade."

Alerio tucked the finished clothing under his arm. He left the shop and at the corner turned left. Behind him, Thomasious stood on the porch of the inn watching the young Legionary stroll up the street.

He knew from one of his little ears which pub the Fireguard Brigade was using tonight. It would be easy to pass on the information to the Lance Corporal. Yet, he worried about getting Sisera killed. Maybe he needed a different prospective. Thomasious stepped off the porch and headed over to speak with Zacchaeus at the Cloth Shop.

Alerio continued up the street and tuned the corner at the Historia Fae Armory.

The door opened before he could knock.

"Your gear isn't ready," explained Tomas.

"It seems, I need to have another conversation with the Fireguard Brigade," Alerio reported. "If it's not an imposition, I'll need to take the duel harness for a few hours."

"If you're paying a visit to the Fireguard District," Tomas replied. "I suggest knee and shine guards and a face mask."

"Why? We don't use them in the Legion," Alerio pointed out.

"Because you carry a big shield in the Legion," Tomas explained. "Unless you want to sneak a shield into the District, I recommend leg pieces. Couldn't hurt. The mask is so they don't spot you on the street tomorrow and shove a dagger between your ribs."

Alerio left the Historia Fae with a large leather bag hung over his shoulder. For the rest of the morning and early afternoon, he wandered the city. From the tightly packed workers' homes to the huge public buildings constructed of granite slabs and decorative brickwork to the large villas of the wealthy, he gawked open mouthed. To a farm boy, it was as if he strolled through a dream.

Eventually, he became overwhelmed by the sights and strolled back towards the inn. Detouring to the east, he slowly walked the edge of the Fireguard District. Rather than the tightly packed but unique houses of brick and painted wood in most of the city, housing in the District was chaotic.

Buildings started in one lot, crossed alleys, and rose two more stories over other buildings. Everything was constructed of raw wood and many structures listed threatening to topple over.

Yet people lived there. Children played and their mothers yelled at them from time to time. Men and women left for work or returned from jobs. Among the people striving to live, rough men occupied doorways, or stood in groups eyeing the workers.

A short time later, Alerio opened the door to his room at the Chronicles Humanum Inn. On his bed lay a small piece of parchment. Four words were scrawled on it; The Wine Trough, Tonight.

Act 3

Chapter 16 - Fireguard District

Workmen returning from a day of hard labor assumed one of two postures. Stooped from a day of heavy lifting or carrying as if the muscles were unable to support the weight of the upper body. Or, straight backed and stiff as they attempted to stretch and relieve the tension in their lower backs. Both postures were accompanied by the same gait. A shuffling of feet from legs too worn out from the day's work to lift their feet fully as they walked.

In the dark of early evening, a cloaked man shuffled into the southern end of the Fireguard District. He held himself in an exaggerated upright posture as a laborer would.

As a farm boy, Alerio was familiar with both postures. After a hard day in the fields, he had assumed both. For entry into the District, the stiff backed worked best for hiding the duel gladius rig strapped low on his back. No one looked closely at the returning workman. It was best in Fireguard to blend in and avoid contact of any kind with strangers.

The Capital City was a wonder of urban engineering. Avenues and streets ran straight, even over the high hills and through the valleys. One could cross the city and never make a turn. The layout was designed so a defending Legion could move rapidly from one section of the wall to the defense of another section.

At first glance, Fireguard's streets seemed to be illogical. Unlike the city's roads, Fireguard's twisted and turned like roots on a tree. Some ended in alleyways, others branched haphazardly, and some stopped abruptly at dead ends. As if the buildings were logs placed and stacked for a camp fire, the District had many passageways. Some alleys were just wide enough for a single person to squeeze through as if they were only there to allow air flow to feed a fire. Maybe it was an example of a different kind of urban engineering.

Alerio had slipped through five of the narrow alleys. At the mouth of each, he stood in the shadows and studied the streets. Shops for vendors selling used goods and fresh produce, eating establishments, and pubs shared the ground floor with apartments. Exterior stairs of rickety wood gave access to apartments on the upper floors. So far, none of the pubs were The Wine Trough and he was half way into the southern end of the Fireguard District.

Impulsively, he skipped through five more alleys and crossed streets giving them only cursory glances. Each street resembled the next and none had the pub where the Fireguard Brigade was supposed to meet. At the mouth of the sixth alleyway, he looked across open ground at a steep wall of dirt.

High above street level, torches blazed ominously every fifty feet along the top of the earthen wall. With little effort, a single Legionary could set fire to Fireguard District by jogging along the top, snatching up torches, and throwing them onto the roofs of the buildings. The District would burn so fast many of its citizens would perish in the flames before they could flee to the clay brick portion of the city.

During the trip through the District, voices of men, women and children had mixed with the shouts of vendors. The noise levels of tightly packed humans, living in close proximally, was almost nonexistent near the earth wall. Maybe, they understood living in the first area to burn was tantamount to a death sentence.

But, there were sounds of laughter and voices echoing off the earth embankment. Looking up, Alerio spied wide porches on the third floor of the buildings. From that height, the view would be over the wall. During the day, an observer could see farms, Legion Posts, and the clay and steel furnaces to the east. At night, it was the only place in Fireguard where the moon and stars were visible.

Alerio walked along the rear of the buildings. There were no doors or windows facing the earthen rampart, yet above, there were porches. He paused and listened below each porch. Loud voices carried down from the first three. At the fourth porch, the voices became muffled as if the speakers were talking in conversational tones. At the fifth and sixth porches, the volume increased to a level matching that of the other drinking establishments.

Chapter 17 - The Wine Trough

Ducking into the alley between the fourth and fifth buildings, Alerio walked to the street. Taking the stairs at the fifth building, he climbed to the third floor landing.

None of the noises from the porches reached the street side of the buildings. A few sounds emitted from the apartments on the third floor, but they were muffled. In fact, the widely spaced doors on the third floor suggested larger apartments. Alerio imagined the advertisement: Large rooms in a tinder box; enjoy the luxury before you burn to death.

Alerio stepped up on the railing of the landing and stretched until his finger gripped the roof's edge. He pulled and swung his body to the side. The first swing carried his legs within two feet of the roof. On the second swing, his right leg reached the roof and he placed a foot on the boards. The other foot followed and he walked his feet up the roof while pulling up his torso. A final pull and his hips crossed over the edge. Now with most of his body on the roof, Alerio was able to slide back until his entire body lay on the roof.

The jump from building five to four was easy for a Legionary. One of the exercises required by the Legion was the broad jump. Whether for fitness or to practice vaulting over an enemy's trench, all Legionaries competed for rations in the broad jump. He landed lightly on building four.

Alerio casually walked across the roof to the rear of the building as if out for an evening stroll. Near the edge, he dropped to his belly, and crawled forward until his ear hung over the roof. From porches on buildings to either side, the sounds of clay mugs clinging and loud voices talking carried into the night. On the porch below him, the voices were muted.

Alerio had figured the porches were prime real estate and for one to be quiet meant it was reserved for a private party. Or cleared for a meeting of the Fireguard Brigade. From below, softly spoken words drifted up to Alerio.

"Collections are up," a man with a rough voice announced. "We have five blocks of clients under our protection."

"What about the Cloth Seller?" a cultured voice inquired. "From the limp, I can see you've had a small issue."

"Once we learn the name of his mercenary," grumbled the rough voice. "We'll take him out and double the old tailor's fee."

"And who will kill the mercenary?" the cultured voice pondered. "It seems to me you had a chance and failed miserably."

"We'll use the whole crew. We'll ambush him," the rough voice replied. "After, it'll be back to business as usual."

"There is no business as usual in our business," corrected the cultured voice. "I will not risk our entire team. So far, this mercenary has tangled with six of our men and we've come up woefully short. No, learn his name and I'll contract with the Cruor for the killing."

A shiver ran down Alerio's spine. The Cruor, Spilled Blood, had a price on his head of seven Republic gold. If the man below knew it, he could exchange the fee for killing him to a reward for finding him.

Yet, the conversation did reveal something. A savvy businessman rather than a bloodthirsty thug led the Fireguard Brigade.

"Ah boss, we can handle one man," bemoaned the rough voice. "I want another stab at him."

"As my chief enforcer, I appreciate your dedication," the cultured voice replied. "But, I can't risk you suffering more than a broken foot. I need you on the streets collecting our coin, not in a mortuary. A dead man can't collect fees. No, we'll hire professionals. It'll be more cost effective."

"Vivianus, you always know best," the rough voice said as a chair scraped and the sound of someone tapping with a cane faded.

"Don't we already pay the Cruor a cut for the territory?" asked a new deep voice. "Why pay them more for something I can do?"

"We do and it's a good working agreement," the cultured voice replied. "You're my bodyguard and I don't want you mixed up in Brigade business. Now, how many more of these morons do I have to placate before I can get back to the villa?"

58

"One more," the deep voice growled. "He's in charge of your gambling house in the District."

"Fine, fine, call him forward," the cultured voice whined. A few seconds later his tone changed as he greeted the new man, "Ah, my favorite croupier. Please have good tidings for me."

"If you mean are we making coin? Then, yeah, our earnings from the gambling house are ahead of last year," a silky voice replied.

"Excellent my good man," the cultured voice said. "What can I do for you?"

"We had to rough up a few cheaters," the silky voice replied. "Now the City Guard is snooping around. Can you bribe them or scare them off? Anything to keep them out of our business."

"I'll see what I can do," the cultured voice promised. "And let me also tell you how pleased I am by your dedication to our enterprise."

"Okay. That's all I need," silky voice said brushing off the compliment. A chair scrapped marking his departure.

The cultured voice was silent for a moment before stating, "I don't care for the man's attitude. I'll have to look around for a replacement. My croupier is starting to think for himself."

"He could disappear," offered the deep voice.

"Not until I find someone else to run the gaming," cultured voice said. "Now, I've had enough. Let's go."

Alerio pushed back from the edge of the roof. He backtracked to the front of the building, moved to the gap, and jumped over to building five. He descended quickly taking the stairs to the street two at a time. On the street, he quickly crossed to the other side and disappeared in the shadows of an alleyway.

Five men climbed down the stairs from the third floor of building four. At the bottom, four of them shifted into a star formation surrounding the man in the middle. With a guard ahead, one behind, and a man to either side, it wasn't a far reach to identify the center man as being important. The mask over his face further confirmed his significance.

Alerio focused on the faces of the four guards. One, he figured was the deep voiced guy. While he couldn't verify the masked man as Vivianus, the leader of the gang, he was positive the personal bodyguard was one of the four.

Using good security, they marched down the center of the street. At a random alleyway, the group shifted to two in front and two behind as they entered the narrow space.

Alerio hung back but paced with the unit. When they turned into the alley, he started to race ahead. Except, the alley wasn't chosen by chance. A man on a crutch, with a heavily bandaged right foot, shifted to block the way. What were the chances a man lounging at the mouth of this passageway had a broken right foot?

Slowing his pace, Alerio approached the entrance causally.

"Use a different route," warned the man blocking the alley.

"Pardon?" asked Alerio as if he were hard of hearing.

To confirm the deafness, Alerio leaned from the waist and cupped his ear with his right hand. "What did you say?" he demanded.

As many people do, when confronted by an unexpected situation, the man looked to the sky, as if to ask the gods, why me?

Jupiter, the God of lightning and thunder, replied. A left uppercut to the man's jaw delivered by Alerio was the answer to the man's prayer. The punch lifted the man off his crutch. The crutch and the unconscious man hit the ground at the same time.

Alerio rushed into the alley. At the next street, he looked for the formation. There was no sign of the five men. This was a dead end street with three alleyways connecting the thoroughfare to other parts of Fireguard District.

One alley ran southwards towards the tradesmen compounds. The west alley headed to the section of the city with middleclass homes. On his right was an alleyway heading northwest. In that direction were the villas of the wealthy. Alerio raced to the right.

Chapter 18 - Villas of the Influential

Alerio didn't locate the five men until he sprinted down six more alleyways. Emerging from the final alley at the edge of Fireguard, he spotted the men. Only four were crossing the dark road.

One guard had dropped out of formation and stepped to the side of a building. He delayed in turning to watch the exit from the District as he stared at the men crossing the road. Maybe he was thinking he should be paid more and wanted to ask for a raise. Or maybe he wanted to go with the others to bask in the splendor of the neighborhoods with the large villas. The rear guard didn't get a chance to explain his motivation.

When he finally turned, he came face to face with a cloaked figure. Alerio's fingers laced together behind the man's head, and with force, pulled the head downward. As the rear guard's face dropped from the pressure, Alerio raised his armored knee. The resulting collision wasn't an even match. The guard's face indented and his brain shutdown from shock and pain.

Alerio let the limp body fall and started to cross the road. By now, the unit was down to three men. Somewhere ahead, another of the guards had dropped out. Lurking in the shadows, he waited to stab anyone attempting to follow the gang leader.

The street was empty and dark except for pools of light from lanterns. The lights hung from the sides of craftsmen compounds at the start of the street. Further up the hill, as the walls grew higher to reflect the increasing size of the villas, the light from the lanterns left wider zones of darkness.

Alerio dashed across the road leaving the Fireguard District behind and entering the edge of the city. He hugged the tradesmen building and moved to the intersecting street. After pulling off his cloak and tying it around his waist, he slid the mask down over his face. Just before stepping into the street, Alerio reached over his shoulders and drew both gladii.

While the sentry was armed and ready to engage a tracker following the masked man, he wasn't ready for an armed Legionary. He led with the point of his short sword, but it deflected off the leather armor. The only damage was a slit in the leather. The damage to him occurred when two gladii slapped him on either side of his head. He fell to the clay brick pavers with blood streaming from both ears.

Alerio sprinted to the next intersection. The three remaining men were strolling down the middle of the road as if taking in the evening air. Alerio followed the men as they faded and reappeared in the lantern light. The gladii were sheathed and Alerio untied the cloak and tossed it over his shoulders.

He followed them by staying close to a villa's wall. They were walking causally northward. As near as Alerio could remember, the City Guard's headquarters were three blocks to the west with the Capital Building across a boulevard and two blocks beyond it. The three men reached another cross street and turned left.

62

When Alerio arrived, he found the street crowded by people out for an evening stroll. Vendor carts sat in the center of the street selling grilled meats and vegetables, vino and ales. Alerio loitered at the corner.

Just as the three men reached the next cross street, one stepped to the side of the road. As the last two turned right, the sentry stared down the block directly at the intersection where Alerio stood.

Unable to follow without being seen, Alerio stepped out from the wall, turned away from the sentry, and wandered over to a food cart.

"Sausage?" asked the merchant holding up a delicious smelling piece of meat on a stick.

Alerio ignored the vendor as he walked behind the cart and joined the flow of people walking westward. As he approached the other side of the street, he ducked out of the flow, and jogged down the pavers. Now he was running on the street parallel with the last two men.

The next street lead to the City Guard compound before intersecting with the boulevard across from the Capital Building. He didn't break stride but continued on to the end of the next block. There, he slowed as he made a left turn.

Tall walls of huge villas loomed over the dark street. As he approached the next cross street, Alerio stopped and peered around the corner. Two men were strolling towards him. He couldn't tell if they were the men he'd followed from The Wine Trough. Not until the tall, broad shouldered man spoke.

"Is there anything you need me to do tonight?" the man asked in a deep familiar voice.

"No. I have some writing to do before I turn in," the shorter and more slightly built man replied in a cultured voice. "Are you going out?"

"Once I check the guard assignments for tonight," the bodyguard answered.

"Ah, to be young on a night like this," the cultured voice said. "Thank you for your service tonight."

The two men reached the street where Alerio squatted next to the wall. They turned left. Alerio eased up once their backs were to him. He gave them a few paces before following them westward. If they crossed the wide boulevard, his chase would end. There was no way to follow in the open space.

They didn't cross the boulevard. At the end of the looming wall, the men turned left and approached the gate of the villa.

"Good night, Senator Ventus," the bodyguard said.

"Good evening to you, Master Gabrielus," stated Senator Ventus, also known as, Vivianus, the leader of the Fireguard Brigade.

Alerio backed away from the corner. When he felt safe, he spun and jogged down the street. Sweat broke out on his forehead. The sweat wasn't from the night's activity. It was from being involved in the politics he had tried to avoid.

Chapter 19 - Thomasious Harricus, Proprietor, Writer and Gossip

Thomasious Harricus was a lifelong resident of the Capital City. As a young man, his father and grandfather hired tutors from the east. While they served in the Republic's Legions, they wanted to be sure Thomasious had an education and, options other than a career in the military. Based on the superb education, young Thomasious envisioned a future as a scholar and, maybe later, as a politician.

His father also had a dream. After his final term of enlistment, the senior Harricus' only desire was to open an inn in the Capital. He went as far as having a classical building designed. Plus, a compound populated with corrals, stables, out buildings, a cook shed and a bathhouse.

During his last year as a Legionary, he led two Centuries on a quest to eradicate a tribe of northern barbarians. Except when they arrived, it wasn't a single tribe standing in their way.

Five years earlier, the Republic had pushed the tribes off their land and driven them deeper into the northern territory. The Consuls' decree cited state security as the reason for advancing the Republic's borders. While the government profited from the newly conquered land, one family in particular grew wealthy from harvesting lumber, mining iron ore, and taking barbarians as slaves from the lands. The source of their wealth was shut off when all the northern tribes banded together and pushed the Legion back across the original border. During one of the battles, Thomasious' father was killed.

Thomasious in his grief and anger went to see his grandfather. At the old man's farm, he professed his hatred for the barbarians and informed the old Legionary of his intention to join the Legion. During a night of intense conversation, his grandfather begged the young scholar to wait six months. If, after that time, Thomasious still wanted it, the old man would buy him a position as a Tribune in the northern Legion.

On Thomasious' trip back through the city, he passed ten Cavalry Officers who were in the city as escorts for their Legion's General, Major General and Colonel. At first, he envied the romance of their duties and assignment. Then, it began to rain. A cold, hard driving rain that lashed the young Officers as they attempted to set up a ten-man Legion tent in the howling wind.

In his warm and dry apartment, Thomasious started a fire with the kindling he kept in his room. As he shrugged off his cloak, his eyes locked onto his father's plans for an inn in the city. Anger guided him. He marched to the plans, snatched it from the desk, and began wadding up the parchment. He intended to add it to the fire when a drop of cold rain fell from his wet hair onto his cheek. Then, he remembered the cavalrymen camping on a public square in the Capital City.

Their senior Officers would be wined, dined, and put up in villas of the influential. The escorts, the junior Officers and senior NCOs, would be left to fend for themselves in the crowded city. Thomasious stood staring at the fire with the crumpled plans in his hands.

His damp hair dried before realizing he still held the plans. Gently, he laid the plans on his desk and began smoothing out the wrinkles. Once it was mostly flat, he selected a quill and began to draw on the plans. By morning, the out buildings on the site plan remained untouched. The classical design of the inn, however, had been transformed. Most inns in the city fell into two categories. The ones for sailors, Legionaries, and workmen were located near the dock warehouses. These inns crowded bodies into group sleeping rooms with little privacy, less security, and no services. The other type of inn was closer to the Capital building and offered amenities equal to the coin a visiting dignitary was willing to spend. A fancy, high value inn with the classical columns was his father's dream. Thomasious had a different idea.

Three days later, he was back at his grandfather's farm discussing a loan. Within a month, construction started on a piece of ground in the tradesmen area just south of east gate. As the bricks were laid and the building rose, Thomasious named it the Chronicles Humanum Inn.

There was a reason the scholar used the name. Not only would Thomasious run the inn, he would listen to his guest, the Legionary Officers and senior NCOs. They enjoyed talking after a day of escorting senior Officers to high level meeting with Senators and senate secretaries. In the evenings, while they talked, he would ask innocent questions. From these conversations, he wrote sharp political commentaries in chain scrolls as the Clay Ear.

Sometime in the first year, a lad showed up asking for a handout. Thomasious discovered from the beggar a tale about a shipping Merchant's wife who was enamored by a rogue with a gambling problem. He hand-copied the story on four scrolls and told the street urchin to find four friends who could sell the scrolls at the wealthiest villas. To his surprise, the lad returned at dusk with twelve Republic coppers, and four additional street kids. Each had a story overheard while maids went about their tasks outside the villas. Thusly, the Clay Ear began to create and distribute the enormously profitable and very much in demand gossip scrolls.

Chapter 20 – Thomasious Harricus' Father

Three years after opening the Chronicles Humanum Inn, a huge northern barbarian stomped into the great room.

"Harricus?" asked the large man shaking a shaggy mane of blond hair.

The innkeeper's senses came to full alert. His father had been killed fighting one of these northern brutes and this one was asking for him by name.

"Who wants to know?" challenged Thomasious.

"Harricus. I will speak with Harricus," growled the barbarian.

"Why do you want to speak with Harricus?" demanded Thomasious.

From a large sack slung over his shoulder, the barbarian pulled a sheathed gladius. Thomasious braced preparing to fend off an attack if the brute drew the sword. He didn't. After laying the weapon on the marble counter top the barbarian stepped back.

"My name is Erebus," explained the barbarian. "I seek the son of the man who saved my life; to him, I return his father's gladius."

"Let me fetch us beverages," Thomasious offered. "And you can tell me how my father saved your life."

They sat at a table with clay mugs of vino. With Thomasious' hand resting on his father's gladius, he listened.

Erebus told of the fighting retreat from the first battle on the northern frontier. Erebus was a scout for the Legion. When the tribes descended on the outnumbered Centuries, the Scout caught a spear in his upper thigh. Being from a tribe to the east, he wasn't related to the northern tribes. The tribes had fought border wars for eons so Erebus was an enemy long before he volunteered to help the Legion.

As he lay on the forest floor, bleeding and unable to move, a Legionary rushed to his side. He screamed when the spear was pulled out and again when the Legionary hoisted the Scout onto his shoulder armor.

The Legionary line fought and stepped back. At any moment, Erebus expected to be tossed aside. But, the Legionary continued to shout orders, fight, and organize the Centuries, all while carrying the Scout.

The Legionaries fought sword-to-sword, spear against shield all the way down a steep hill. Above them, scattered on the slope, lay dead and dying Legionaries and barbarians. Yet, Erebus remained on the broad shoulders of the Legionary until reinforcements arrived and beat back the barbarians.

Even then, Erebus wasn't cast aside. He was carried to a Legion hospital tent. When he healed, the Scout went looking for his savior. He located the Legionary in the midst of another battle. Before Erebus could reach Thomasious' father, a barbarian's sword crushed Harricus' helmet and dropped him to the ground.

This time it was the Scout carrying the wounded Legionary as the Legion fought and stepped back. At the hospital tent, Harricus woke up just long enough to make a request.

"Take my gladius to my son," the Legionary whispered before his life force left him.

It had taken Erebus a year to get his separation papers from the Legion and two more years to walk to the Capital City to complete the task.

"Where will you go now?" Thomasious asked.

"I have no plans," admitted Erebus.

"Stay and work at the inn," offered Thomasious.

"If you are half the man Harricus was," replied Erebus. "It'll be an honor."

Chapter 21 - Sage Advice from the Clay Ear

Thomasious Harricus balanced running the inn with the political and gossip writings of his alto ego, the Clay Ear, by sticking to a schedule. Late into the evenings, he was the friendly proprietor and questioning host. Early afternoons, he was the Clay Ear with the poison and biting quill. During the day, he was the booking agent and supply manager for the inn. As part of the schedule, every morning he woke early, poured a mug of wine, added water, and went to the empty great room. There, he'd sit and watch the city awaken while he collected himself for another day.

With a mug of watered vino in hand, Thomasious walked through the sleeping inn. He pushed opened the double doors expecting to find an empty great room. It wasn't empty.

In a corner table without a view, the young Lance Corporal sat with his head cradled in his hands.

"Rough night?" Thomasious inquired as he pulled out a chair.

"Master Harricus. What do you know about Senator Ventus?" replied Alerio without lifting his head.

"The other night he was arguing with now deceased Senator Faunus," Thomasious stated. "If you're looking for more, I'll need a point of reference."

"Why would a Senator of the Republic also be head of the Fireguard Brigade?" questioned Alerio. Also in the measured, I really don't want to say this tone, he explained. "Vivianus is Senator Ventus and he runs the Brigade. Is that a good starting point?"

"You claim the honorable Senator Ventus is the crime boss Vivianus?" Thomasious challenged. "And how would you know this?"

"I followed him and his bodyguard, Gabrielus, from the Wine Trough," said Alerio. "Followed them from the Fireguard District to his villa. No doubt, Ventus and Vivianus are the same man."

Thomasious was silent for so long Alerio looked up to see if the innkeeper was asleep.

Last night, when Alerio returned to the inn from tracking Senator Ventus, or Vivianus, he stowed away his armor and stretched out on the bed. After tossing and turning, he got up and got dressed. No one was around so he took this seat and tried to figure out what to do with the information.

"I almost didn't believe you," admitted Thomasious. "But, you knew the northern bodyguard's name. Gabrielus is at the Senator's side to and from the Senate and at all social functions. Something odd does occur to me."

"Something, I hope, like how to get Zacchaeus and me out of this war with the Fireguard Brigade," ventured Alerio.

"Zacchaeus' a crusty old merchant," Thomasious confided. "He'll survive. It's you who needs advice. As the reclusive Clay Ear, I would advise you to run. But that's not what I was thinking about."

Alerio waited as Thomasious sat as still as a clay brick. Finally, the innkeeper nodded his head as if he'd reached some sort of decision.

"I once considered joining the Legion," confessed Thomasious. "But, after seeing what the Legionaries endured, I realized it wasn't for me. Instead, I built this inn to give junior Officers and NCOs a quality place to stay. For my duty to the Republic, I use the Clay Ear to keep citizens informed about what goes on in the Senate."

"That's all very interesting Master Harricus," said Alerio. "but what does it have to do with this situation?"

"My father was killed when the northern tribes pushed back the Legion," Thomasious said with his voice cracking from

71

emotion. Alerio started to express his condolences, but Thomasious held up a hand to keep the young man quiet. "When the Republic lost the lumber and iron ore from the north, one family suffered the biggest financial losses. By the time the war began, the family had put their eldest son in the Senate. When the Legion established a defensive line in the flatlands beyond the barbarian's mountains, the family petitioned the Consuls for more men and money for the northern Legion. They wanted the mines and forests back but the Senate and the Consuls resisted the political and economic pressure."

"I'm guessing it was Senator Ventus' family," ventured Alerio. "So he turned to crime to keep his coffers full of coin. It makes sense."

"By the time the barbarians pushed the Legion back, the Ventus' had invested in shipping and trading," Thomasious stated. "Financially, they were secure. Of course, they missed the prestige of having massive amounts of coin rolling in yearly. But, according to my sources, Senator Ventus is very wealthy."

"Could he be raising money for a Legion?" asked Alerio. "A Legion to take back the northern region."

"This is the odd thing I was referring to," explained Thomasious. "Two years ago the Consuls asked the Senate to debate the issue of retaking the north. It split the Senate down the middle and lines were drawn. Senator Faunus, who was killed, was pro invasion. Senator Ventus, whose family gained wealth and power from the region, led the opposition. The final vote from the Senate to the Consuls' question was no to restarting the northern campaign."

"Wouldn't Senator Ventus' family still have ownership of the mines and the land?" Alerio surmised. "If the Republic reclaimed the region?"

"His parents are dead so the grants would all transfer to him. And that's the puzzling aspect of this," Thomasious said. "Ventus seems ambitious. His speeches are well attended. He's popular with the citizens. With the extra coin from the north, he could bribe his way to being President of the Senate. As it is, he seems comfortable chairing a few committees. As a matter of fact, Senator Ventus is a sponsor of this week's games and festival."

"What games?" asked Alerio. "What festival?"

"The Consuls have ordered a celebration of Janus," Thomasious explained. "In three days, the area outside the east gate will be transformed from pasture land to festival grounds. You know with the usual competitions, plays and acts. Every citizen will be there. I understand, the commanders of the central Legion have been invited to be Marshals of the games."

"A festival honoring the god of change and new beginnings," Alerio inquired. "Is it an annual event?"

"No. This is the first time the Consuls have recognized the deity with a festival," replied Thomasious. "There are openings in the sword fighting tournament. As a gladius instructor, would you consider entering?"

"No, Master Harricus," Alerio replied as he pulled up his right sleeve to display the double line of scars. "These are from Daedalus of the City Guard. I can't be publicly announced or the next time, someone will put the scars on my heart."

"Funny you should mention Daedalus," Thomasious stated. "Senator Ventus' bodyguard Gabrielus and the Corporal trained together when the northerner came to the city. Rumor has it, Gabrielus' father is a King of the Insubri. As a teenager, he was sent to the City as a hostage to be sure his father respected the newly formed northern border."

73

"A northern royal hostage is the bodyguard for a Senator of the Republic?" gasped an astonished Alerio. "You know Master Harricus, I may be just a simple farm boy. But, even I know the difference between a sheared sheep and a scrawny goat."

"What is the difference?" asked Thomasious.

"In a few months, one will grow back thick, rich wool," stated Alerio. "while the other, in a few months, will still be a skinny goat."

"I don't understand," complained the innkeeper.

"Breeding Master Harricus, it comes down to breeding," explained Alerio. "No matter how an animal looks, it doesn't change the creature's nature."

"I'll see what I can find out about Senator Ventus' activities," promised Thomasious. "And get some information on his opposition in the Senate. And what specific issues they disagree on."

Act 4

Chapter 22 - Heat, Time and Muscle

Alerio strolled away from the Chronicles Humanum Inn, two blocks up the road, he rounded the channeling defensive wall, and headed for the eastern gate. He'd changed into his new clothing. After eating breakfast, he set out for a day of exploring. The City Guardsman, noticing the finely tailored tunic and not sure of the young man's social status, saluted as he passed.

The road outside the gate ran Republic straight. In the far distance, he could see the tents of a Legion Transfer Post. Closer to the city, workmen dug post holes and hammered in pegs as they built the rough planked stands for the games and festival. Although he gawked at the construction, the festival honoring Janus wasn't his destination.

A quarter of a mile outside the city, Alerio turned right and walked to the top of a rise. From the knoll, he could see the wide Tiber river as it meandered to the sea. Sailing ships and rowed vessels moved towards the city's docks with raw materials, or sailed away from the docks carrying goods to cities throughout the Republic.

A stream running toward the big river showed marks left by picks and shovels on the plain surrounding it.

What had once been a natural tributary, with steep banks, was now a broad flat of exposed clay. A dam created a small lake and only a trickle was allowed to flow down a narrow serpentine channel. Workers carried buckets of water and slabs of clay from the excavated area.

The heavily loaded workers disappeared from view behind a stockade wall. All around the hill and the land to the east, the wooden wall blocked the view of what lay inside. A hint was the tops of high brick domes appearing above the walls. The domes were the purpose for Alerio leaving the city.

He walked down the hill and entered the open stockade gate. In front of each dome, workers mixed clay, sand, and straw while liberally sprinkling the elements with water. Once the mixture was pliable, it was pounded into forms. When each of the six squares in a form was full, another worker would scrap off any excess wet clay. The form with the six raw clay bricks was then carried into a dome.

"Heat, over time, bakes the bricks into manmade stones that will last for hundreds of years," a familiar voice stated from behind him. "Any savage can blend clay, sand and straw. Turning the soft clay into solid building material is a talent."

"Good morning, Master Kellerian," Alerio said while turning around to greet the broad shouldered armorer, "What brings you out this morning? Certainly not clay bricks?"

"Not bricks, Lance Corporal Sisera," Tomas stated while laying a hand on Alerio's shoulder. He guided the young man around the domes.

"Steel brings me here this morning. Like clay bricks, anybody can gather the raw materials. And like bricks, it takes heat and time to make steel," the armorer explained. "But, there is another element beyond skill. You need muscle to make steel."

On the other side of the huge brick drying domes, Alerio and Tomas found an open field dotted with relatively tiny domes. These domes, much smaller than the kilns for bricks, were constructed of bricks with clay packed between and over the bricks. A round clay tube ran from the base of the domes to goatskin sacks stretched between stick frames. The sticks were mashed together forcing air from the goatskin sack into the clay tube. With each movement, flames rose from the tops of the small domes.

"Iron ore is dropped into each dome," said Tomas. "Charcoal is added and encouraged to burn hot by the bellows. The ore is heated until the iron forms a blossom in the bottom of the dome."

"And the blossom is steel?" guessed Alerio.

"No. What comes out is a mess of impurities surrounding a core of pure iron," explained Tomas. "Come on, I'll show you steel."

Beyond the small domes, flat metal slabs were stationed around the floor of an opened air hut. Men with iron hammers took turns pounding on ugly misshapen hunks of black material. As they hammered, pieces flew off until a solid, but much smaller, piece of iron remained.

"That's iron," advised Tomas. "It's relatively soft and you wouldn't want to fight with a gladius made of wrought iron. It would snap or bend on the first strike."

"So there's more to the process?" asked Alerio.

The armorer nodded and led them through the hut. They circled around a brick wall and walked into the heat of a thousand suns.

Alerio almost stumbled from the intensity of the heat. Two brick squares resembling wells were the source of the heat. Each square had a low dome supported by four columns. Three clay tubes ran out a long distance to giant bellows. The distance from the furnace gave the two men on each of the bellows some relief from the heat.

"Charcoal," shouted a large man. In response, two men rushed in and shoveled broken chunks of charcoal into the wells. "Air," the man yelled and the bellows began pumping.

Flames rose until the area between the bed of the wells and the low roofs resembled the center of hades itself. The bellows pumped, the air flowed, and the fire changed colors reflecting zones of heat.

The large furnace foreman walked around the wells watching and judging the quality of the flames. He seemed satisfied and stepped back.

"Turn," ordered the furnace foreman. Two men grabbed long iron poles. They put the tips into the flames and, with surprisingly gentle pushes, they rolled clay eggs a quarter turn.

The eggs were as big around as a man's chest and as long as an arm. Once the eggs had been turned, the foremen shouted, "Charcoal."

While the men raced forward to brave the heat and feed the fire, Tomas guided Alerio past another brick wall. After the waves of heat, the midmorning air seemed cool and a shiver ran through Alerio.

They entered another open-air hut. Broken clay eggs littered the floor, their exteriors blackened from the intense heat of the wells. A thin layer of metal coated the cavities in the center of the broken eggs.

Open topped furnaces sat on each side of the hut. Workers pumped air into the charcoal, and while hot in the center of the wells, they didn't emit the intense heat of the wells where the eggs were baked.

Two stations in front of each well had balls of metal on slabs of hardened iron. Two men took turns striking the balls of metal until the balls began to flatten and stretch. Every so often, a worker would pick up the metal with tongs and hold it in the center of a furnace. When they pulled it out, the metal glowed red hot. It was again laid on the hardened iron slab and the pounding continued.

"That's steel," announced Tomas pointing to the metal so hard it took two men to pound it into a shape.

"What else was placed in the egg with the iron?" asked Alerio. "It had to be an exotic ore. Or something rare for the alchemy to work. What changes soft iron into steel hard enough to make a quality gladius?"

"Come with me and all shall be revealed," Tomas whispered as if the additive to create steel was a closely guarded secret.

They left the noise and rhythm of men beating metal and walked around a divider wall. Alerio's nose was assaulted long before he saw what a team of men was doing. One squatted pounding dried animal bones into powder. Another took scoops of the ground bone and sprinkled in finely mashed charcoal. A final man took a ladle of urine and sprinkled it over the powders. He mixed the items together. Then he smeared the paste around a misshapen piece of iron.

"Ground bone and charcoal?" asked Alerio in disgust. "That's the secret to turning iron into steel?"

"And cow's urine. One mustn't forget the urine," Tomas stated with a self-satisfied smile on his face. "In the intense heat of the clay egg, the iron absorbs the mash. Somehow, it makes steel."

"I don't understand," admitted Alerio as he glanced around at the workers.

"You said it yourself," Tomas replied.

"Said what?" asked Alerio

"Alchemy, Lance Corporal Sisera, it's alchemy," said Tomas. "Now I've got to ask the foreman which eggs have the best steel. You can tag along if you like."

"Thank you Master Kellerian for the lessen and the offer," Alerio said. "But, I learned enough mysteries of the universe for one day. I think I'll head back to the city."

"Bring your duel rig to me when you're finished playing with the street gang," Tomas teased as he walked back towards the egg baking station. "So I can get it fitted on the armor."

Alerio waved at the armorer and took a route that hugged the stockade wall. It would keep him far away from the waves of heat. Once out of the clay ovens and steel furnaces area, he headed back towards the city.

Chapter 23 - Street Crime and The City Guard

Alerio stood transfixed at the crossroads of the north-south and the east-west boulevards. The fountain in the center of the thoroughfares' roundabout proved to be more breathtaking up close. While the view from far down the boulevard made the statues of the horses appear spectacular, standing and craning his neck allowed for a full view of the magnificent sculptures. Adding to the experience, a spray of mist blew off the jets of water. It felt as if he were standing near a natural waterfall instead of in the center of the Capital.

After circling the fountain five times so he could gaze at every angle of the statues, Alerio headed north towards the Capital building.

Inside the huge building were chambers for the Senate and the two Consuls who ran the city and, by extension, the Republic. Tree lined walks and grassy areas surrounded the building for two blocks in every direction.

Across from the Capital grounds and also two blocks long were the City Guard Headquarters. As it should be for security reasons, the Guard needed only to cross the broad boulevard and the grassy area to reach the Government building. There they could defend the government officials and, by default, the Republic from attack.

Alerio strolled the length of the landscaped grounds and continued on for another block. Across the boulevard were the walls of Senator Ventus' villa. The visible part of the villa rising above the walls was constructed of brick with clay shingles on the roof. Few of the massive homes used brick for the second floor. While bricking the entire villa was impressive, it was also expensive.

A carriage gate opened onto the boulevard and two men-at-arms stood at the opening. Both guards were big and blond obviously from the northern territories.

Alerio didn't see the Senator or, his bodyguard Gabrielus and he didn't stay around to watch for them. The Lance Corporal simply eyed the villa as he turned off the boulevard.

A block later, he took a left on a wide street where the walls of large villas created a canyon. At the end of the street, he could see the Capital grounds and the Capital Building.

Vendor carts occupied the roadsides at the end of the street. Some carts had braziers with roasting meats, others with bread and cakes, while others sold wine.

Alerio was half the distance to the last cart when two men began arguing with a vendor on the corner. Not wanting to get involved, he crossed to the other side of the street.

One of the men pulled an iron knife and threatened the vendor. His accomplice began calling other vendors over to witness the dishonesty of the vendor. Five of the sellers deserted their carts to get a better look at the altercation and to hear the story. The voices of the arguing man and the vendor reached a high pitch as each got hotter and more animated. More vendors left their carts to see the show. Alerio continued his stroll down the far side of the street.

Ten youths raced from around the corner and suddenly, the empty carts had customers. Except, the lads weren't paying. They grabbed as much food as they could carry and dashed towards Alerio. The absentee vendors began shouting and calling for the City Guard.

From the manicured lawn of the Capital grounds, four-armed City Guardsmen raced to aid the vendors. But, the young thieves weren't sticking around. Alerio didn't want to get involved and was fine when the last lad, his hands holding the ends of a hot metal rod that ran through a whole roasted ham, ran by. Alerio laughed as the ham was bigger than the lad's chest.

The Guards crossed the street and the vendors all pointed at the retreating boys. One vendor indicated the men who were arguing. Another motioned for the Guards to stop Alerio.

"He's part of the gang," the vendor announced. "I saw him laughing at the theft."

The two arguing men spun, shoved aside a vendor, and raced towards Alerio. Out of instinct, he put out a foot and tripped one of them. The man sprawled face first on the brick pavers while his companion continued to run.

"Stay there," a Guard ordered as he and two others tried to sort out the vendor's stories. It seemed they all had a different version and wanted to be the first to explain. The result was unintelligible mad chatter.

The fourth Guard had his gladius in hand as he approached Alerio and the man on the ground.

"Don't move," the Guard ordered.

Alerio had no reason to resist. He was an innocent bystander and was sure the City Guard would understand.

Then, four more City Guardsmen appeared on the Capital grounds. A Corporal ran beside them and suddenly Alerio had a reason to resist.

Corporal Daedalus knew Alerio's face and name. He also knew about the bounty of seven Republic golds for Alerio, dead or alive, offered by the Cruor Syndicate. As a matter of fact, Daedalus had tried to collect the reward during a sword completion.

Alerio's right foot shot out kicking the Guard's blade to the side. Two quick steps brought him inside the gladius' tip and within elbow's distance from his chin. Alerio's forearm connected with the Guard's chin and the man jerked back and plopped down on his backside.

Seeing the City Guardsman dumped on his butt, the man on the ground jumped to his feet and ran towards the end of the street. Alerio was right on his heels.

From behind, Alerio heard the City Guardsmen yelling for the fleeing men to halt. What he couldn't see was Corporal Daedalus shaking his head as he attempted to recall where he'd seen the young man in the quality tunic before. As he stopped to consult with his Guardsmen, the Corporal recalled a snot nosed kid who, rather than die properly, had embarrassed him in an arena. And he remembered the seven Republic gold bounty. The only drawback, he couldn't remember the kid's name.

"Private. Once we get this sorted out," Daedalus directed one of his guardsman. "I need you to go to the western Legion Transfer Post. Find Corporal Gratian. Ask him for the name of the kid I fought at the tournament."

"The one where you were hurt?" asked the Private.

"Yes. The one where I was hurt," Daedalus replied obviously annoyed to be reminded of the incident. "Tell him I want to send my apologies to the kid."

"It'll take me a week to get there and back," the Guardsman stated.

Before the Corporal could order the man to rent a pony, three vendors descended on him. As he unwound the story of the theft, Daedalus forgot to inform the Private of the timely importance of the inquiry.

Chapter 24 - The Firebreak District

Alerio could have easily outpaced the man, but the guy seemed to have an escape route in mind. A block from the City Guardsmen, he ducked into a narrow alleyway. About half way through the alley, the man stopped, climbed a low wall, and leaped to the other side. Alerio mimicked the action and soon they were running between the back walls of villas.

A delivery cart blocked the way. In three high steps, the man walked over the cart and jumped off the other side. Alerio did it in two strides and had to slow up to keep from overtaking the man. They dashed across a street and were hailed by a Guardsman standing a half block away. Ignoring the Guard, they ran into a twisting alley, jumped another wall and continued to run.

The man was breathing heavily and beginning to slow down. Alerio changed his gait to a Legion jog, the pace Legionaries used to eat up miles while in training or heading to battle. A few alleyways later, the fugitives emerged behind a tradesman's compound. The smell of freshly shaved oak filled the air and Alerio spotted wood shavings, slats, and completed barrels through an open gate.

At the corner, they turned onto a street and Alerio saw their destination. The Firebreak District resembled Fireguard. Buildings of raw wood haphazardly constructed with narrow streets and narrower openings between the structures. With the maze of Firebreak in sight, the man's energy rebounded and he broke into a sprint. Alerio matched him step for step.

They were soon deep into Firebreak. As if transported from the paved streets and urban setting of the Capital City to a border town, they were now surrounded by weather beaten three story tenement buildings that loomed over the crowded streets. Poorly dressed women, children, and men wandered up and down the road. Also, leaning against the buildings were hard looking men armed with iron knives.

"You shouldn't be here," the man leading Alerio said. He was bent over gasping for air. Between hurried pants, he stated, "It's not safe for a farm boy here."

"What makes you think I'm a farm boy?" Alerio inquired.

"We see your kind all the time," the man explained. "Grain fed, bursting with muscles, and eyes as big platters. Gawking at the buildings, fountains, and the number of people rushing about, it's easy to spot a first time visitor to the Capital."

"You figured me out," Alerio lied. "It's my first time in the city. I need to get to the east gate and get back to the farm. But as you know, the City Guard is looking for me."

"This is the Firebreak District and not a good place for you," the man warned. "You're better off taking your chances with the Guard."

Chapter25 - Following the Path to Stata Mater or Mars

As they spoke, four men separated from the building walls and stepped into the street.

"What have you got here Salvator?" asked one of the rough men as they approached. "A new convert?"

"No. Just a kid who took a wrong turn," Salvator replied. "He's leaving."

"Seems to me he's dressed nice. So he must have a few coins for the needy," another of the four observed.

"Convert to what?" Alerio inquired as if he hadn't noticed the men.

"I am Epulone Salvator follower of Stata Mater," he explained. "And you should run."

An Epulone was a priest who specialized in blessing major festivals, feasts, and games. To have someone standing in the dirt street of the wooden tender box of Firebreak and claiming to be one of the exulted Priests was funny. So Alerio laughed.

"Let me guess Epulone Salvator," Alerio said with a big grin on his face. "The stolen food was for a feast honoring the Goddess. And what gifts do Stata Mater bestow on the Republic?"

Before Salvator could reply, one of the four thugs demanded, "Give me your coin purse, farm boy."

"First off, don't say farm boy like it's a nasty term," Alerio instructed. "Secondly, the Priest and I are having a conversation. And you are interrupting."

"So the food is for a feast?" Alerio asked the priest. "To celebrate what, exactly?"

"Today we celebrate Stata Mater's gifts to the Firebreak District," Salvator said with pride. "She is the mother who prevents fire."

Looking around at the raw wood of the buildings, Alerio agreed, "A Goddess who guards against fire deserves a feast. Daily wouldn't be too often."

"The food and wine were gathered from the brick part of the city," stated Salvator. "Befittingly for followers of Stata Mater. Don't you think?"

"I said give me your coins," the thug screamed in anger.

"You are a rude man. Hold on," Alerio said to the thug with a smile. "You'll get your turn." Then refocusing on Salvator, he explained, "I don't think being chased by the City Guard shows much respect."

"It's all in the interpretation," Salvator said in defense of the theft. "Stata Mater will appreciate the concept."

The four thugs stepped in closer to appear more imposing. It worked on the Epulone as he began fidgeting nervously.

"Epulone Salvator. I believe it's time for you to leave," Alerio suggested taking pity on the Priest. "We're about to see who is favored most by Mars, the God of war. These gentlemen or me?"

Salvator took a step away but a fist to his back threw him forward. He stumbled into Alerio who caught the Priest and stood him upright. The thugs pulled iron knives to further intimidate their victims.

The mugger who punched the Priest sneered, "Not so fast Salvator. I think the lads and I should get an invitation to your feast."

"Do you know any songs?" Alerio asked Salvator.

"A song?" asked the Priest as he gazed around at the iron knives and the leering men. "You expect me to sing at a time like this?"

"A chant then, one to your goddess," suggested Alerio. "You claim to be an Epulone. So prove it. Give us a chant."

Chapter 26 - Chanting and Killing

Salvator swallowed, lifted his head and began to chant.

"Stata Mater, Stata Mater
When embers soar
With hearths alight
And kindling scores
The heat at night
Stay the flame, Stata Mater
And guard us from the fire"

"Stata Mater, Stata Mater
When Lightening Claps
And the groves spark
And a branch taps
The sky fire mark
Stay the flame, Stata Mater
And guard us from the fire"

"Stata Mater, Stata Mater
When lanterns crash
And hot oils spread
And straw grasps
The flowing dread
Stay the flame, Stata Mater
And guard us from the fire"

"Stata Mater, Stata Mater
When candles fall
And flames stay bright
And parchment calls
The wicked light
Stay the flame, Stata Mater
And guard us from the fire"

"Nicely sung," Alerio said. "Now chant it again."

As Salvator opened his mouth to chant another rendition, Alerio kicked the Priest's legs out from under him.

"Sing Epulone," urged Alerio as he reached to the small of his back.

The long curved knife whipped out from behind Alerio's back and drew a deep red line across one of the thug's breast. The man fell away clutching the gaping wound.

Salvator hit the ground with enough force to drive the air from his body. At first he didn't understand what happened. But as the first thug staggered back, he realized the farm boy had removed him from the fight by kicking his legs. He restarted the chant when the deep screeching noise of the farm boy singing, as if an iron bar were being drug across a metal plate, reached his ears.

"When embers soar, With hearths alight," Alerio chanted while the blade continued around and downward. *"And kindling scores, The heat at night."*

89

The knife sliced opened the skin and sinew of the second thug's left and right wrists. It happened so fast the third mugger didn't have time to react.

"*Stay the flame, Stata Mater,*" Alerio sang as the blade reached the bottom of an arc and began to curve upward, "*And guard us from the fire.*"

The upward sweep of the knife gutted the third mugger. From belly button to mid chest, where the sternum deflected the blade, the man opened like a flower. If the pale pedals parting revealed a blossoming blood red flower.

"*When Lightening Claps, And the groves spark,*" Alerio chanted before grunting.

While his three cohorts in crime fell from the farm boy's blade, the fourth mugger lunged upward from thigh high. His blade sliced the farm boy's side from hip to the small ribs.

"*And a branch taps, The sky fire mark,*" Alerio sang louder as the burning pain ripped up his side, "*Stay the flame, Stata Mater.*"

The fourth man controlled his blade. From the upward cut that slit Alerio's side, he angled for a power slash that would cross the wound and open it to the bone.

In mid pivot, Alerio felt the knife's edge open the gash in his side. His left hand up in a guard position hovered at shoulder height. His right, holding the knife high as it finished gutting the third mugger, continued up and out of position to engage the thug. With his torso still turning away from the third man, Alerio's flank lay undefended for the second slash.

"*When lanterns crash, And hot oils spread,*" Alerio chanted as he slapped the hilt from his right hand into the palm of his left. "*And straw grasps, The flowing dread.*"

Backhanded, Alerio drove the entire length of the blade through the fourth man's neck. The thug's eyes widened in surprise. He stared at the farm-lad until awareness vanished from his eyes and he sank to his knees.

"*Stay the flame, Stata Mater,*" Alerio sang as he jerked the blade free. "*And guard us from the fire.*"

Salvator's neck twisted as he followed the path of the long curved knife. When the farmer stepped over him, he lost the blade for a moment. When he located it again, the blade was slashing the throats of the other three muggers.

"Good song," said Alerio as he cleaned the blade on a dead thug's shirt.

"It's a chant of hope and protection," advised the Priest. As the blade vanished behind the young man's back, he added, "You're not a farm-lad, are you?"

"No Epulone. I'm a Lance Corporal of the Legion," admitted Alerio as he placed a hand over the wound on his side. "You wouldn't happen to have a piece of clean cloth?"

Chapter 27 - Thirty-three City Blocks

"We better got off the street," Salvator suggested as he scrambled to his feet. "Usually the City Guard doesn't come into Fireguard. But four dead are enough bodies to get their attention."

"Lead the way Epulone Salvator," Alerio said.

"If you are a Legionary, why did you run from the City Guard?" asked the Priest. Then, he paused and got very serious, "Or are you from the High Priest, sent to crush my sect of Stata Mater?"

"I can assure you I am not an agent for the High Priest," promised Alerio. "As far as the City Guard, there's no problem. I have a history with Corporal Daedalus and he is a problem. So I ran with you."

"Now you're bleeding all over the street," observed Salvator. "Follow me."

Three alleyways from the scene of the fight, Salvator ducked into a narrow opening. Alerio followed. They moved bent over under the basement of a building. At a ladder, they climbed.

The smell of fresh ham greeted them at floor level. A candle lit table took up much of the room. Around the table, but standing in the shadows, were people.

"Epulone Salvator," a voice said with obvious pleasure. The lad was about twelve and he bravely stepped into the light. Both of his hands were wrapped in damp cloths. "You escaped," he said with glee. "We didn't know whether to eat or to wait for your blessings for the feast."

"What's the difference between a meal and a feast?" asked Alerio.

"Intention mostly," replied Salvator. "If you're hungry, a scrap of food can be a meal. If you say a blessing of thankfulness before eating, it's considered a feast."

"So which is this?" Alerio asked while pointing at a table laden with the food stolen from the vendors. "A meal or a feast?"

"Well, which is it?" Salvator inquired of the youth.

"A feast Epulone," the lad announced. "We waited for you and the blessing."

"Then in fact, it is a feast," replied the Priest. "But first we need to attend to our guest."

Alerio's tunic was pulled off and a length of cloth wrapped around his ribs and hips. There was nothing to be done about the torn and blood splattered tunic. He ate sparsely and silently.

Despite Salvator's command of language, his followers were common workers with no education and no training in the art of conversation. Families descended from royalty and the very wealthy looked down on farmers and craftsmen. In turn craftsmen looked down on merchants. Not to be outdone, merchants looked down on apprentices and day workers. And day workers looked down on slaves. The slaves, Alerio guessed, held animals in contempt.

While the talk around the table was unintelligible, the food was delicious. The feast went on until the light faded and the followers of Stata Mater began leaving.

As he finished, Alerio pushed off the wooden crate that served as a chair. The room spun and he almost toppled onto the few leftovers on the table.

Salvator rushed to his side saying, "You should rest and gather your strength."

"I need to get to the docks," Alerio stated as he shrugged off the Priest's hands. "There are people near the docks, who can help me."

"The lad can lead you to the south end of Fireguard," Salvator explained while pointing to one of his flock. "From there, if you stick to the alleyways, you can avoid the City Guard until you reach the stockyards. There, you'll deal with private guards and they shouldn't bother you. Unless you loiter."

"Sounds simple enough," Alerio said. He hadn't toured the west side of the city so he depended on the Priest's directions.

"Your biggest challenge is crossing the boulevard near the west gate," advised Salvator. "The City Guard patrols the area heavily watching for thieves robbing the warehouses or the stockyards, and trying to escape out the gate, or into the city."

"Thank you from the guidance, Epulone Salvator," Alerio said weakly. He was sleepy and feeling sluggish. If he laid down here, he was afraid he'd be stuck in Firebreak for days until he recovered.

"Guidance is what I do," replied Salvator. "May Stata Mater watch over you and keep you in the dark."

The youth helped Alerio down the ladder. At the alleyway, the lad stuck his head out to see if the way was clear. Immediately, he jerked it back.

"City Guards," he whispered. "Searching the alley."

"Is there another way out?" Alerio asked.

"Wait here. When they leave, go right," advised the youth. "Four streets and alleys over, turn left. Fireguard ends five blocks from there. Wait here."

The lad took three deep breaths before vaulting through the opening. Alerio heard him yell at the guardsmen. Footsteps pounded by the narrow opening then faded.

Following the lad's directions, Alerio crawled through the opening. By the time he reached the end of the alley, he was settled into a comfortable Legion jog. Except, the run wasn't comfortable as his side sent waves of pain through his body with each footfall.

Two, three and when he reached the fourth street, Alerio turned left while maintaining the pace. At a couple of intersections, he slowed for heavy pedestrian traffic. At the end of the fifth block, he dropped into a walk and staggered. Weaving off the street, he moved to a building to get his balance.

The bandage was soaked through on his left side. Even at night, in the weak illumination of a lantern's light, it was obvious to anyone looking, it was blood staining the tunic.

Alerio shook his head in an attempt to clear the cobwebs. The straight roads and walls ahead of him stood in sharp contrast to the twisting and turning of the Firebreak District behind him. He felt as if he stood on the threshold between order and chaos. Between…

He shook his head while trying to remember how long he stood leaning against the building. Alerio had twenty-eight more blocks to go. If unwounded, he could do it easily. In his current state, he worried about finishing the trip at all.

Legionaries run. Hurt, missing an arm, bleeding or sick, Legionaries run. So while Epulone Salvator recommended sneaking through alleyways, it didn't fit with the Legion mindset. Alerio pushed off the boards of the building and marched out of Firebreak. After ten steady paces, he broke into a jog. Twenty choppy steps later, the pain became a numb throbbing in his side and he entered the paved streets of the Capital City in full stride.

Alerio's pace had eaten a third of the city when his nose revealed the next area. The aroma from the stockyards of closely packed cows, sheep, goats, ponies, and horses assaulted his senses. For a farmer, it smelled like home. As his nose twitched at the recognizable aromas, his mouth became dry. A trough with stagnate water covered in slime rested just inside a pen.

Using one hand to hold himself on the top rail, he used the other to brush away the slime. After dunking his head twice, he took in a mouthful of the putrid water, flushed it around, and spit it out.

95

"You there," shouted a man. "Get away from the pens."

Alerio eased away from the pen and turned. As if drunk on cheap vino, he staggered along the line of pens.

"I said to get away from the pens," the same voice yelled.

Alerio was trying to get away from the pens. Unfortunately, every time he stepped to his left, his right foot shot out to maintain his balance. The only thing keeping him from veering off to the right was the top rail of the pens. And his progress forward was from him pulling hand over hand along the rail.

He finally left the crutch of the rail when the head of a club shoved him away from the fence.

"Move along," the male voice ordered. "Or the next time it'll be the club. Not just a poke."

Ahead, the lanterns on the east-west boulevard seemed to sway as if rocking in a storm. The night was calm with only a light breeze. It was Alerio's unfocused eyes and the staggering of his body that created the illusion.

His body wanted to close down and all he desired was to lie down for a short period and sleep. Somewhere in the back of his mind, he heard an echo from the past.

"Quarter rations, half rations," the Legion instructors had yelled. "Or full rations, it's up to you. Finish what you start or go hungry. The enemy is out there. Are you hungrier than your enemy? If not, they will kill you. Now get up and finish the drill."

The brick pavers on the street felt cool on Alerio's cheek. Not far away, the lights along the boulevard and the west gate glowed steadily in the night. He didn't remember lying down on the road.

Five City Guardsmen marched down the avenue and Alerio watched the changing of the guard at the gate. If he had continued on, he would have stumbled into the patrol.

After the guardsmen vanished around a building, Alerio crawled to his hands and knees. Blood rushed to his head and pain radiated from his side.

"Are you hungrier than your enemy?" he whispered as he staggered to his feet. "Are you hungrier than your enemy?"

He realized it was a race against his body. Between shock and blood loss, Alerio had a narrow thread of control between consciousness and collapsing in the street. Angling away from the guard shack at the west gate, he crossed the avenue at the Temple of Portunus. By bouncing off of the trees on the temple grounds and acting as if he were in a life sized children's game, Alerio bounded from side to side always moving forward.

At the southern edge of the temple grounds, he found the footing on the pavers preferable to the grassy lawns of the temple. He was familiar with this section of the city. His destination lay seven blocks ahead. Straight down the road, past the Legion Transfer Building, and a block and a half from the southern warehouses. All he needed to do was put one foot in front of the other.

The villa was still a block away. However, the Legion Lance Corporal knew having traveled the entire length of the Capital City, and bleeding with every step of the way, he would make it.

"I am hungrier than my enemy," Alerio mouthed.

Chapter 28 - Blood of an Ally

Alerio leaned against the solid wood of the gate and pounded. Resting his head against the gate to catch his breath, he pounded

97

again before sinking to the ground. Just before the darkness closed in around him, he reached back and pulled the long knife from the small of his back. It lay in his outstretched hand as his final thoughts snapped off.

"Drink this," a voice ordered as his body was raised to a sitting position.

A salty and bitter beverage poured into his mouth and he swallowed. It burned all the way down. A pulling on his side at the site of his wound made him look down. Neat stitches of thread ran the length of the slice.

"Thank you," he said looking up at a lean man holding a clay mug.

"Can you explain where you acquired this?" the man asked as he sat down the cup and picked up the knife with the yellow strip on the black hilt.

"From the Dulce Pugno," Alerio explained. "I claim the rights of an Ally of the Golden Valley."

"It has been rendered," replied the man as he set the knife on the table and picked up the cup. "Drink it all."

Alerio gulped down the liquid.

"What's in this?" he asked.

"Mostly honey," the man replied.

"But honey is sweet and this is," Alerio faltered while seeking the proper words.

"I said mostly honey," the man replied. "The rest are bitter herbs and powders for healing. You'll sleep for a few hours. Is there any other service you require Ally of the Golden Valley?"

"Some information," Alerio said as his eyes began to close.

"When you awaken," the man said.

But Alerio didn't hear the reply, he'd gone out again.

Alerio opened his eyes and glanced around the room. His tunic now cleaned and mended lay on the side table. He yawned and stretched. Surprisingly, there was little pulling against the tightness of the stitches. He could feel the injury but it was as pliable as if it were weeks into the healing process. Peeling the wrapping from over the wound, revealed a yellow paste over the skin and stitches. After rolling out of bed, he slipped the tunic over his head.

Alerio opened the bedroom door and was met by a young man. Without a word, the youth guided him to an office.

"I am called Favus," the man sitting at a desk said in greeting. "And you are Lance Corporal Alerio Sisera, an Ally of the Golden Valley."

"Thank you for the medical attention," Alerio said pointing to his side as he walked into the office.

The man at the desk was the same man who had given him the healing drink.

"A man matching your description is wanted by the City Guard, and the Cruor. Also, the Fireguard Brigade seeks an unknown mercenary," Favus reported. "Please have a seat."

"I know about them," admitted Alerio. "What do you know about Senator Ventus. And, his connection to the Fireguard Brigand as Vivianus?"

"If you have put the connection together, I have no other information," the man said in the sing song accent of the east. "Gabrielus, the Senator's man, is training with the City Guard."

"Nothing unusual there," said Alerio. "Gabrielus and Corporal Daedalus were trained as youths by the same master sword instructor."

"Under instructions from the City Guard, Gabrielus and thirty northern slaves and freemen are training Legion drills with shields and gladii," Favus explained.

"Why would the City Guard be training three squads of barbarians?" asked Alerio. "What are their plans?"

"I can provide information," Favus said. "The conclusions are for you to decide."

"Thank you for the information," Alerio said then added. "And the medical treatment."

"About the wound, cut and pull the stitches in two weeks," Favus instructed. "Until then, rest and refrain from exercise and fighting."

A strange look came over Favus' face as if a dilemma had presented itself. As quickly as the strange look appeared, it faded and was replaced by a smile.

"However, you are an Ally of the Golden Valley and a Lance Corporal of the Legion," Favus said as he reached into a box on his desk. "Take this. Before you fight, wrap the wound tightly."

Favus held out a twelve-foot-long black silk scarf. As he handed it to Alerio, his sleeve fell up displaying a long scar on the side of his forearm.

"From experience, I can recommend the silk wrap," Favus advised. "It'll be light soon and we can't have you leaving without taking a package. It is, after all, the purpose for your visit to our trading house."

"How long was I asleep?" inquired Alerio, "If it's just dawn."

"You arrived the night before last," Favus reported. "We woke you for liquids and medicine over the period. But, you were unable to take solid food. You may find yourself hungry."

"Again thank you," Alerio said.

"Now you must go before daylight," Favus ordered. "Or stay until dark if you are unable to travel."

Act 5

Chapter 29 - Hunting the Clay Ear

Alerio held the package of goods against his chest using both arms. Any other time, he would have balanced it on one shoulder. The wound in his side prevented carrying it high so it rested on his chest and he had to lean around the package to see the road.

The awkward carry proved useful as he approached the Chronicles Humanum Inn. On the front porch, four City Guardsmen stood in the lantern light talking with Thomasious.

"If I see him," the innkeeper assured the guardsmen. "I will certainly alert you. But, he hasn't been around for a few days."

Alerio ducked his head behind the package as the guardsmen turned.

"Delivery, Master Harricus," Alerio called out from the street.

The City Guard ignored the deliveryman as they descended the steps.

"Take it around back," ordered Thomasious with an edge to his voice. "How many times do I have to tell you people? Deliveries are made around back."

One of the guardsmen laughed at the tone of the irate innkeeper. Alerio waited for the men to pass before heading for the side gate.

"Well, well, well if it isn't Lance Corporal Sisera," Thomasious said as he met Alerio in the rear courtyard. "What have you there?"

"It really is a delivery," Alerio informed the innkeeper. "From the Golden Valley trading house, purveyors of rare and exotic goods."

Thomasious reached out and took the package.

"This is a pleasant surprise," Thomasious said as he carried the package into the inn.

"I am sorry about that," Alerio stated.

"About what? The package?" asked Thomasious. "Anything from a trading house of their standing is always welcome."

"No, Master Harricus. I was referring to the guardsmen on your stoop at first light," explained Alerio. "I'll of course pack my things and leave the city."

"Whatever are you talking about?" Thomasious asked as he untied the package, reached in, and lifted out a bag of rare tea. "Excellent blend. What else have you brought me?"

"The guardsmen. They're hunting for me," Alerio said. "I heard you say, I haven't been around for a few days. I'll just pack and get out of your way."

"Ah, honey from the Golden Valley," Thomasious exclaimed while holding up a small amphora. "They weren't looking for you Lance Corporal. They were seeking the elusive Clay Ear. It seems his story about a prominent citizen living a double life as a crime lord bothered some people. I believe the people were actually one person, Senator Ventus."

"You wrote about that?" Alerio asked in alarm. "Having a Senator of the Republic angry at you could prove fatal."

103

"Oh, I didn't write it," Thomasious explained as he held up a skin of excellent vino and a wrapper of pungent cheese. "The Clay Ear wrote it. Oh, and he also wrote about the attack on Senator Faunus being an organized assassination. That caused yesterday's visit from the City Guard."

"Aren't you pushing the boundaries?" asked Alerio. "A Senator has a lot of power at his disposal. As I just learned, Gabrielus and three squads of northerners are training with the City Guard. Ventus could easily send a trained unit after you, if he ever learns the truth."

"Senator Ventus has a private army of warriors being trained in the city?" Thomasious said softly as if thinking out loud. "I wonder what game the Senator is playing?"

"I don't know and unfortunately, my movements around the city are restricted," Alerio explained. "I was recognized by Corporal Daedalus."

"Why is that a problem?" asked Thomasious as he pulled out a long wrapped item from the package. "Ah, wild boar sausage spiced with eastern herbs. Excellent."

"There's a price on my head by the Spilled Blood," confessed Alerio. "Daedalus knows about the seven Republic gold reward and my name. It's why I thought the City Guardsmen were looking for me."

"You've managed to tangle with the Fireguard Brigade and the Cruor and you've only been in the city a few days," Thomasious exclaimed. "For a young Lance Corporal, you do enjoy mixing it up with dangerous people."

"Not intentionally, Master Harricus," Alerio assured him. "I'll just pack and leave so you don't get into more trouble. Wait, what about Zacchaeus? His time is up."

"I had the old Cloth Seller send the Fireguard Brigade a double payment with a note stating the mercenary was hired by a broker," explained Thomasious. "Zacchaeus assured the Brigade he was diligently seeking to contact the broker to find out the transit mercenary's name. Not to be indelicate, but where have you been."

"I met some new friends," Alerio replied while pulling up the tunic and peeling down the bandage. "We had a disagreement."

Thomasious leaned in and studied the neat line of stitches. From what he could see, the medical attention had been superior to most civilian doctors. In the Republic, only Legion surgeons were capable of sewing a cut with that much precision.

"I see you found a Legion doctor to treat you," Thomasious surmised. "I was just sitting down to breakfast when the guardsmen arrived. Care to join me for a light repast?"

"Master Harricus, it would be a pleasure to dine with you," Alerio replied. "But could I skip the light part and get two breakfasts?"

"Hungry are you?" Thomasious asked.

"Put it this way," explained Alerio. "If you have a sacrificial bull out back, I'll gladly do the ritual killing, butcher it myself, and eat the entire bull."

"Let me talk to the cook," Thomasious said. "I believe we can accommodate a starving Legionary and save the bull for a proper ceremony."

Chapter 30 - Persuasive, if Misleading Speech

Alerio slept through the day and didn't awaken until early the next morning. His side was painfully stiff and he favored it until he ran into Erebus on the way to the bathhouse. Seeing the servant in the lantern light, Alerio straightened up trying to hide the wound.

"Good morning sir," the northerner said in greeting. "I'm afraid the fires have yet to be stoked."

"Not a problem Erebus," Alerio replied. "I'm just going to clean up. No time for a bath."

He didn't want to tell the servant about the wound. Yet, something did occur to him.

"You're from the north," ventured Alerio. "What do you know about Gabrielus, Senator Ventus' bodyguard?"

"I'm from the northeast," Erebus corrected and added while spitting on the ground. "Gabrielus, the pig, is the younger son of a northern King. My people are thinkers, farmers and hunters. Gabrielus' tribe are wild boars to be slaughtered on sight."

"Well, that isn't exactly what I was asking," Alerio explained. "What do you know about Gabrielus' dealings in the city?"

"He is an Insubri Prince. Every northern tribesman in the city owes allegiance to him," Erebus reported. "And, he makes a point to enforce their loyalty."

"How does he do that in the Capital City?" inquired Alerio.

"Late night visits from loyalists," explained Erebus. "Anyone seeking to separate from Gabrielus gets a beating to remind them of his royal lineage. Gabrielus, the slime, hides behind his Senator for protection so the City Guard ignores the beatings."

"Thank you for the information," Alerio said as he stated to walk away. "I'm going to clean up."

"I'll bring you a mug of strong wine," Erebus stated.

"Why? I'm only doing a quick wash," Alerio remained the servant.

"The wine is for your pain," explained Erebus. "I served with the northern Legion. I recognize when a Legionary is favoring an injury, Lance Corporal."

The sun had yet to rise when Alerio walked into the great room. Instead of having time alone to think, he found Thomasious sitting with four scrolls. One, a large scroll for gossip stories, the other three were long chain scrolls.

"Good morning, Sisera," Thomasious said as the innkeeper rinsed the nub of a quill in a mug of water. "You look healthier than yesterday morning."

"Gabrielus has loyal subjects in the city," blurted out the Legionary. "It's as if units of northern warriors were housed in the city."

"I know that, it's not something polite people admit," stated Thomasious. "Why do you think it's important?"

"Three squads of northern troops, trained and protected by the City Guard," Alerio said listing his concerns. "Under the command of Gabrielus, a northern Prince, and financed by a Senator of the Republic. None of this troubles you?"

"If you put it like that, yes, it does paint a troubling picture," admitted Thomasious. "But, this is the Capital of the Republic. We have Legions nearby. If Gabrielus and his merry band revolt, they'll be up on crosses before the next sunrise. We've experienced slave revolts before and they never succeed."

Alerio pulled out a chair and sat down slowly to protect the wound. Everything Thomasious said made sense.

"What's with the scrolls first thing in the morning?" asked Alerio, "I thought the Clay Ear waited until afternoon to wield his mighty quill."

"Another Senator died last night. This one at home and in his bed," Thomasious said. "It seems to be a robbery gone wrong. In light of two Senators dying within a week, the Senate is calling for a special session. I'm preparing my scrolls early with background. This morning, Senator Ventus is giving a speech to the public before going into the session. I can fill in the details later."

"Was the dead Senator pro Ventus, or against the Senator?" asked Alerio.

"As it happens, Senator Ferox had a long and storied history of debating against Ventus," Thomasious replied while making a face as if his stomach had soured. "With Ferox dead, Consul Marcus Regulus in the west and Consul Julius Libo in the east, Ventus is one of the senior Senators in the city. In fact, after the President of the Senate, he is second in charge of the Republic. At least until one of the Consuls return."

"He is a dangerous man," offered Alerio.

"The Republic has survived for almost two hundred and fifty years," Thomasious assured him. "We tossed out the King and installed a Republic. I can't see one man harming us after all that time."

"I'd like to hear the speech," admitted Alerio. "But you know my situation. Are you going?"

"No, I've got a business to run," Thomasious said. "However, the Clay Ear will have lots of little ears around to gather the pertinent facts. It'll be a good show. Ventus will no doubt feed the crowd. It assures a large turnout and puts citizens on his side."

"I've never seen a Senator give a speech," Alerio said wishfully. "It must be amazing."

"Maybe there is a way for you to see it," Thomasious said. "Let's go see Erebus."

The woman in the crowd moved four urgent steps away from the cloaked and hooded stockyard worker. Cow and horse merda, and gods only knew what else, clung to the hem of his cloak. She wasn't the first or the last to move away from the stink rolling off the man's clothing.

Thankfully, Alerio's nose had grown accustomed to the aroma. By the time Erebus finished shoveling fresh manure and having a couple of horses empty their bladders on the cloak, Alerio's sense of smell deserted him.

After some jostling between groups, he found himself standing with other stockyard workers and men from the tanner's compound. If anything, the dead skin and urine smell from the tanners was worse than the stockyard men, but only by a little. The happy group of nose blind workers had an empty ring around them as citizens with less aromatic employment gave them a wide berth.

There was almost trouble when the team passing out free bread avoided the offensive smelling group. Two of the big stockyard men strutted over and secured enough loaves for everyone. The problem was averted and the crowd chewed idly while waiting for the Senator to make his appearance.

High overhead, the roof of the Capital building gave the impression of floating in the sky. It seemed as if the roof would drift away with the clouds, if not for the eight soaring columns. As if decreed by the fates, the marble columns widened at the base anchoring them to the marble porch. A section at the center of the pouch bowed out creating a stand for a speaker. Eight steps, on either side of the stand, descended from the porch and the Capital building to where the crowd chewed and waited.

Alerio broke off pieces of his loaf. He found it adequate if he ignored the rough ground grain and the lack of salt in the bread. Apparently, Ventus had saved a few coins by buying cheap. Of course, he had a multitude to feed so Alerio hadn't expected bread as good as his mother made.

A trumpet blared and the crowd of citizens shifted in anticipation. When it blew again a cheer went up from the throng. A tall, thin man strutted out from the building, crossed to the porch to the round jutting area, and held up his arms for silence.

"Citizens of the Republic, good morning to you," the man announced in a booming voice. "May I present a fellow citizen, a man of the people despite his wealth and exulted position. A hard working, family man, a man who everyday fights for the people in the Senate of the Republic. A man who cares about you and about the future of our great Republic. Citizens, I present to you, Senator Ventus."

The crowd screamed unintelligently at first but soon, the cheering solidified into a chant, "Ventus. Ventus. Ventus..."

As the chant reached a fevered pitch, Gabrielus, the Senator's bodyguard marched out of the building and onto the porch. He stopped and scanned the crowd. Surprisingly, Gabrielus was dressed in Legion ceremonial armor with a Tribune's insignia over his shoulder.

Right behind the bodyguard, the Senator strutted out of the building. He didn't go directly to the speaker's stand. Ventus pranced to one end of the porch, waved and pointed as if acknowledging friends in the crowd before moving to the far side. There he repeated the antics of a popular politician. Before

110

the cheering died down, the Senator swaggered to the speaker's stand.

"My fellow citizens. Did you enjoy the bread?" he asked and waited for the cheering to resume and fade. "Citizens of this great, no citizens of our great Republic, should have bread every day."

The cheering started again. He's getting a lot of mileage out of the bread thought Alerio. In Legion training, the instructors had repeated threats and praise in equal parts. After a few weeks, the more astute Recruits noticed the pattern. For the rest of their lives, it was hard to verbally manipulate them with insincere words and repeated phrases. Most of this crowd hadn't been through Legion training.

"I speak with you today of a tragic lose. My beloved colleague, Senator Ferox, was assassinated last night," Ventus announced. He paused to let the news sink in and for the murmuring to cease. Continuing, he stated, "Coming soon after the assassination of our beloved Senator Faunus, who was knifed down in the streets of this very city. Along with his wife, Senator Faunus fell to evil and vile, yet well-trained blades. Believe me, when I promise the Senate of the Republic will uncover the butchers and bring them to justice. But, the murders were more than just the killings of public servants. Here me on this."

The crowd stilled waiting for Ventus to announce more salacious language. This was entertainment, drama of the highest order, and everyone wanted to hear so they could tell the story to their friends later.

"Our Republic is under attack," Ventus shouted. "Under attack, I say. Forces of darkness are moving across our city, no, across our Republic. We in the Senate have been charged to do everything necessary to protect our citizens. And we will do everything necessary to protect our people and the Republic."

Fists were raised in the air. The crowd cheered encouragement and enthusiasm for their Senator. He promised to pursue justice in the Senate and the people appreciated his dedication. In the midst of all the adoration, Alerio wondered why the two dead Senators had been with the party opposing Ventus.

"A festival honoring Janus is scheduled to start tomorrow," the Senator explained. From the downward tone of the crowd, it was easy to see cancelling the popular event would disappoint the citizens.

"I struggled mightily, in the face of my two dead brothers, with whether to support the festival or not," Ventus explained. "So I asked the gods. Early this morning, I sacrificed a lamb to my family's household god. After the slaughter, I read the entrails."

The crowd, now silent, was bent forward to hear the will of the gods from the Senator. Alerio pondered the sacrifice of a lamb. At his father's farm, they sacrificed strong working animals or beasts with status. Gentle lambs were only slaughtered when the family was celebrating and wanted something special for dinner.

"After my readings, I can tell you, citizens of the Republic," Ventus announced. "I am marching into the Senate and with the sweat of my brow and the strength of my right arm, I will fight for the celebration of Janus. We will honor the god and you will have your festival. I swear it."

Ventus spun around quickly, set his shoulders, and march into the Capital building as if he were going into battle. Gabrielus, in his ornate armor, trailed behind the Senator.

Emotionally it was a good play. Substance wise, the speech was empty of facts. Alerio followed a group of men to the stockyards. As they walked, the conversation was mostly about the festival and the coin they would make from selling sacrificial animals. Some spoke of the forces of darkness in the city. No one knew what they were, but those speaking about the darkness agreed something had to be done.

Alerio presented a note from Thomasious to a stockyard man and left the area leading two goats. It was his cover; a stockyard man delivering a purchase to the Chronicles Humanum Inn.

Chapter 31 - Little Clay Ears

"And what did the good Senator have to say?" Thomasious asked. "What did you learn?"

They were standing in a stable. Alerio held up a hand for the innkeeper to wait while he shrugged off the cloak. Erebus took the cloak and marched the smelly garment to a tub of boiling water.

"Senator Ventus has a taste for lamb," Alerio related. "And he is going to fight to keep the festival for Janus on schedule. Also, there's a dark force spreading across the city. And he is going to do what every is necessary to fight it."

"So all political speak with no substance," Thomasious summed up the report. "I didn't expect much else."

"Oh, one curious fact," added Alerio. "Gabrielus was dressed in armor with the rank of Tribune. How could he have rank, he's not a citizen of the Republic?"

"If Ventus bought him a commission in the City Guard," responded Thomasious. "He could wear it within the confines of the city limits. Outside, any Legion Officer could charge him with subversion or being a spy."

"What have your little clay ears said about the speech?" asked Alerio.

"Nothing yet," replied Thomasious. "I have them situated along the routes Senators take to their homes. Maybe a couple will talk out loud after the Senate session. Right now, I have a request for you."

"Master Harricus, what can I do for you? Alerio asked.

"Go to the bathhouse and wash," said Thomasious. "Because lad, you stink."

Alerio, because the City Guard had come by twice asking for the Clay Ear, was eating lunch in a storage room off the hallway. He watched as Thomasious' urchins passed the door on their way to report to the innkeeper. After delivering their tidbits of information, they passed the door again on their way to the cook shed for a meal.

Sounds drifted in from the great room where customers dined and drank. Between visits from the little clay ears, Thomasious stood behind the marble counter drawing mugs of ale and wine.

"Is Lance Corporal Sisera staying here?" asked a familiar voice.

"Sergeant Chlotharius. Good to see you again," Thomasious replied in greeting. "Here have a mug of wine. It's on the house. You know, the young man stopped in but said he had other accommodations. Probably with a lass, you know how those young Legionaries are."

"Thanks Thomasious," the Sergeant of Legionaries replied. "I haven't time for more than one. We've been ordered to sail. I'm going through the city rounding up my lads. I just stopped in to say hello before we row out."

"Your ship is doing the eastern patrol," declared Thomasious. "Shouldn't you be in port for a couple of weeks after the last cruise?"

"That's the usual schedule," the Sergeant confirmed. "From what I hear, someone floated the idea that it would have taken fifteen trained men to kill Senator Faunus and his Legionary bodyguards. Seeing as the only trained units nearby are Legionaries, the Senate has ordered all military units to leave the city."

Alerio wanted to shout out there was another military unit in the Capital. They weren't Legion, they were northern barbarians, but he held his tongue.

The sounds of chairs sliding back reached Alerio as other NCOs came in and rounded up members of their units. By evening, there wouldn't be a single Legion unit in the Capital City or a Legion ship docked at the piers.

While Thomasious checked out guests, the line of little ears grew. Finally, they filled the narrow hallway leading to the alcove and the innkeeper's desk.

"Go eat and come back," Alerio said from the doorway.

The hallway cleared quickly and the line shifted to the cook shed. When the last Legionary assigned to a unit was gone, Thomasious strolled back to his alcove.

"An unusual form of martial law," the innkeeper said. "Now where are my little ears?"

Alerio leaned out of the storage room and pointed down the hallway. The rear courtyard of the inn was crowded with children. Some eating, other playing and a few were sleeping.

"Let's go find out what the Senate is up to, shall we?" suggested Thomasious.

For the rest of the afternoon, they held meetings with groups of children. Each child was allowed to talk before being released.

At the end of the interrogations, a picture of the Senate session emerged.

"Let's hear what you got from the little ears," Thomasious ordered.

"Senator Ventus opened the session with a plea to hold the Janus festival. It was overwhelmingly approved," Alerio reported. "Then, Ventus brought up the deaths of the two recently deceased Senators."

"Where was the President of the Senate during these discussions?" asked Thomasious.

"He yielded the floor to Ventus at the opening of the session," Alerio said. "One of the little ears reported hearing a Senator complain about it. Is that normal?"

"The President of the Senate is the leader of the governing body," Thomasious replied. "For him to yield the entire session to Ventus was the same as making Ventus the President. What else?"

"Ventus asked to be named a temporary Consul," Alerio reported. "But the Senate voted it down. After that, they passed the Legion restraint bill to clear the city until the murders could be investigated."

"And that leads us back to the question," Thomasious asked. "What is Senator Ventus' end game?"

"I have some advice for the Clay Ear," Alerio warned. "Don't publish any of this. Not a story, not a gossip piece, not a biting political commentary. The City Guard and the barbarians control the city. You are not safe."

"That's nonsense," responded Thomasious. "I'm a citizen of the Republic. I have my rights."

Chapter 32 - The Qart Hadasht

With all the Legionaries assigned to units ordered to leave the city, Alerio wasn't sure of his own travel status. So he left the inn and walked to the Legion Transfer building.

"Lance Corporal Sisera," he reported. "I'm checking on the ship to the southern Legion."

"It's delayed," the Transfer NCO replied. "If things aren't settled in the next few days, we'll organize a march south. If the Senate reopens the port, you'll sail. If not, we'll put together a Century and supply wagons and you can march with them."

"How long is the march?" asked Alerio.

"Roughly eighteen days," the Legionary replied. "The march isn't the problem. It's having you and the other transferees waiting around until we have enough men to make it feasible."

"When do you want me back?" asked Alerio.

"In a couple of days," the NCO replied. "The Centurion should have made a decision by then."

As Alerio turned for the door, a squad of City Guardsmen marched by. He eased back and waited for them to pass.

"There's an amphora of merda for you," the Transfer NCO said while pointing at the squad.

"The City Guard?" inquired Alerio.

"No. The Qart Hadasht launch the guardsmen are meeting," the NCO replied. "The Senate chases off Legion ships and invites in an enemy Ambassador. It's just not right."

"For The Festival of Janus?" asked Alerio.

"Who knows?" the NCO replied. "I have too many friends buried along the coast because of those cūlus to care."

Alerio left the office and wandered to the warehouses. Using the long buildings and the crowd of workers as cover, he eased up to get a look at the docks.

A smallish ship rowed up the river and smartly pivoted in mid-channel. He had to admire the seamanship when the boat sped towards the pier, and just before reaching the pilings, the rowers reversed oars. The ship went from slicing the river water and leaving a wide wake to gently nudging against the dock.

The launch was narrow with carved images on the fore section and the aft tail. And, it was a true tail. The stern rose until it curved over the pilot where it ended in a point. It reminded Alerio of a scorpion's tail.

Five large brass shields lined each side of the ship. But twenty oars had raised when the launch reached the dock. If Alerio figured correctly, the ten shields were for Qart Hadasht Marines meaning the ship had ten rowers and ten warriors in its compliment.

As dockworkers caught and secured lines to anchor the boat, a coach pulled by a team of four big horses rolled up. The first person to emerge was Gabrielus resplendent in his Tribune armor.

The northerner marched to the City Guard squad and amazingly began issuing orders. Soon, the squad was in line facing one direction. The bronze shields from the ship were pulled down and ten men in brown armor marched off the ship. They came abreast of the City Squad, halted, and turned sharply to face the guardsmen. In a move screaming of intimidation, the Qart Hadasht squad had turned so they were just a foot from the guardsmen's faces. Additionally, they were taller which forced the City Guardsmen to stare at the Qart Hadasht squad's chests. On command, they stepped back in unison for five paces.

Gabrielus signaled someone on the boat before turning and waving at the coach. Senator Ventus stepped down from the carriage as a tall man dressed, in an ornate robe, stepped onto the dock from the Qart Hadasht launch.

The two men met at the center of the ceremonial lines. They exchanged hugs as if they were longtime friends before linking arms and strolling to the coach. Ventus and the Ambassador disappeared into the carriage and the two squads trotted forward to flank the vehicle.

When the coach and the squads left the docks, Alerio was surprised to see the Senator's bodyguard still standing on the pier. Gabrielus watched the carriage for a long time before turning and walking to the Qart Hadasht boat.

A tall man with long blond hair appeared on deck. When Gabrielus stepped onto the ship, they embraced. Looking closely, Alerio notice the same short nose, high cheekbones, wide set of the shoulders, and matching height. If not brothers, they were certainly related.

The man on the boat was maybe a couple of years older but leaner as you'd expect from a northern tribesman. While they spoke, the tribesman patted Gabrielus' armored chest and both men laughed. When they sat down and began eating, Alerio eased back from the corner of the warehouse before sprinting away.

He didn't break stride until he reached the door of the inn's great room. Rushing to the counter and waving frantically for Thomasious Harricus to follow, Alerio turned and pushed through the double doors.

"What seems to be the trouble?" asked Harricus as he walked into the rear courtyard.

"Senator Ventus is meeting with an Ambassador from Qart Hadasht," Alerio blurted out between gasps of air. "That fits with his agenda," Harricus explained. "I finally collected enough information to figure out his plan."

"You mean why he's killing off his opposition?" asked Alerio.

"Now look who's talking treason," teased Harricus. "Senator Ventus is a free trader. He believes the Republic will be better served by making peace with the tribes on our boarders. And by making trade deals with neighboring city states and Empires like Qart Hadasht."

"Master Harricus, my father's farm is fifteen miles from the border," Alerio explained. "If not for the Legion, and I mean active heavy infantry, the northern and western tribes would attack and kill every citizen between my father's farm and the Capital City. How can you make peace with barbarians like that?"

"Well, the barbarians are savages, I agree," Harricus replied. "But there's no connection between trading with ocean going cities and the barbarians. Maybe if we made friends and expanded our trading partnerships, we'd have more resources to use for defense against the barbarians."

"There is a connection," Alerio stated. "Gabrielus met a northern barbarian on the Qart Hadasht launch. If the Ambassador is here to talk peace, why does he have a northern tribesman with him?"

"This is getting beyond the privy of a simple scribe and innkeeper," Harricus admitted. "Fortunately, my inn has been serving junior Officers for enough years that a few have risen to Command status in the Legions. Let me send a message to Colonel Nigellus. He's in town as a Marshal for the Festival of Janus and should be available."

"What can I do?" asked Alerio.

"Go watch the games. I expect Champ wouldn't get back to me until he finishes his duties at the Festival," Harricus explained.

"You call a Colonel of the Legion, Champ?" asked Alerio in horror.

"When I met Nigellus, he wasn't the third man in charge of an army," Harricus said with a laugh. "Champ was a broke Centurion with the southern Legion. He supplemented his income by arm wrestling for coin. I believe there are still a few Republic silvers due on his room bill. So, he's Champ to me."

Chapter 33 - The Festival of Janus

Alerio was torn. While he wanted to see the festival celebrating the god of beginnings, gates, transitions and endings, he couldn't chance being seen by the City Guard. It seemed he was doomed to miss the opening blessings. In his room, he looked at the dark cloak and realized he could watch in relative safely from one vantage point.

Before the sun reached its zenith, Alerio shuffled into the Fireguard District. On the street before the earthen berm, he climbed to the third floor, walked through a hallway, and into The Wine Trough.

The pub was crowded, but Alerio managed to find a seat on the porch. It only cost him four silvers to buy out a table occupied by three young men. They left with wicked smiles on their faces. For a few heartbeats, he worried he'd see the three again when he left after sundown. But the festival grounds and the crowds drew his attention to the activities outside the city.

Four Epulones stood around a bull with swords. The crowd stood back as the Priests began stabbing the beast. Alerio knew livestock, and in all his days on the farm, had never seen a bull stand perfectly still for anything. This sacrificial bull was so drugged it was a wonder he could stand. Eventually, the bull didn't. Amid sprays of blood and the hacking of the Epulones, the noble animal gave up his spirit to Janus and toppled over. While the crowd cried out in delight, a rope was tied around the bull's legs and he was hauled away by a team of mules.

Butchers stood by and the sacrificial bull was soon in pieces small enough to roast. While the slaughter was taking place, the four Epulones separated and ran to every corner of the festival grounds.

Most people avoided the near naked, blood covered Epulones. Some folks in need of a blessing, reached out to swipe fingertips of sacrificial blood off the Priests. They promptly stuck their fingers into their mouths and sucked off the blood. Alerio assumed they were either hungry or needed Janus to begin, gate, or transitions something in their stomachs.

Once the Epulones had finished marking everything on the festival grounds with bull's blood, they raced to the reviewing stand. As the Priests raised their hands, men on the stand waved their acknowledgement of the Epulones' blessings.

Senator Ventus and the Ambassador occupied the center of the stand with other dignitaries spread out on either side of them. Three Legion Officers stood on the far left. They would be the General, the Major General, and the Central Legion's Colonel. If the big Officer was Nigellus, Alerio could easily see why he won arm wrestling contests.

As Alerio sipped a mug of wine, Senator Ventus remained standing. While his arms waved and his mouth moved, he was too far away to hear any of the words. Despite Alerio's limited experience, he decided this was the best way to view a political speech.

Bored with watching the antics of the Senator, Alerio shifted his attention to the competition areas. He shivered at the thought of the archery range and smiled at the staggered javelin targets. A blush ran down both arms when he ogled the gladius arena. Maybe someday he would compete. But until he cleared the Cruor bounty, he was limited in his public exposure.

The speeches ended and the Legion Officers walked down from the stand and separated. Each would act as ceremonial Marshal for different competitions before relinquishing the duties to the real Marshals of the games.

Squads of Legionaries were stationed in strategic areas. If anyone got out of hand, they would be subdued, maybe beaten a little before being delivered to the Medical tent. The busiest vendors were the sellers of vino and ale so by evening, the Legionaries would be busy policing the festival.

As the competitions began, Alerio watched as gamblers streamed to and from the betting tents. A Legion NCO wandered between squads, stopping to chat with one before moving on to another squad. Just before the competitions began, the NCO turned full face towards Fireguard District.

Alerio immediately recognized Corporal Gratian of the Capital City's Western Transfer Post. Apparently, the Central Legion had moved additional Centuries to the festival area. Corporal Gratian was known as an NCO who cared about his men. And, as a man who enjoyed wagering and deal making. Alerio chuckled as he tried to imagine what deal Gratian had made to finagle a duty assignment at the Festival of Janus.

Corporal Gratian, true to form, finished checking on his men before heading to the betting tents.

Alerio watched the gladius fights, the archery shots, and the javelin throws. Tomorrow, the horse and chariot races would begin as well as the ranked competitors in the former games. He decided The Wine Trough was a good venue for viewing. Promising himself to come back for the second day of the festival, he stood and headed for the exit.

Pausing on the top of the stairs, Alerio glanced down at the dark street and the black holes of the alleyways. Somewhere down there, three young men looked to relieve a stranger of his purse. Alerio thought about teaching them a lesson but he was under a time constraint and needed to get back to the Chronicles Humanum Inn. The best deterrent against crime is a show of force. He quickly dropped his cloak, drew both gladii, and put the cloak back on. If the three were brave enough to mug a man brandishing two gladii maybe they deserved a lesson.

There is no sense in carrying two swords if your enemy doesn't know you have them. At the bottom of the stairs, Alerio began twirling the blades. With spinning steel on either side of him, he causally walked down the center of the street.

He located the three and walked by with a nod of his head. They responded by shrugging as if to say you won this time. In fact, Alerio's demonstration had possibly saved the lives of the three young men. They just didn't realize it.

Chapter 34 - Colonel 'Champ' Nigellus

Alerio arrived at the inn and headed straight to the baths. After a quick clean up, he went to his room and put on the military tunic. It was the first time since enlisting he'd dressed in something besides armor for a Legion event.

"It's a nice look on you," commented Harricus as Alerio marched into the great room. "Come join me."

The innkeeper was sitting in the silent room with a mug of wine.

"This place hasn't been this empty, since the day before I opened the inn," continued Harricus.

"I'm sure you'll be busy once the Senate allows the Legion units back in the city," Alerio said trying to console the proprietor.

"Oh you misjudged my meaning," Harricus replied. "I gave my staff the day off to enjoy the festival. Even hired a few workmen to do some needed repairs. Me? I'm relaxing in the evening for the first time in years."

A stallion, especially one accustomed to dominating on a battlefield, creates chaos wherever it goes. The first to sense the alpha equine were the penned livestock. Horses whinnied, mules hew-hawed, lambs bleated, and even the hardheaded goats bleated out a warning as the big warhorse trotted into the rear courtyard. If the animal sounds failed to alert you, the stomping of massive hooves and the deep chested snorting and exhaling of a large horse in a confined space was sure to get your attention.

"Champ has arrived," Thomasious announced with a relaxed smile. "Come on, I'll introduce you."

Alerio followed innkeeper. By the time they reached the courtyard, Erebus was walking from the stables.

"Good evening Colonel," the barbarian said as he approached the horse and rider.

The stallion began to dance sideways while shaking his massive head.

"Erebus. Good to see you again," the rider replied. "Careful, he's a little jumpy. Doesn't care for the crowds in the city."

125

"That makes two of us," Erebus replied as he marched straight to the stallion.

The horse nipped the air three feet above the stableman's head.

"That will be enough of that," scolded Erebus as he reached up with both hands.

In one hand, he balanced an apple on an open palm. The other hand reached for the bridle and as the warhorse took the apple almost gently from the palm, Erebus pulled the horse's head down to eye level.

"It's alright lad," Erebus said soothingly to the stallion.

The horse responded by dropping his head and nudging the stableman in the chest. Although a large man, the nudge drove Erebus back two steps. Taking a half step, the horse remained in contact with the stableman.

"I'll give him a rub down while you're here," Erebus offered as he scratched the big head affectionately. "I don't imagine the grooms at the fancy inns you stay at do it properly."

"I believe you're right Erebus," the rider said as he pulled a foot from the stirrup, swung the far leg over the horse's neck, and dropped lightly to the ground.

"Thomasious Harricus. You old scoundrel," boomed the rider. "Are you still antagonizing the women of the Republic with your spicy stories?"

"Are you still skipping out on your bar tabs?" replied Harricus.

"The Tribune was supposed to pay that," answered the rider.

"Well he didn't. You still owe me five silvers," Harricus spit out.

"That's good," the rider stated as he walked to the innkeeper. "It means my tab is still open."

The rider towered over the innkeeper. He had to bend down to embrace Harricus.

"Don't touch me," Harricus ordered as he quickly hugged the rider before pushing him back. "Thank you for coming."

"Your message sounded urgent," the rider replied. "Why don't you tell me about it over a mug of wine?"

Erebus dropped his hand from the bridle and turned his back to the stallion. As Harricus led the rider into the inn, the warhorse docilely followed Erebus towards the stables. The scene was reminiscent of two relatives returning home for a visit.

"And who are you?" the rider asked as he peered over the mug of wine.

"Lance Corporal Alerio Sisera, gladius instructor. Formerly of the eastern Legion," Alerio replied. "In transit to the southern Legion, sir."

Alerio finished reporting and slammed a fist into his left chest.

"Colonel Nigellus of the Central Legion," the rider responded. He looked from the Lance Corporal to the innkeeper before adding. "All day long, I put up with poppycock politicians, Priests with body odor, crowds of drunks, and foreigners who make my skin crawl. So why am I here? Other than to enjoy this delicious wine?"

He was taller and almost as heavily muscled as the younger Legionary. There was a briskness to his movements and his manner of speech correlated to his position as third in command of a Legion. At no time in Alerio's short military career had he been this close to a command level senior Officer. Now he stood drinking excellent vino in the great room of an inn in the Capital

127

City with a Colonel. After the short introduction, Alerio stood holding his mug while standing at the position of attention.

"Colonel Nigellus, do you remember the time General Florus stopped by for a drink?" Harricus asked.

"I was a newly commissioned Centurion. After buying my armor, I was embarrassingly short of coin," Nigellus replied. "I was drinking on a tab and in walks the General. I remember as if it were yesterday. You sent a mug of your finest wine to General Florus with my compliments. Then, you introduced me to him."

"And how did the General respond to a new, untested Centurion?" prodded Harricus.

"He was gracious. And while I stammered, he guided the conversation making me feel relaxed," Nigellus replied. Slowly, he looked at Alerio who stood stiffly holding an almost full mug of wine. With a smile spreading across his sun creased face, the Colonel said, "Lance Corporal Sisera, stand at ease. The southern Legion you say? I served there. It's a fine posting. Take some time to learn boat handling and mooring. It'll serve you well in the future. Now that we're all friends Thomasious Harricus, can we get to the purpose of this gathering?"

"As you know, Legion units have been temporarily banned from the Capital," Harricus explained. "What you may not know is three squads of northern barbarians have been sanctioned by the City Guard."

"That's impossible," the Colonel responded. "The Guard is technically part of the Central Legion except they're under the direct control of the Senate. Only citizens are allowed to join the Legion."

"Oh it gets more improbable," Harricus exclaimed. "A barbarian Prince has been commissioned as a Tribune in the Guard by Senator Ventus. The same barbarian met with a fellow tribesman on the Qart Hadasht launch while the Senator was showing our city to the Ambassador."

"You speak of high treason, innkeeper," Nigellus warned sternly.

"That's what Lance Corporal Sisera keeps telling me," replied Harricus. "Nevertheless, it's true. Tomorrow, while the festival is going on, the Senate is meeting to discuss a treaty with Qart Hadasht."

"But Consuls Regulus and Libo are in the field with their Legions," Nigellus said in shock. "The Senate will never pass a treaty without the Consuls."

"They can if Senator Ventus is voted in as an interim Consul," Harricus offered. "With the City Guard and the barbarian squads backing him, the Senate will do anything he asks."

The sound of a horse moving fast on the street in front of the inn reached them. It stopped and footsteps on the front risers echoed from the stomp of riding boots as someone pounded up the stairs. Nigellus, Sisera and Harricus turned as a dusty Legion courier burst through front door.

"Colonel Nigellus. A missive from the General," the Legionary stated as he crossed the room while digging into a shoulder bag. "He said to wait for your reply."

Nigellus took the parchment, unfolded it, and studied the words.

"Harricus, I need writing implements," Nigellus said.

"In the alcove behind the counter," the innkeeper replied. "You know where it is."

But Harricus was speaking to the Colonel's back. Nigellus was already vaulting the marble counter.

In the time it took Alerio to drink down his mug of wine, Nigellus with an arm extended, handed the courier a reply over the counter.

"Stop at the Legion Cavalry tents on the Festival grounds," the Colonel ordered. "I want you to have an escort on the way back to the General."

"Yes, sir," the courier replied as he shoved the parchment into his bag. "Is there anything else Colonel?"

"No. Away with you," Nigellus ordered before pointing at Alerio. "Lance Corporal Sisera. I have a mission for you."

"Yes, sir, I'm at your disposal," Alerio replied while snapping to attention.

"I want two squads of Legionnaires in the City before sunrise," Nigellus spoke rapidly as if thinking out loud. "I'll write you a note. Find a Sergeant and..."

"I know Corporal Gratian of the Western Transfer Post," Alerio volunteered. "He's at the Festival."

"Alright. Locate Gratian and have him trickle in two squads," Nigellus ordered while handing over a second parchment. "Here's my authorization. Harricus can you hide them here?"

"Of course but the City Guard will never let armored Legionaries in, even if they come through the gate one or two at a time," the innkeeper suggested. "We'll need Tomas Kellerian to armor them."

"I know Kellerian. He's a patriot and was once a fierce Legion Centurion," Nigellus said relaxing for a second as he remembered a different time. "He was one of my instructors when I joined. I believe I still have bruises from his gladius training lectures."

"What did the General say?" asked Harricus. "If it's not a secret."

"Tribes along our western and northern frontiers are gathering," Nigellus reported. "And reports from the east state the Rebels are increasing their attacks. It's as if they were coordinating their movements."

"Or someone, or some Empire is orchestrating an attack on the Republic," suggested Harricus. "An Empire like Qart Hadasht?"

"Sisera. Tell Gratian, I want four squads in the City," Nigellus ordered after weighting the new information. "I'm speaking to the Senate before the session starts and I want Legionaries at my back."

"Yes, sir. By your leave Colonel?" Alerio asked.

"Yes, go and get my Legionaries, Lance Corporal," Nigellus replied. Turning to Harricus, he said, "Tell me more, Clay Ear, about what's going on in the Capital."

As Alerio pushed through the double doors, the innkeeper began explaining everything he knew about the murders of Senators Faunus and Ferox. And, Senator Ventus' entanglement with the Fireguard Brigade gang.

In his room, Alerio stripped off the green military tunic. Before slipping into the gray ill-fitting tunic, he coiled the silk scarf around his waist and hips to protect his wound. Once dressed, he pulled on the duel rig and topped the outfit off with the dark cloak.

Chapter 35 - The Festival by Night

The sacrificial bull plus other delicious roasting meats were slowly turning over low fires. In the morning, almost the entire city of nearly one hundred thousand would pour from the confines of the walls and join in the Festival of Janus. They expected to eat, drink, and celebrate the god of beginnings, gates, transitions, time, doorways, passages, and endings. It would turn ugly fast if there wasn't enough sacrificial meat for everyone to enjoy the feast.

While the bulk of citizens would come tomorrow, the festival grounds were far from deserted. Performers, vendors, competitors, and attendees who had traveled to the event were camped around the fringes. On the far end, the Legionaries assigned to the festival had pitched their tents.

"Halt," challenged the Legionary on guard duty. "This is a restricted area citizen."

"I am Lance Corporal Alerio Sisera. Get me the Sergeant of the Guard and Corporal Gratian," Alerio stated. "I have a message from Colonel Nigellus."

The Legion had been fighting to protect or expand the Republic for over two hundred years. From one end of the Republic to the other, only military discipline had allowed them to win battles or come back stronger than before after a defeat.

Even in a temporary camp where the duty was watching citizens celebrate, the Legion's ethos was strong. At the mention of their Colonel, they responded with the night's full guard command.

The Sergeant of the Guard, the Corporal of the Guard, and the Duty Centurion plus a four-man quick response team in full armor arrived shortly after the guard's shout.

"Name and unit," demanded the SOG.

"Lance Corporal Sisera. Formerly of the eastern Legion," Alerio replied while holding out the note. "I'm in transit to the southern Legion. This message is from Colonel Nigellus."

"Can anybody vouch for him?" asked the Corporal of the Guard as he took the message and handed it to the Sergeant. Then he ordered, "Take off the cloak."

The Sergeant and the Centurion were huddled under a brazier studying the note by the flickering light. They looked up at Alerio as the cloak fell away.

"What's that on your back?" asked the SOG.

"A duel gladius rig, Sergeant," explained Alerio and added to prevent a lesson in left handed swordsmanship. "I'm a weapons instructor. The second gladius is for my students."

"That's not Legion regulations," the Corporal said leaning around to eye the rig. "Looks like civilian junk or maybe barbarian gear."

"Colonel Nigellus needs four squads in the city by morning," explained Alerio, "He sent me to..."

"Shut up. I'll let you know when to speak," the Sergeant ordered. "All we have is a note saying a Lance Corporal Sisera speaks with my authority. Signed by someone as Colonel Nigellus. Now I don't know who might want us to run afoul of the City Guard. Or go against Senatorial orders but I'm not about too without some kind of confirmation."

Alerio stood helpless under the stern gazes of the seven Legionaries and their Officer. It was a standoff with no solution until a voice called out from between the tents.

"Recruit Sisera. Are you causing trouble, again?" called out Corporal Gratian.

He marched into the light of the guard post and right up to Alerio. A hard slap to Alerio's right shoulder rocked him.

"This is Recruit Sisera. The man who defeated Daedalus in our games last year," Gratian explained.

133

"You vouch for this man?" asked the Centurion

"Yes, sir. Sisera's one of my favorite kind of farmer," Gratian announced.

"What kind is that, Corporal Gratian?" asked the Officer.

"One who can fight, sir," Gratian replied. "One who can fight."

The Officer waved the parchment from Nigellus in the air.

"Gratian you're lead NCO on this," the Centurion ordered. "Get the Colonel what he needs. I don't care what it takes. I'll okay it with your Centurion and we'll back you. Now people, don't we have guard patrols to perform?"

As the guard command broke up and dispersed in every direction, Gratian took Alerio's elbow and guided him back towards the Corporal's Century.

"It's not Recruit anymore," Alerio explained as they walked. "I'm a Lance Corporal and a gladius instructor."

"Well look at you," Gratian teased. "The eastern Legion must be desperate for NCOs."

"It had more to do with the Raider Century I was assigned to," Alerio began to explain as they reached an intersection between six tents.

"What does the Colonel need?" asked Gratian.

"The Colonel is speaking at the Senate tomorrow. He's afraid the City Guard may try to prevent him from getting there. So he wants four squads of heavy infantry in the city before morning," Alerio replied. "I don't think the City Guard will allow you to just march in."

Gratian cocked his head and looked askew at Alerio. "With the Raiders were you?" the Corporal asked before turning away and speaking loudly. "Century on the street for orders. Now people."

Two heartbeats later shouting from the squads' Lance Corporals had everyone in the tents moving. By the time Alerio counted to fifteen, sixty Legionaries were standing in the road.

"First, Second, Fourth and Fifth, get dressed in your war gear," the Corporal ordered, "Third and Sixth, you're support. Round up ropes, ladders, and breaching gear. Squad leaders on me."

As the Legionaries went to collect their equipment, six Lance Corporals converged on Gratian. From the shadows, a Sergeant appeared but only waved a go ahead.

"What's up, Corporal?" one asked.

"We're going to sneak forty heavy infantrymen into the Capital," Gratian said with a smile. "Right under the City Guards' noses."

"We could march through them," one suggested. "I can't see the Guard stopping us."

"No. Colonel Nigellus wants backup not fighting in the streets," Alerio said. "He's speaking at the Senate tomorrow and wants his Legion around him."

"He'll have it," another vowed.

Gratian huddled the squad leaders together and began issuing specific instructions. After the last Lance Corporal rushed off to organize his squad, the Sergeant wandered over.

"Anything I can do?" he asked.

"I could use a diversion at the east gate," Gratian said. "A small riot of drunken Legionaries should do it. Any orders Sergeant?"

"You'll have your riot," promised the Sergeant. "Get to the Colonel and protect him. That's all the Centurions said."

The Sergeant left to collect men from other Centuries for the riot and Alerio turned to the Corporal.

"How are you going to sneak four squads and their gear into the city?" he asked Gratian.

"We're going to walk in, Lance Corporal Sisera," Gratian replied. "Now here's what I need you to do."

Chapter 36 - Securing Transportation

The eastern gate was normally slow late in the evenings. Although a few wagons left each night while farmers delivering food to the Capital arrived, the traffic only required a couple of guardsmen. With the Festival entering a full day of competition in the morning, wagons, riders, carts and individuals on foot exited the City or waited in a long line to enter.

Alerio waited, shuffled forward, and waited again as six City Guardsmen searched every vehicle. After being inspected, a Corporal collected a tax, and passed them through the gate. Five wagons, two carts and six walkers later, Alerio stepped up.

"Reason for entering the city?" asked a guardsman.

"I am staying at the Chronicles Humanum Inn," answered Alerio. "Just heading back for a mug and my bed."

The guardsmen studied his face in the torch and lantern light. Alerio feared the Guard was on the watch for him and he was prepared to lie if the guardsman asked for a name. Thankfully, there was no further questioning; the guardsman simply waved him through the gate.

Alerio waited until he was a block from the gate before picking up his pace. Six blocks later, he turned left and maintained the speed for another three blocks. He actually didn't slow down. His forward momentum ended when he collided with the thick wooden door with the iron bands.

"Master Kellerian," he announced as he rapped the knocker on the door. "I must speak with you immediately."

An iron strip slide back and Tomas mumbled, "When I was young, like you, I didn't sleep at night either. But now that I'm older and wiser, I value my rest. Come back in the morning."

The iron strip slid closed. Alerio stepped back and looked at the façade of the Historia Fae. There was no way to climb in so he marched back to the door and knocked again.

The strip slid back and the armorer warned, "Every time that knocker beats on my door, the cost of your armor goes up by five, no make that seven coppers. Go away."

"Centurion Kellerian. I have orders from Colonel Nigellus," Alerio said quickly before the iron slide could close.

"Nobody has called me that for twenty years," Tomas stated. "It reminds me. Reminds me of sleeping in the mud, bleeding barbarians, and eating corn mush and dried goatskin. I still have that taste in my mouth."

The slid closed and the noise of locking bars being removed followed. When the door opened, Tomas stepped out and looked down at Alerio.

"And what can this retired Legionary do for the Colonel?" he demanded.

"He's sneaking in four squads of heavy infantry," Alerio began. Tomas grabbed his arm and jerked him across the threshold.

"Not on the street," the armorer scolded. He closed and secured the door then shoved Alerio into the shop. "The Guard has ears everywhere. Now, why does the Colonel need forty Legionaries?"

"He's speaking to the Senate before they go into session tomorrow," Alerio reported. "And he doesn't trust that the City Guard will allow him passage to the Capital building."

"Why would the Guard prevent a Colonel of the Legion from speaking to the Senate?" inquired Tomas while shaking his head in puzzlement.

"Senator Ventus is going to ask the Senate to promote him to interim Consul. Then he wants to make a treaty with Qart Hadasht's Ambassador," Alerio replied. He was filling in details and lumping everything into a narrative to entice the armorer to help. He concluded with, "And the Tribes are gathering on our borders and Colonel Nigellus suspects they're being supported by Qart Hadasht. So, he has to get to the Capital building and warn the Senate. He fears Senator Ventus may use the Guard to stop him."

"So how can I help?" asked the armorer.

"At first I was going to ask you to armor the squads," Alerio replied. "but there was a change in plans. Corporal Gratian, who's in charge of the infiltration, is having the squads bringing their own gear. I was hoping you had an idea of how forty sets of Legionary armor, helmets, and shields could be transported secretly from Fireguard to the Chronicles Humanum Inn?"

"Aromataque et Saccharo," Tomas announced with a smile.

Chapter 37 - Aromataque et Saccharo

Retired Centurion Kellerian bolted the door after the young Lance Corporal left. Despite what he'd told Sisera, he did miss the Legion and the comradeship of his fellow Officers. Before heading to the rear of the Historia Fae compound, he stopped at the fish scale armor and lifted it off the stand.

In short order, the gate on the compound opened and Tomas flicked a whip over the heads of the mule team. They jerked forward and the wagon bumped over the curb and into the street. He jumped down and secured the gate before climbing back into the wagon.

Three blocks later, he turned east on the boulevard. Four blocks from the east gate a patrol of four City Guardsmen approached the wagon.

"What are you doing out this late in the evening, Master Kellerian?" asked the Lance Corporal still ten feet in front of the mules.

"Heading the long way around to the tanners," Tomas replied. "Giving the mules a little exercise."

"It's an odd time to be doing business," another Guard suggested. "Maybe we should have a look in the wagon."

"Sure, have a look. But be careful of Aromataque," Tomas warned.

The Guard patrol was three feet in front of the mules when the mule on the left stretched out her neck and snapped at the guardsmen. Even as they danced away, she attempted to pursue them across the street. The only thing preventing the mule from attacking the guard patrol was the anchor of her teammate on the right.

"I was going to suggest you cross beside Saccharo," Tomas said. "Aromataque is the reason I do business at night when the streets are empty. Still want to look in the wagon?"

Aromataque was twisted half way around in her harness and baring her teeth at the guardsmen. They inched along sideways until they were past the rear of the wagon.

"No, it's fine Master Kellerian, you have a good night," the Lance Corporal said as they walked away.

"Yo, Aromataque et Saccharo, move it. You stubborn mules," Tomas ordered while snapping the whip over the team's head.

The laughter of the guardsmen faded as they walked away and talked about the angry mule. Tomas turned the team and wagon onto the next street on the left and guided them towards the Fireguard District.

Behind him, men began yelling and shouting at the east gate. The guardsmen patrol reversed course and ran to help the sentries posted there. Tomas ignored the disturbance and kept a light hand on the reins as the team went from the clip-clops of the paved streets to the dirt and gravel road leading into Fireguard.

Chapter 38 - Two Things

Alerio changed his stride to the shuffling gait as he made his way into the Fireguard District. No one paid attention to him and soon he arrived at the last street before the earthen rampart. He maintained the gait of a weary worker as he climbed the steps to the third floor landing.

Before following the landing around the corner of the building, he pulled a mask over the lower half of his face.

There were five customers lingering over their wine. It was late and after the crowd of festival watchers had left the pub, it was mostly empty. From the looks of the five patrons, they had been nursing their vino for a long time.

"Proprietor. I have a proposition for you," Alerio announced as he stepped around the corner and into The Wine Trough.

"You come in here masked saying you have a proposition for me," challenged the pub's owner. He snatched up a club with one hand and produced a short iron knife with the other. "I can imagine the offer," he ventured with sarcasm.

"I'm meeting associates here this evening and I am willing to pay for privacy," explained Alerio. "The mask and offer are because my business isn't for the public. Now, do we discuss terms or should I go to a pub that wants my coin?"

"Five gold," announced the owner.

"I'll pay you five coppers to replace the business from these fine gentlemen," Alerio offered waving at the customers. "And three silvers for a couple of hours."

"Done. We are closed," shouted the proprietor. He came out from behind the oak barrel counter and began shooing the five drunks out of the pub.

While he emptied The Wine Trough, Alerio stacked five Republic coppers on the bar. By the time the owner finished clearing out the room, Alerio had placed three silvers beside the coppers. As the owner walked over looking fondly at the coins, Alerio dropped a Republic gold on the bar.

"What's that for?" asked the proprietor.

"Two things," replied Alerio. "One is where can I find a Lieutenant of the Cruor? I can locate any number of their street thugs myself. I could ask one of them but it would get messy, and that's no way to open negotiations. What I want is a name and directions to a top guy."

The owner eyed the gold coin. Crime groups valued his discretion and the off-the-grid location of his establishment. He wasn't sure if he wanted to break that trust until Alerio began moving his hand over the gold coin.

"Spurius Kanut," the pub owner announced as he shoved Alerio's hand away from the coins. "The Cruor have a building in the west arm of Firebreak. It's where they collect and count the coins from their businesses. You don't want to go to the building uninvited. Kanut keeps men-at-arms there for security."

"Spurius Kanut. Thank you for the information," proclaimed Alerio as he stepped back while the owner scooped up the coins.

"What's the second thing?" the man asked as he turned to face Alerio. He cupped the coins protectively in both hands.

Alerio shrugged off the cloak, reached over his shoulders and grabbed both gladii. In one smooth motion, the swords came free, and arched over ending up resting on the pub owner's shoulders. The sharp blades lay an inch on either side of the man's neck.

"Like I said, this meeting is private," Alerio stated. "Turn around slowly and lead us into the back room."

Still cupping the coins in his hands, the man was placed in a wooden chair. Alerio looped line around the pub owners' upper body and tied his ankles together. Then as a final act, he wrapped the pub owner's head in layer after layer of cloth he found in the back room.

"After we're gone, you can shrug off the rope, untie your feet, and free yourself," explained Alerio. "If I see or hear you during my meeting, I'll come back in here and cut off your head. Do you understand?"

The mess of cloth around the man's head nodded vigorously. Alerio closed the door, reached out and grabbed a piece of kindling. After wedging the wood under the door, he walked to a brazier on the porch.

In the distance, he could hear the sounds of men's voices rising and fading. Apparently, the uprising at the east gate was in full riot. Using a spade, he selected a small coal from the brazier. Leaning over the porch rail, Alerio tossed the ember underhanded.

The small glowing particle flew from the porch to the near edge of the earthen rampart and over the flat top where it lost altitude. The hot coal nipped the far side of the dirt fortification. The collision ended its flight but momentum carried the hot coal over the edge. It rolled five feet down the steep dirt wall before the ember died.

Chapter 39 - Walking on Air

Corporal Gratian had his Century kneeling in the dark twenty feet back from the steep dirt wall. While he could see lights on the porches glowing from the other side, he was confident the patrons couldn't see his Legionaries waiting in the dark. When the burning ember rolled over the lip of the wall, it's short illuminating roll was as good as an arrow pointing to the breaching location.

Two men carrying long poles ran to bracket the marked area. Following closely were eight men toting three lengths of ladders lashed together. The poles were tied to the ladder and, as the poles raised, the end of the ladder elevated. The last four men on the extended ladder shoved it beyond the length of the poles and higher up the earthen wall.

Three men charged at the ladder and began to climb. Strapped to two of their backs were ten-foot ladders. The third carried three long poles. They all had lengths of hemp rope over their shoulders.

Alerio saw the tip of the ladder before the first Legionary finished climbing to the top of the wall. The man unslung the ladder from his back and set it to the side. Next, he began pounding stakes into the far side of the earthen rampart. Another man appeared and he laid his ladder down so it over lapped the first ladder by three rungs. Afterward, he joined the Legionary pounding in the stakes. Ropes were tied to the newly drive stakes and one man crawled partially forward until his upper body hung over the far edge of the rampart.

Two Legionaries lashed the three poles to the two ten-foot lengths of ladders. Now, the joined and reinforced ladders created a footbridge fifteen feet long. They lifted the ladders, spun them in the direction of The Wine Trough's porch, and dropped them.

Alerio caught the end of the footbridge and secured it to the railing. By the time he finished with the last knot, an armored Legionary with his shield strapped to his back came over the far edge. Quickly, the man strolled confidently to the end of the narrow and flimsy footbridge. He paused while stakes were driven in and ropes tied to the other end of the ramp. A slap to his leg sent the Legionary moving onto the bridge.

Alerio reached up and helped the man step slowly down from the rail. It was human nature to bend and leap from a surface to start a jumping movement. The last thing they wanted was a heavily armored Legionary putting launch pressure on the temporary platform. Helping him down prevented the impulse to jump. The first across joined Alerio and together they helped the next Legionary down. Then, Alerio was shoved aside as the Legionary took his post.

The third man to cross was Corporal Gratian.

"It's like walking on air," he said as the two Legionaries helped him to the porch. "What's the plan, Lance Corporal Sisera?"

"Centurion Kellerian should have his wagon in the alley at the bottom of the stairs," Alerio reported. "It's best not to congregate. Why don't you go down and send the men off two or three at a time?"

"Thinking on your feet, I like it," Gratian said. "Must be the Raider influence. See you later Recruit."

Three men had crossed while they talked. Gratian led them to the door and the landing. He paused just outside the entrance. When two more Legionaries had made it to the porch, the Corporal led them away.

"First Squad is out," the two helpers announced when the last of their men crossed the footbridge. "Second Squad. You have the duty."

They were relieved by two new Legionaries and walked heavy-footed to the pubs exit. Alerio hadn't thought about it but now glanced at the porches to either side of The Wine Trough. Two men stood on one of the neighboring porches. They were standing with their mugs of wine held out in salute. The other porch was empty.

Fourth and Fifth squads crossed and as the last Legionary headed for the exit, Alerio untied the footbridge. Then, he stood staring at the Legionaries on the berm. One signaled for him to push the ladders away from the railing. He did and the end fell into the void between the building and the earthen rampart. But the other end was anchored so the footbridge simply fell away. Two Legionaries pulled it up hand over hand while the third knocked out the stakes. Soon the dirt was smoothed flat so there were no signs of the squads' passing.

Chapter 40 - Nice Evening for a Moonlit Drive

Alerio arrived at the alley as Corporal Gratian sent his two final Legionnaires off into the night. The Lance Corporal and the Corporal grinned at each other in relief. All four squads were in the city and making their way to the inn and their Colonel.

"Can I get a hand here?" asked Tomas impatiently. "That is if you're not too busy planning the conquest of Qart Hadasht."

The armorer stood on the back of the wagon holding a goatskin tarp. In the wagon were layers and layers of neatly placed Legion armor, helmets, and shields.

"Sorry Master Kellerian," Alerio apologized as he jumped onto the wagon.

"I'll see you at the inn Centurion," Gratian said as he moved out of the alley. "Take care of the Recruit."

Before Alerio could respond, the Corporal had turned the corner.

"Knew him before you joined the Legion?" asked Tomas as he lashed down the covering.

"We did a little business on my way through the Transfer Post," explained Alerio. "Are you sure you want me with you. I'm avoiding the City Guard for a couple of reasons."

"Good. It'll give us something to talk about on our tour of the City," Tomas said as he stepped up to the driver's bench. "If we do run across any curious City Guards, you act deaf and dumb. I'll handle them."

Alerio climbed up beside the armorer and Tomas snapped the whip.

"Yo, Aromataque and Saccharo, move it. You stubborn mules," he urged.

The wagon pulled from the alley and Alerio was surprised when Tomas guided the mules in a northerly direction.

"The Chronicles Humanum Inn is that way," Alerio said while pointing to his left.

The wagon completed its turn before Tomas replied, "You are a bright lad. With an intellect like yours, you should be a scholar, not a Legionary."

"Sorry. It's not easy being a deaf and dumb assistant," Alerio said sheepishly.

A man was staggering down the center of the street in a direct line with the mule team.

"Don't do it Aromataque," Tomas shouted, "Ah, hades. Saccharo haw, haw."

The mule on the left had started to angle towards the unsuspecting drunk. At Tomas' command, the mule on the right shouldered her team mate and the wagon moved. The intoxicated man passed safely along the right side.

"The mules are Sugar and Spice?" asked Alerio.

"They are mules," Tomas replied. "I couldn't rightly call them lighting and thunder. It would be insulting to Jupiter and every respectable Legion warhorse. Now. Tell me why you're dodging the City Guard."

They rolled out of the Fireguard District and onto the paved roads of the Capital City. As they traveled, Alerio explained about the bounty on his head by the Cruor and how he needed to confront Spurius Kanut. He went on to describe his fight with Daedalus where the City Guard Corporal attempted to collect the reward in a competition. Finally, he brought the armorer up to date on his dealings with the Fireguard Brigade.

147

Tomas turned after eight blocks and headed the team westward. They talked softly and rolled across the deserted city. Before they reached the left leg of Firebreak District, he guided the team south heading towards the stockyards.

"It sounds like you need to get out of the city," Tomas suggested.

"That's what I've been trying to do," Alerio said. "But the transport has been delayed."

The aroma of the stockyard drifted to them and Tomas took a turn and a few blocks later turned again on the road leading towards the Temple of Portunus.

"I don't want to be too close to the west gate when we cross the boulevard," explained Tomas. "As it is, we may get stopped. Remember, you are a deaf mute so act accordingly."

Tomas and Alerio fell into silence as the east-west boulevard came into sight. As the mules clopped towards the doublewide road, the same patrol as before came marching from the east.

"Still exercising the mules, Master Kellerian?" the Lance Corporal asked then added. "I see you've picked up a passenger.

"Handling raw leather is hard work," Tomas explained as he slowed the mules so the guard patrol would be in front of his team. "I needed someone with a strong back and one who knows how to keep his mouth shut."

"You there. What's it like working with the Armorer to the Gods?" another teased.

Tomas swung around and clubbed Alerio in the shoulder with the whip handle. "He's deaf and dumb," Tomas explained. "As I said, I like my help to keep their mouths shut. With him, it doesn't matter."

148

Alerio opened his mouth in surprise but didn't utter a sound when the whip handle smashed into his shoulder. He peered out from under his cloak at the armorer. Tomas ignored him as he pulled on the reins as if attempting to restrain the mules. In fact, he pulled both to their left.

"Aromataque gee, Aromataque gee," Tomas shouted at the mule before saying to the City Guardsmen. "Sorry. She's getting tired and ill-tempered. Do you want to search my wagon? There's nothing like the aroma of fresh leather, goat urine, and lye to liven up your evening."

Between the thought of smelling fresh tanner's products while avoiding the snapping jaws of the mule, the City Guard decided against searching the wagon. The Lance Corporal motioned for the wagon to move on.

"Have a good morning, Master Kellerian," the Guard said.

As the wagon crossed the boulevard, they could hear the guards talking about how mean it was to strike a deaf mute so hard. It just confirmed the guardsmen's opinion that Kellerian was a tough taskmaster and none of them would like working for him.

Along the quiet road bordering the Portunus Temple, Alerio whispered, "That hurt."

"I know," admitted Tomas. "But it had to be convincing."

"Now I understand what Nigellus meant," Alerio replied.

"Nigellus was a good student," commented Tomas. "He knew how to take a hit. What did he say?"

"Pretty much the same thing," answered Alerio. "Sort of the same thing."

They reached the harbor intersection and Tomas turned the wagon to the left. Six blocks later they crossed the north-south boulevard.

The sky was pitch black and other than the widely spaced lanterns, there was little light. A single lantern marked the intersection before the city's defensive wall. Tomas turned left towards the Chronicles Humanum Inn.

Chapter 41 - Colonels Deal in Discipline, Death, and Intelligence

"Colonel Nigellus. Corporal Gratian reporting as ordered, sir," announced the NCO as he marched into the great room of the inn.

"Corporal. Glad you could make it," replied the Legion Officer. "What have you brought me?"

"Sir, First, Second, Fourth and Fifty squads," Gratian stated. "Heavy infantry of the Central Legion. Our armor is in transit but we're ready to go."

"I like your spirit Corporal," Nigellus said. "But, I think we have time to wait for your equipment. Have the men get some rest. It's going to be a busy day tomorrow."

"Yes, sir," the NCO said as he slammed his right fist into his left breast.

Nigellus returned the salute, turned his head and spoke to Thomasious, "I've heard people say the Republic is doomed. Our young people are soft and aren't hard enough to face the struggles we did building it. That young NCO brought forty Legionaries into a closed city and was ready to go into battle without his armor. If he's an example of our young, the future is in good hands."

"It's not the young I worry about," replied the innkeeper. "It's the old and scared. The ones who want to stop progress and seek safety behind treaties with our most vicious enemies."

"Senator Ventus and his compatriots haven't succeeded yet," Nigellus reminded him. "I have intelligence from the General. It should be enough for the Senate to stop the treaty."

"I hope so Champ," Thomasious said softly. "I hope so."

The two men sat, each keeping his own counsel, while in the courtyard, forty Legionaries gambled, slept or chatted in the chill of the evening. A Legionary was sitting on a barrel with a cluster sitting around him listening as he softy sang a song. One figure paced between squads offering words of encouragement or advice.

Corporal Gratian, usually the first to take a chance and always up for a bet, couldn't relax. Being the senior NCO for a clandestine mission going against the wishes of the Senate wasn't what had him worried. Paramount for the Legion Corporal was the safety of his men.

A long time later the rumble and clatter of a mule team and a wagon came from the side of the inn. Erebus unlatched the gate and swung it open. Tomas urged the mules through the opening and pulled them to a stop in the center of the courtyard.

"Alright people. That wagon isn't going to unload itself," a relieved Corporal Gratian announced. "Fifth squad collect your gear. Forth squad stand by."

Tomas and Alerio climbed to the wagon's sides and unlashed the goatskin cover. Hands reached in and pulled out armor and shields.

"Just take the top layer," Tomas instructed. "You can sort out who belongs to what away from the wagon."

The packing was so precise; all four squads quickly had it unloaded. Alerio noticed a few items laying on the floorboards.

"Is someone missing their gear?" he asked as he glanced around at the Legionaries.

"Yes, Lance Corporal Sisera. You and I are missing our gear," Tomas explained as he pulled out a set of new armor. "Here. This one is yours. I'll need it back to adjust it to the duel rig, but for now, it'll have to do."

After handing off the armor, a helmet and a shield, Tomas reached back into the wagon. He lifted out the fish scale armor.

"I thought maybe I could test it," Tomas ventured.

He was standing on the far side of the wagon and a group of Legionnaires had gathered around him to see the fish scale armor.

"Well. Don't stand there gawking," Tomas complained. "Help me strap this on."

As hands reached to hold the armor with the small plates and others to secure straps, Colonel Nigellus appeared in the doorway. He stood looking around at the squads strapping on their armor; he wasn't seeing them. His mind was turning over a problem.

"Lance Corporal Sisera, Corporal Gratian," the Colonel called out. "A moment of your time, if you please."

He started to turn when a voice addressed him from the far side of the wagon, "You'd think, a Centurion would be included in a war planning session."

Tomas stepped out from behind the wagon. His helmet tucked under his left arm leaving his right free to salute.

"Centurion Kellerian, reporting for duty, sir," announced the armorer.

"You still look as if you could beat a Recruit into the sand," Nigellus replied.

"I still can Colonel," confirmed Tomas.

"In that case, Centurion Kellerian, do join us," stated Nigellus as he spun on his heels and marched back into the inn.

Once Kellerian, Gratian, and Sisera were seated at a table across from Nigellus and Harricus, the Colonel started speaking.

"Lance Corporal Sisera. You saw this barbarian on the Qart Hadasht boat?" he asked.

"Yes, sir, he met with Gabrielus," answered Alerio. "On the boat at the pier."

"The one thing I don't have is intelligence on the enemy's plan," Nigellus explained. "I would like the opportunity to have a talk with the barbarian. Any ideas?"

"Give me five Legionaries to take the boat. And we'll deliver him to you," Alerio assured him

"Wouldn't it be safer to take an entire squad?" asked Corporal Gratian.

"We can sneak six men from here to the harbor," Alerio explained. "Moving eleven and we're sure to be seen."

"That's an odd take on the manpower requirements for the mission," challenged the Colonel. "Usually heavy infantrymen prefer going in stomping with a healthy dose of bloodletting. What unit were you with in the eastern Legion?"

"Legion Raiders, sir," Alerio explained. "Centurion Stylianus and Sergeant Horus' command."

"Alright. Corporal Gratian pick five men to accompany Lance Corporal Sisera," the Colonel ordered then added. "Make sure they're strong swimmers."

Centurion Kellerian knew the Republic lacked a large navy and most of their warships were for coastal patrols. Chasing and engaging pirates on the water was dangerous. He agreed with the suggestion to use expert swimmers. Still, putting a young Lance Corporal in charge worried him.

"Ah Colonel, shouldn't we have a more experienced NCO on the mission?" Kellerian suggested.

"Lance Corporal Sisera, do you need a more experienced NCO?" Nigellus asked.

Alerio stood up and bent his head forward to display the crescent shaped scar on his head.

"I killed four Rebels before I started Recruit training," he explained. "And I was part of a two-man rescue mission in a warehouse full of Rebels. I wouldn't think a snatch and grab of a barbarian off a boat guarded by rowers would provide much of a challenge."

"He doesn't lack for confidence, does he?" the Colonel asked Kellerian.

"Or experience. I withdraw my objection," Tomas replied.

"Five expert swimmers, I'm on it sirs," Corporal Gratian said as he stood. "Come on Lance Corporal Sisera. I'll introduce you to your team.

Act 6

Chapter 42 - Fire Watch

Alerio lead the five Legionaries out of the inn, past the Cloth Seller's, the Apothecary, and the Candle Maker's compounds. The group crossed the road near the city wall and entered an alley. Keeping off the roads, they weaved between merchant compounds following the defensive wall southward before it gently wrapped around towards the west. They veered away from the wall at the south gate to avoid the guardsmen. Once over the boulevard, they slipped back nearer the wall.

When they moved behind the Golden Valley Trading compound, Alerio thought he saw the shape of a man squatting on the roof of the house. But it was dark, the light low, and he figured his eyes were playing tricks on him. Two blocks later, the Legionaries arrived on the southern end of a warehouse.

The six-man snatch team eased along the façade of the warehouse. At the other end, Alerio held up a hand to halt the team. He leaned around the corner to get a glimpse of the harbor and the piers.

"Who are the best talkers?" Alerio asked the Legionaries.

"You looking to parlay you way onto the boat?" a Legionary asked.

"You're one, who else?" demanded Alerio.

"I talk a pretty good game," another responded.

"Alright. There are two merchant ships at the dock," Alerio instructed. "We're going to march out acting like City Guardsmen. One talker to each of the merchant ships. I want the fire watch on those boats engaged in deep and philosophical discussions with you."

"You want us to just talk?" one asked in surprise.

"It's better the ships' watches be talking to you," explained Alerio. "Instead of calling for City Guardsmen when the sword fight breaks out on the Qart Hadasht launch."

"That will only leave us four bodies to take down the ship and snatch the barbarian," complained another Legionary.

"Actually, you and you are my snatch team," Alerio said as he tapped the shoulders of the two biggest Legionaries. "The barbarian is on the aft section. When we board, you two charge directly for him. Get him off the boat and on the way to the Colonel. Don't stop for anything. Once the barbarian is clear you talkers break off from the fire watches and escort the snatch team."

"There's going to be Qart Hadasht sailors on that boat," the one Legionary without an assignment pointed out. "And Lance Corporal Sisera, there are only you and me to clear and hold the deck."

"I know, that's why I picked you," Alerio replied.

"You picked me for a suicide mission?" the Legionary asked with pain in his voice.

"Actually, I picked you because you were singing in the courtyard," admitted Alerio. "I fancy a song when I fight. Think of a good song for us. Now, four to the front, the talkers in the rear with me. Everyone ready?"

Four of the Legionaries reached out. They patted the singer on his shoulder armor as if to offer condolences. Next, they formed up.

"Forward march," Alerio ordered and the six Legionaries stepped off.

At the first merchant ship, Alerio shoved a talker out of formation. The Legionary strolled towards the ship.

"Yo, where do you hail from?" he asked as he walked up the ramp.

"Beneventum," replied the sailor on fire watch.

"Where you there when Pyrrhus attacked the city?" the Legionary inquired. "That was what, fifteen years ago?"

"No. The Greek attacked closer to eight years ago," the watch replied. "I was in the city when General Dentatus marched in victoriously after the battle."

"That must have been a sight," the Legionary said as he sat beside the man. "Tell me about it."

The voices faded as Alerio and his team moved closer to the second merchant ship. A shove sent the next Legionary towards the ship's ramp.

"When do you sail?" asked the Legion talker.

"Right after the Festival," the fire watch replied. "My Captain and First Mate went to see it."

"And left you here to watch the ship?" asked the Legionary in surprise.

"Yup, I've got the duty," the sailor replied sadly.

"I know the feeling. My Centurion put me on guard duty," the Legionary commiserated. "I really wanted to see the games and, you know, place a few bets."

"I too enjoy wagering a few coins on the games," the sailor admitted.

The talk of gambling faded as the remaining four Legionaries approached the pier where the Qart Hadasht launch was docked.

"By twos, double time march," Alerio ordered.

The four picked up their pace as the singer fell back with Alerio to allow the bigger snatch team to charge onto the launch.

Their shields hit the Qart Hadasht fire watch who was standing on the ramp. He bounced off the shields, the edge of the ramp, and tumbled into the water. Another sailor sleeping on the deck got stomped unconscious as the two big Legionaries raced down one side of the ship.

At the aft section, the barbarian sat up but was hammered down by one of the big shields.

"It'll be easier to carry him if he's asleep," advised one of the snatch team.

"You carry and I'll tie his hands," the other suggested.

So far the snatch and grab had gone smoothly. Except, the boat rocked, the Legionaries' hobnailed boots made the deck wood ring, and the fire watch in the water began to yell. All this caused the forward hatch to begin vomiting Qart Hadasht sailors. They poured through the hatch from below deck half-dressed and brandishing wicked knives and long heavy clubs.

The Legionnaires noticed something odd about the sailors. Beyond being hunched over, their sloping shoulders went from huge arms and deltoids directly to their ears. They had no necks. As well, they didn't shout. Rather they squawked and made grunting noises that rose from deep in their throats.

"Trolls," the Legionary beside Alerio whispered before shouting. "Troll! There are trolls guarding the Qart Hadasht boat."

Alerio set his shield down on the dock, reached over his shoulders, and unsheathed the two gladii.

"Trolls or rowers, it doesn't matter. As long as they bleed and die," Alerio informed him. Then, he suggested, "Now would be a good time to sing."

"Now Lance Corporal Sisera?" the Legionary asked with a quiver in his voice. "You want me to sing now?"

Two of the odd sailors had reached the snatch team. The unencumbered Legionary used his shield to drive one into the deck. But, all the big shield did was shove the short but massive sailor back. He stabbed at the second sailor and despite drawing blood, his gladius was beat down by a club.

The Legionary holding the barbarian defended his partner's left side with his shield. As the sailors shoved and beat silently at the snatch team, Alerio took a step forward.

"Sing now! Sing loud," ordered Alerio as he ran across the ramp and leaped at the two Qart Hadasht sailors.

Chapter 43 – Hold The Line Lads, Hold The Line

"Hold the Line Lads, Hold the Line," the Legionary sang in a basso voice.

"Who are they? We shout.
They're in the valley to murder our families.
We're here to kill, those homicidal savages.
Hold the Line Lads, Hold the Line."

"Who is she? We shout.

159

A brown eyed girl looking for a rescuer.
You're the right Legionary, to be her deliverer.
Hold the Line Lads, Hold the Line."

"What if I die? We shout.
They'll cut us down from left to right.
Second line up, fill the gaps and fight.
Hold the Line Lads, Hold the Line."

"Know what I think? We shout.
In a melee brawl, it's not political debate.
It's gladius muscle, as Gods test your fate.
Hold the Line Lads, Hold the Line."

"Why did I join? We shout.
Cause Sergeants care for you just like.
Your mommy did, on cold winter nights.
Hold the Line Lads, Hold the Line."

The bottoms of Alerio's boots slammed into the sailors' hips. They were short and stocky yet the angle of collision bent them sideways. The two sailors blocking the snatch team flew across the deck. Alerio landed on his back. But not for long, he popped up and spun to face the rest of the advancing rowers. Suddenly, the two shields of the snatch team flanked him.

"Don't defend me," he sneered. "Your only job is to get the barbarian to Colonel Nigellus. This is my job."

Alerio began weaving figure eights in the air with his gladii while stepping forward.

"What if I die? We shout. They'll cut us down from left to right," he sang as his blades came closer and closer to the mob of sailors. *"Second line up, fill the gaps and fight. Hold the Line Lads, Hold the Line."*

The closest two sailors realized the danger and backed up into the other six. For a moment, the Qart Hadasht rowers bunched together freeing a narrow path to the ramp. Just as the snatch team reached the end of the ramp, the sailors let out inhuman screeches and surged forward. The snatch team was driven back.

From the ramp, the singer rushed forward and smashed into the rowers' flanks. They staggered to the side from the shield's impact and the path to the ramp reopened.

"Who is she? We shout. A brown eyed girl looking for a rescuer," Alerio and his Legionaries sang. *"You're the right Legionary, to be her deliverer. Hold the Line Lads, Hold the Line."*

The snatch team reached the ramp and the Legionary singer backed up using his shield to seal off access from the ship.

Alerio chopped a sailor's hand off and for a heartbeat he looked into the face of the rower. The man opened his mouth and let out an animal sound from deep in his throat. That's when Alerio noticed the rower's tongue had been cutout. As the man sank to the deck holding the stump, Alerio drove his other gladius from near the deck upward and split the chin of another sailor.

"Know what I think? We shout," Alerio sang as he stomped a foot and neatly peeled off a section from another's sailor's scalp. *"In a melee brawl, it's not political debate. It's gladius muscle, as Gods test your fate."*

From the two Legionaries racing down the merchant ships' ramps, the snatch team with the barbarian, and the Legionary singer, he heard, *"Hold the Line Lads, Hold the Line."*

But the final words of the song were sung from near the corner of the warehouse as they raced away with the barbarian captive. Another sound followed the fading notes. City Guardsmen were calling out as they descended on the harbor.

161

Alerio pulled in his elbows as hands reached for him. The remaining rowers had circled him and were trying to grab on and drag him to the deck.

"Who are they? We shout. They're in the valley to murder our families," he sang as he used the hilts of the gladii to punch and gouge at the sailors. *"We're here to kill, those homicidal savages. Hold the Line Lads, Hold the Line."*

His attack rocked back a sailor leaving a gap in the circle. Alerio bent his knees and, catching the rowers off guard, he vaulted out of their clutches. In two hopping steps, he reached the ramp.

Three sailors paused then made a decision. They ran for the ramp. Alerio snatched up his shield and sprinted for the corner of the warehouse. Behind him, the rowers were roaring as they reached the dock.

Six City Guardsmen met the rowers.

"What happened?" one asked.

When the mute sailors attempted to push aside the guardsmen, they were beat down. One guardsman saw a Legionary running with a shield flying behind him.

"There," he shouted directing the other four. "One's getting away."

The guardsman left the unconscious sailors and ran toward the warehouse.

At the west gate a trumpet sounded one long note. The guardsmen who beat the sailors and chased after Alerio had come from the east-west boulevard. One roving patrol from the north-south boulevard angled toward the docks. What Alerio couldn't know was another patrol from the south gate responded to the trumpet. When they reached the Golden Valley trading house, they split with two guardsmen going behind the compound while the other three kept to the road.

Alerio sprinted down the line of warehouses. When he cleared the last building, he was confident he'd gotten away. As he reached the corner of the Golden Valley's walls, two guardsmen holding lanterns rounded the far corner. He turned towards the road in front of the trading house, but three more guardsmen appeared.

From between the warehouses, four guardsmen approached and searched every dark corner as they came. Alerio looked hard at the city's thirty feet high defensive wall, realized he couldn't scale it, and resigned himself to surrounding.

A noise drew his attention. As if someone had dropped an armload of kindling against the wall, the wood tapped, tapped, tapped from high up on the trading house wall to waist high.

Chapter 44 - An Ally in Need is an Ally Indeed

"Climb Legionary," a voice whispered from atop the trading house's wall.

Alerio slipped the shield's strap over his shoulder and slung the big shield onto his back. As the heavy infantry shield settled, he jumped and clutched at the rope ladder. It took effort to climb hand over hand until he could get a foot on the first narrow rung. Once he had footing, he made short work of scaling the wall.

"Excuse me," the man said politely.

He was squatting on the flat narrow top of the wall. Despite his precarious perch, the man reached around Alerio and began pulling up the ladder. Once he gathered the entire length, he dropped the flexible ladder down the interior side of the compound's wall.

"After you," invited the man.

Alerio glanced at the guardsmen as the two groups converged on the grass below him. Quickly, he swung his legs around and used the ladder to reach the interior courtyard.

The man jumped, fell for half the distance before grabbing one side of the ladder. It slowed his fall enough so when he released the rope, his final drop required only a slight bend to his knees to land safely.

"Welcome back to the Golden Valley trading house," Favus said in greeting.

The merchant glided across the ground with almost no movement to his upper body. When he stopped a couple of feet from the Legionary, it was as if he had been standing there the entire time.

"I appreciate the assistance, again," Alerio replied.

"Are you injured?" Favus inquired.

"A few cuts and a lot of bruises," replied the Legionary. "Nothing that requires medical attention."

"I am pleased," Favus exclaimed. "Because I need to speak with you. And I want to show you something. Follow me."

From standing still in front of the Legionary, the merchant ghosted to a dark open doorway in the rear of the trading house. Alerio had to rush to catch up. As he jogged across the courtyard, it occurred to him the merchant might be more than a trader in exotic goods. Favus might be an assassin of the Dulce Pugno.

Inside the storeroom of the trading house, Favus guided him to a two-course wide brick stairway.

"I can lower a rope and pulled you up," Favus offered as he nimbly took the first five steps.

"Unnecessary," Alerio assured him as he unstrapped the shoulder armor. "Is it alright to leave the armor here?"

The man who had helped him over the wall took the shoulder, the chest and back pieces.

"It'll be here when we've finished," the merchant explained as he started up the stairs.

The former farm-lad followed the merchant as the steps doubled back four times before Favus stopped. He reached out and pushed a cover. Stars appeared in the opening and Alerio realized they were just under the roof of the trading house. Soon they were on the roof tiles and squatting beside each other on a flat piece of slate.

They stayed like that for a long time before Alerio broke the silence.

"It's a beautiful view of the Capital City," Alerio said.

"Look over to the northeast between the four lanterns," Favus ordered. "Watch as they blink out and quickly relight."

He held a stick level and used it to guide Alerio's eyes to a place across the city. Sure enough, the lanterns went dark momentarily before resuming a steady glow.

"Those are your five Legionaries on the street before the inn," Favus stated. "They avoided the guardsmen and should be back with your Colonel shortly."

"Thank you. That takes a load off my shoulders," Alerio confessed but a questioned occurred to him. "How did you know the Colonel was at the inn?"

"The same way I knew you plucked the Insubri Prince from the Qart Hadasht ship," answered Favus. "The same way the Clay Ear gathers information. I have spies throughout the city."

"I'd expect nothing less from the Dulce Pugno," Alerio stated testing to see the merchant's reaction.

"Ah my friend, we don't use that term in the city," Favus replied.

As Favus didn't deny being an assassin from the Sweet Fist, Alerio tried a harder question, "Did you accept a contract on Senator Ferox?"

"We do not discuss our customers. Not who the customer is or what they purchase," the assassin explained. "However, I can assure you, we did not take a contract on Senator Faunus."

"Of that I'm sure," Alerio said with confidence. "Senator Faunus' assassination was a bloody street brawl. Hardly an elegant execution of a secret contract."

"Thank you for realizing that," Favus said accepting the compliment to his skills. "Senator Faunus is why I wanted to speak with you in private."

"I'm here. And based on the numerous City Guard patrols I can see," Alerio stated. "I'm not going anywhere for a while."

"Trading houses of the Golden Valley do not get involved in local politics," Favus explained. "In most cases, a change in leadership makes no difference to our trade. We trade with the Republic, the Rebels opposing you, the Greeks, and the Qart Hadasht Empire. The groups we do not trade with are the northern and western tribes. They take before trading and kill before negotiating. Until they provide safe trading, we deem it fitting to assist you."

"Assist me how?" asked Alerio. "Kill Vivianus? Take out Gabrielus? Either would be appreciated."

"No. The Senator is the Senate's business," Favus informed him. "The barbarian Prince Gabrielus is a different story. I may be

166

able to provide proof of his involvement in Senator Faunus's murder."

"How? The reports say nothing was stolen, even the ropes and staff of his office were found on the body. There's nothing to connect Gabrielus to the crime," Alerio declared. "As much as I appreciate the offer of help, I'm afraid the word of a merchant wouldn't be enough to tie him to the assassination."

"Senator Faunus' wife was once a Priestess of Luna," Favus explained. "To honor the moon Goddess she served, she wore an amulet. Hidden under her blouse should have been the trinket; a gold half-moon against a blue sky of crushed sapphires with moonstones as stars. It depicts Luna driving a two-yoke chariot pulled by a team of charging bulls across the sky. The amulet was a gift from the Senator when he was a Tribune. She never went anywhere without it. It was not found on her body."

"How does locating a piece of jewelry help?" asked Alerio. "And how do you know about the missing jewelry?"

"The Clay Ear didn't know? My source was in the Senator's home, not waiting at the wash racks," a self-satisfied Favus stated. Then he continued, "The Insubri like shiny trophies. If the amulet was taken during the attack, one of the killers will have it."

"If Gabrielus' men ambushed the Senator," Alerio ventured before pausing. "Are you saying Gabrielus has the amulet?"

"I am not saying he definitely has the amulet," admitted the merchant. "What I know is the Insubri Prince has a chest in his room full of trinkets. If he is in possession of the Luna charm, it will be in that chest."

"Will you get it for me?" asked Alerio hopefully.

"There is a legal term; chain of custody. If I were to hand you the amulet, who is to say it wasn't me who murdered the Senator," advised Favus. "No, Ally of the Golden Valley, I can't touch the charm. On the other hand, I can return you to the inn."

"How? There are active patrols across the city," Alerio reminded the merchant.

"We have a delivery for the grandstand at the festival leaving shortly," explained Favus. "A harness on one of the horses could come loose. When the wagon driver stops to adjust it, a stowaway could slip out of the wagon, and steal away into the dark."

Chapter 45 - Trolls

The snatch team of Legionaries had crossed the boulevard as the alarm went out. With City Guards rushing around, they were forced to duck into an alley. Fortunately, all the guardsmen eventually headed for the harbor. Moving quickly through the shadows, the five men and the barbarian Prince remained undetected as they crept back to the inn.

"Where's Lance Corporal Sisera?" Gratian asked as they came through the side gate.

"We have the barbarian," the two big Legionaries offered.

They shoved the prisoner forward as if to provide evidence.

"Take him to the Colonel," Gratian ordered while motioning the two Legionaries towards the inn. Then he grabbed another member of the team and demanded, "Where is Sisera?"

"He ordered us to leave," the Legionary replied. "He said our only job was to get the barbarian to the Colonel."

"But where is he?" insisted the Corporal.

"The last time we saw him," another reported. "He was on the boat surrounded by trolls."

"Surrounded by what?" an astonished Gratian asked.

"Trolls, Corporal. The Qart Hadasht boat was guarded by trolls," repeated the Legionary.

"He's right," another confirmed. "Trolls right out of mythology."

"Why didn't you help him? How did you get away?" Gratian inquired. "Weren't you also surrounded by, by the trolls?"

"No, Corporal. I was on a merchant ship talking to a sailor from Beneventum," replied the Legionary. "But they were trolls, I can assure you."

Gratian beckoned the three remaining members of the snatch team over to where the lantern light was brightest. He studied each man's armor, shield and helmet. There wasn't a blood splatter on any of the three.

"And, where were you?" he asked another one.

"Talking betting with an old sailor," replied the Legionary. "He has some interesting ideas on picking winning chariot teams."

Gratian held up a hand to stop the man and asked the third member, "And, what were you doing while Sisera was surrounded by trolls?"

"Singing Corporal. I was singing," the Legionary stated.

Before the NCO could ask another question, Centurion Kellerian shouted from the backdoor. "Corporal Gratian. Front and center."

"We'll talk later," he said to the three confused Legionaries. Then he jogged for the inn and disappeared through the doorway.

"Trolls? Did you say Lance Corporal Sisera was killed by trolls?" asked a Legionary as he and several others gathered around the snatch team.

"Yes. Trolls. Thickly muscled like oxen with no necks," one replied. "And they didn't speak. Just screeched and growled as they clawed at him."

"That's an ugly way to die," a newly arrived Legionary ventured. "They probably ate him."

His declaration was agreed upon unanimously by the crowd. Then, each Legionary went to tell the tale of the trolls to his squad.

Chapter 46 - A Colonel Trumps an Insubri Prince

Corporal Gratian rushed down the hall. He pushed through the double doors and entered the great room. His two big Legionaries flanked the barbarian. The three were standing in front of a table. Thomasious Harricus and Colonel Nigellus sat at the table looking at the barbarian. Centurion Kellerian paced the floor off to the side. Everyone turned at the sound of the doors swinging open.

"Sirs. Corporal Gratian, reporting as ordered," he announced.

"Gratian. Did all the team make it back?" Nigellus inquired.

"No, sir. Lance Corporal Sisera is missing," the NCO said. He kept his tone professional yet his true emotion showed through as he bit off each word.

"Any wounded?" the Colonel asked.

"No, sir. No medical attention or equipment repairs required," he replied while scanning the last two members of the snatch team.

These two at least displayed some blood splatter. Although it wasn't what he'd expect after an assault.

"Our barbarian here refuses to talk with me," the Colonel advised. "I wanted you here so there was no confusion."

"Confusion, sir?" inquired Gratian.

"Yes, Corporal. I don't want my orders misconstrued," Nigellus explained as he shoved back his chair and stood. He turned to face the prisoner before continuing, "In the morning, you will take the barbarian to the nearest open park and crucify him. Is that clear?"

"I understand sir. If I might make a request?" asked Gratian. "I'd like to saw off his feet before he goes up on the wood."

"But he'll bleed out and die," the Colonel complained. "I want him to suffer."

"He'll suffer, sir," the Corporal promised. "We'll tie off his thighs to stop the blood loss. Of course, we'll need to tie the tourniquets painfully tight around his thighs to stop the bleeding at his ankles. If that's enough pain for you, sir?"

"It's agreeable to me. Centurion Kellerian. Your opinion?" asked Nigellus.

"Colonel, treatment like that is savage," the Centurion said with horror in his voice. "Crucifixion is one thing. But you'll have the Corporal mutilate, ah, what's your name?"

Everyone stopped as they waited for the barbarian to reply. Five heartbeats later he did.

"I am Prince Peregrinus of the Insubri," he announced. "I am not afraid to die."

"The crucifixion wouldn't kill you. Unless I leave you up there for several days," explained Colonel Nigellus. "No, Prince. The Corporal will cut you down after a few painful days. You won't die. But, if you want to walk around, you'll need to learn to balance on stumps."

Peregrinus tilted his head and stared down at his feet. When they saw him wiggle his toes through the ends of his sandals, they knew he was prepared to talk.

"Tell me Prince Peregrinus. Who is Gabrielus to you?" asked the Colonel.

"He is my brother," the barbarian blurted out. "Taken to your Republic when he was just a teen."

"You see. Talking to me is preferable to the alternate," Nigellus said evenly. "Why were you on the Qart Hadasht ship? What did you and your brother discuss?"

Peregrinus looked out the front windows of the inn. Outside, the moon had set. The dark had deepened as it did every morning before dawn's first rays. As if having decided something, he turned back and smiled.

"I accompanied the Ambassador here to wait for my warriors," Peregrinus proclaimed. "Once Qart Hadasht has control of the city, the Insubri will take control of the surrounding territory."

"And how does Qart Hadasht plan to control the Capital City of the Republic?" inquired the Nigellus. "The Ambassador's ceremonial squad couldn't hold a tradesmen's block of real estate against the Legion."

"But Colonel, there are few Legionaries in the city," Peregrinus reminded the group. "After a signal, the Qart Hadasht navy will deliver more than enough troops to capture your city."

"Signal? What signal?" demanded Kellerian. "Tell me now before I start removing body parts."

"I don't know the nature of the signal," Peregrinus exclaimed. "Just that a signal will alert the ships waiting off the coast."

The port of Ostia was located nineteen miles to the southeast. Where the Tiber dumped its yellow, brown water into the blue ocean, the Republic had established a port for large merchant ships and the patrol boats of the navy. A signal would have to be seen miles out to sea in order to signal the Qart Hadasht's ships.

"A swift courier could reach high ground after a hard ride. From there, the ships could see a signal fire, if they knew where on the mountain to look," Thomasious Harricus ventured. "But why wait to attack? Unless they want the city as empty as possible."

"They could close the gates locking out a majority of citizens and festival attendees," Kellerian added. "But what would they do with the city and a countryside occupied by the Insubri?"

"Install a puppet ruler," Thomasious announced. "One elected by the Senate, agreeable to the Insubri, and friendly towards Qart Hadasht. In other words, Senator Ventus."

"Innkeeper, I'm hoping this flight of fancy you're weaving is just that, a story," proclaimed Colonel Nigellus. "In the event it's not, it's more important now that I speak with the Senate than it was before. Also, there's the issue of stopping the Qart Hadasht navy."

"Colonel, we have patrol boats docked at Ostia," Gratian offered. "If they had enough warning, the navy could commandeer merchant ships and blockade the Tiber channel."

"With the change of horses, it'll take too long to get to Ostia," the Colonel said. "Plus, we'll lose time getting a man to the cavalry detachment, mounted, and on the way. It'll take half the morning. By then, the signal will be active."

"Give me three strong rowers and I'll make the trip in less than half that time," proclaimed Thomasious. "Erebus will be my fourth oarsman."

"Master Harricus, I didn't realize you included being a sailor among your many talents," acknowledged the Colonel.

"As a young scholar, I studied the science of boat making and mastered the art of rowing," responded Thomasious. "Also, as a younger man, I tested the theories by taking young ladies out for cruises on the Tiber. I can happily report; I was successful in all my endeavors."

The Colonel stared at the innkeeper with an odd look on his face. Finally, he spoke to Gratian, "Corporal pick three men with rowing experience and have them stand by."

As Thomasious Harricus rose from the chair there was a commotion among the Legionaries in the courtyard.

Chapter 47 - Troll Bait, Not Today

Alerio pushed through the double doors. To Corporal Gratian's delight, despite the dried blood coating the Lance Corporal's armor and helmet, the young Legionary was alive and seemed healthy.

"I can prove Gabrielus killed Senator Faunus," Alerio exclaimed before realizing who he was talking too. "Sirs, I apologize for the outburst. Lance Corporal Sisera reporting."

"What's that you said about Gabrielus murdering Senator Faunus?" asked Centurion Kellerian.

"Maybe not him personally, but one of his trained barbarian squads. The Senator's wife carried a trinket of Luna. It's missing," Alerio replied. "I have it on good authority, Gabrielus may have the amulet in his trophy chest."

"Colonel. We know Gabrielus is supported by Senator Ventus. He promoted the barbarian to Tribune in the City Guard and allowed the open training of three squads of barbarians," Kellerian said. "Having proof of the murder will help discredit the Senator. It's one less vote you'll need to stop the treaty."

"If you walk into the Senate holding a charm, Senator Ventus will challenge you and the authenticity of the jewelry," advised Harricus. "Let me get word to the High Priestess of Luna. She'll be able to confirm and verify the amulet belonged to the Senator's wife. No one will question the High Priestess."

"Harricus. Send word and have her meet me at the Senate," Nigellus instructed as he walked to the granite slab. He vaulted the counter and disappeared into the alcove. Reappearing a short time later, he held out a parchment, "Here's a note to the Centurion at Ostia. It directs him to act in concert with acting Tribune Harricus to form a blockade of the Tiber. Oh, and congratulations Tribune Harricus on your enlistment."

"I'd stay and buy everyone a drink to celebrate," Harricus stated. "But I've got to go and save the Republic. After sending a note to the High Priestess, of course."

Harricus jumped the counter and went to his desk. After writing quickly, he ducked into a supply closet before vanishing out the rear door. Once in the courtyard, he whistled one sharp note.

"Helier. Are you up there?" the innkeeper called out.

From the roof of the stable, a high pitched voice replied, "Yes, Master Harricus."

"Well, come down here," Harricus ordered. "I have a job for you."

A lad of about thirteen rose from the dark. The lantern light caught his thin frame as he walked to the edge of the roof. Dropping to his belly, Helier swung his legs over the side and wrapped them around a center post. Half way to the ground, the lad's decent stopped.

"What about the trolls, Master Harricus?" Helier asked. He was hugging the post as if deciding whether to finish the climb down or to go back up.

"Trolls? What are you talking about lad?" Harricus demanded.

"I heard the Legionaries. They said the trolls have fangs and sharp claws five inches long. And Master Harricus," Helier admitted. "I'd feel safer on the roof."

What Thomasious Harricus wanted to do was jerk the kid off the pole and scream, "There aren't any trolls." But he was in a rush so he settled for the obvious.

"Lad, you are surrounded by forty Legionaries of the heavy infantry. The most terrifying fighting force in the world," Harricus exclaimed. "Trolls wouldn't stand a chance against these men."

Three Legionaries wandered over and stood beside the innkeeper.

"Master Harricus is right lad," one bragged. "The heavy infantry fears nothing. Not trolls, giants, or cyclops."

"What about specters," Helier asked with a little more bravado in his voice.

"Specters and will-o'-the-wisp are a problem," another of the Legionaries admitted. "You can't stab them with a javelin or cut them with a gladius. They…"

"Get down here," Harricus ordered while interrupting the Legionary. "I'm in a hurry and I need you to run an errand. Now Helier!"

The boy slid to the ground and walked to the innkeeper.

"Take this note and this Empire gold to the High Priestess at the Luna Temple," explained Harricus as he handed the lad three items. "The gold is an offering. The note goes to no one except the High Priestess. And this silver coin is for you. Mostly so you don't run off with the gold. This is a serious situation. Can I trust you?"

Helier took the items and shoved them into an old pouch crisscrossed with patches.

"You can count on me," the boy assured Thomasious.

"That's why I called you," he replied while looking up at the roof of the stable. "Instead of the other three hiding up there." With a grin that spread from ear-to-ear at the honor of being selected, Helier sprinted for the side gate.

Act 7

Chapter 48 - Two Teams, Two Missions

"Sisera. What do you need to procure the amulet of Luna?" asked the Colonel.

"A couple of men to fight our way in or out," Alerio responded. "One should be an Officer, or an NCO, to act as a witness as to where we found the amulet."

"Gratian. Besides the rowers, pick your most eloquent Lance Corporal. And, your best single combat swordsman to accompany Sisera. I need you and Centurion Kellerian with my formation," commanded Nigellus. "Sisera, make no mistake, I want that trinket."

"If it's there, Colonel, you'll have it," promised Alerio. "By your leave, sir?"

"You and Corporal Gratian are dismissed," Nigellus said. Then he added, "Corporal, get the teams together for Lance Corporal Sisera and Tribune Harricus. Once they're away get back here. We have a lot to discuss."

Chapter 49 - A Swordsman, an Orator, and Rowers

Corporal Gratian pushed through the double doors and jogged to the courtyard.

"Squad leaders, on me," he announced before turning to Alerio. "Are you hungry?"

"Yes, Corporal. Famished as a matter of fact," Alerio replied.

"Who has extra food?" Gratian asked.

Four Legionaries sitting at four separate cooking pots jumped up. They all wanted to hear about how he survived the trolls. Each squad had assigned a cook for the evening. It was a competition as to which squad would feed the Lance Corporal and hear his story.

"Over here," one called out.

"I make the best camp stew in the Legion," another bragged.

"If you like boot leather," challenged another cook. "Come dine with us Lance Corporal, our stew is better."

A Legionary walked out of the dark and approached Alerio. He waved down the others.

"Lance Corporal Sisera. Come eat with my squad," the Legionary offered. Alerio recognized him as the singer from the snatch mission. "If it weren't for you, I don't know if I'd have survived. All the stews are the same but with Fourth squad, you'll have bigger portions. Both of your talkers are also Fourth and they owe you. So you'll be among friends."

Alerio nodded his approval at the invitation. As the two Legionaries strolled away, four Lance Corporal's converged on their Corporal.

"I need three rowers," he began. "Long haul oarsmen for an important mission."

"Private Demetrius. His father's an ocean fisherman," First squad's Lance Corporal reported. "The lad grew up rowing into waves and through swells. He's got strength and stamina."

"Private Celer. He's from the eastern mountains," Fourth squad's Lance Corporal explained. "He grew up paddling in

179

mountain streams. You ever try paddling a boat loaded with meat from two days of hunting up a mountain stream. He wouldn't let you down."

"I would advise you to select Private Pontus," Second squad's Lance Corporal announced. "Pontus has a deep affection for the sea. Although a farmer's son from the flat lands, the Private spends every chance he can on boats. His future ambition is to become captain of a merchant vessel. I believe he'll reach his goal. So, Private Pontus is a clear choice for your mission."

"Alert Pontus and your right wing anchor," Gratian said.

"Pontus, I understand. But why my second in command?" asked the Lance Corporal.

"Because Lance Corporal Iacchus, you're going on a different mission," advised Gratian. "Now I need a swordsman. I'm thinking Private Nereus from Fifth squad. Any objections."

"Merda, Corporal. You're sending the Wet One out on a mission?" Fifth squad's Lance Corporal asked. "Do you realize when we're in the city, the squad rotates a watch on him?"

"I don't think his issues will be a problem on this mission," the Corporal replied. "Get the rowers to Tribune Harricus. Iacchus. Collect Nereus and report to Lance Corporal Sisera. The rest of you, see to your men. We're not sure what we'll face in the morning so I want the men rested and ready. Any questions?"

The four squad leaders broke up to collect the men assigned to the missions. Corporal Gratian walked back into the inn to meet with Centurion Kellerian and Colonel Nigellus.

Chapter 50 - The Tiber Team

Thomasious stood by the stables speaking with Erebus.

"We'll us two sets," the innkeeper explained. "Rig up two of the big storage boxes."

"It might work," replied Erebus. "If the overnight shift is lax. If not?"

"We fight our way out," Thomasious declared. "This is too important to waste time with bribes or a long questioning session."

As Erebus went to rig up the boxes, three tall and lanky Legionaries walked up.

"Tribune Harricus. We're your rowers," one reported.

"Excellent. See my man behind the stables," Thomasious ordered. "Two men to a box. Store your armor in the boxes. You'll have to leave your shields. Where we're going, it shouldn't be an issue."

"Yes, Tribune," the three replied as they stacked their shields off to the side. Then, they disappeared into the dark beside the stables.

A short time later, a man in a robe holding the ends of long poles on his shoulders came from the stables and entered the courtyard. Behind the man was a large box suspended from the poles with another man holding the other ends of the poles.

Behind the first litter came a second box slung between poles and carried by the other two rowers. Tribune Harricus stepped into the gap between the two litters.

As the convoy rounded the side of the Chronicles Humanum Inn, every Legionary in the courtyard watched. They couldn't figure why their best oarsmen were tasked with being porters. However, Legionaries see and do odd things in the name of the Republic. They figured this was simply another example of a weird mission.

The two litters reached the north-south boulevard and turned. Blocks later, they approached the southern gate. Harricus picked up his pace and arrived at the gate ahead of the first litter.

"Master Harricus, good morning," the City Guard said in greeting. "Where are you heading so early? Most people are going out the east gate to attend the Festival of Janus."

"Guardsman. When I was a lad, I couldn't wait for festival days. I always got up early in anticipation," Harricus explained. "Now that I'm an adult and a businessman, I still get up early. I get up early to buy fish and pig to sell to the festival attendees. It's not the same kind of joy."

"I understand," the guardsman agreed. Then turning to his partner said, "Open the gate."

The double doors swung open and Thomasious Harricus lead the procession through the gate. They marched out beyond the defensive wall following the dark road into the black of early morning.

Chapter 51 - Pig Farmers, Fishermen and the Tiber

Ahead in the dark, lanterns lit the right side of the road. Outlined by the lights were the fronts of fishermen's huts. In the back of the huts was the river.

Huts might be giving the temporary hovels too much credit. There were two kinds of buildings on the riverbank. Because the Tiber flooded in the spring, some years only a couple of feet and others times ten to twelve feet, the construction types dealt with the rushing water in two ways. One type resembled the city harbor. Structures of massive brick work and natural stone constructed to withstand the raging water. Or, in the case of the fishing village, hastily built huts that were easily replaced when the water receded.

As the rowing team reached the huts they could see men preparing boats for the day's fishing. Thomasious didn't stop. Past the last hut, a larger structure loomed out of the dark. It was open sided. A high roof supported by thick columns of brick hung high over a raised floor of stone. On the riverside of the building, the floor sloped until it dropped to meet the river. Beyond the building, pigs snorted and rutted for grubs in the quiet of the morning.

"Builder! Master Builder," cried out Harricus as he stepped up to the raised floor.

The thick spine and wide ribs of three partially constructed boats rested on cradles. Piled around each frame were wood shavings, and lengths of wood with one end shaped and squared while the other end was still in its rough natural form.

From a quarter of the building blocked off by a goatskin curtain, a large man emerged. He yawned looked around the shop before narrowing his eyes and focusing on the innkeeper.

"Harricus? What in the dēfutūta hades are you doing here?" demanded the boat builder. "You may be out dancing the night away. But, decent working men are trying to get a full night's sleep."

"I can't explain. I don't have time," announced Thomasious. "I need to rent your baby. Right now, and I'm paying."

The builder turned and yelled into the tented section of the shop.

"Get up," he yelled while pulling back the curtain. "Launch baby and get my darlings fed."

183

Five workers tossed back blankets and jumped to their feet. One lit a lantern. He jumped off the far side of the structure and the illumination showed a wall of logs. From behind the logs, pigs began to snort.

"He'll feed my darlings their morning mush," explained the builder as he joined the other four workers. "This afternoon, fishermen will bring them fish heads, guts, and tails."

"I don't have time to savor the dietary regimen of your pigs," Harricus reminded him. "I need to be in Ostia. There's a Qart Hadasht fleet coming and I have to stop them."

"If you're not kidding or drunk Thomasious," the builder stated as he and his workers pulled the cover off a fourth boat. "There's no charge as long as you bring her back to me undamaged."

Every craftsman, at least those with true passion and artistic talent, have a personal project. One where their everyday product is taken to an extreme.

Potters, who mass product durable amphorae, have magnificently sculptured vases of exquisite, thin walled clay in the back of their factories; Metal workers, who hammer out hot steel to form deadly gladii by the dozens, have sculptures of steel with the hard metal so curved and flowing as to resemble leaves on a plant tucked away behind the forges; Coopers, who shave geometric edges on slats to make water tight barrels, have oak carvings of figurines with hands so real as to resemble miniature people stored in the corner of their compounds; and boat builders, who shave and fit lengths of wood to construct wide working boats, have narrow swift boats under wraps in the corners of their buildings.

The builder peeled back the cover to reveal his baby. It was long and narrow. Six bronze oarlocks lined with fine leather to protect the oars allowed for six tightly packed oarsmen. Carvings along the rails displayed scenes of Neptune lording over sea creatures. Baby was so different from the average workboat, one could safely call her a work of art.

While the builder and three of his workers rolled baby down the slope to the river's edge, another worker selected long oars. These weren't carved. The oars were polished and oiled to protect them from absorbing water.

"You can use two of my workers," volunteered the builder. "She'll fit six rowers."

"We have Legion gear to carry," Harricus informed the builder. Pointing to Erebus and the three Legionaries, he explained, "These four will do."

Two workers waded into the water and stabilized the boat. After lifting their gear out of the boxes, the Legionaries began to pile the armor pieces and helmets into the front of the boat.

"No. No. No. Place the weight in the center of the boat," corrected the builder. "You don't want her bow or stern heavy. She's designed to skim the surface so you'll want to keep the weight balanced. Take off your robes."

These last words he uttered while pointing a gnarly finger at the rowers. With a nod from Thomasious Harricus, they pulled off their robes. As the builder walked to each, he grasped their shoulders and tested their weight by lifting them off the ground.

"You, front right," he directed Erebus to a rowing station before selecting another man. "You to the left front."

The final two were placed at the rear rowing stations and the builder turned to Thomasious.

"Take care of my baby, innkeeper," the builder said a little sadly. "I'll expect a room and dinner the next time I'm in town."

"Breakfast in bed and a pitcher of morning wine will be delivered to your room Master Builder," Harricus declared as he stepped into the boat.

A gentle shove propelled the custom boat from the ramp and it drifted into the swift current.

"Ready. Stroke," Harricus said as he lowered the rudder into the water.

The boat lurched to the right as Erebus pulled his oar harder than the other oarsmen.

"Hold water," directed Harricus.

The rowers placed their blades in a stable position in the water. The bow, aided by the rudder and the current, drifted back to the centerline of the river.

Chapter 52 - The Tiber Run

"Gentlemen, we need to reach the port as soon as possible," explained Harricus. "We'll not get there without teamwork. So, on my count, stroke and let it run."

The four oarsmen dipped their oars once then held them out of the water. As designed, the boat surged forward letting the rowers get a sense of the effect of a stroke.

"Stroke. Stroke. Stroke. Let it run," Harricus directed.

This time with three even rows, the boat picked up speed and the rowers felt their timing improve. They waited with blades hanging above the water.

"Stroke," began Harricus and this time he continued the command again and again.

As the rowers fell into a rhythm, the Tiber rolled to the left before gently curving into a long right-handed arc. Many powerful strokes later, the mighty river straightened and, almost as if built by Republic construction crews, it ran directly for the sea and Ostia.

Chapter 53 - The Port of Ostia

Harricus turned his head and tried to see over the trees for a view of the hills to the northwest. His attempt was foiled by the riverbank and the tall growth. He feared that somewhere out there a man was rushing to light a signal fire for the Qart Hadasht ships. Returning to his crew of rowers, he continued the mantra of stroke, stroke, stroke to keep them in rhythm.

The sun had risen and he could see sweat gleaming off the taunt muscles of the oarsmen. Although bone weary and breathing like a herd of sacrificial bulls, they didn't let up as the boat raced for the port.

"Let it run," he announced as they arrived the mouth of the Tiber.

While the oars hung unmoving over the water, he studied the docks on the ocean side of the left bank. Most of the smaller boats were beached on the shore. Only the large merchant transports with grain and goods to unload used the docks. After running his eyes along the Port of Ostia he located a Legion standard in front of a collection of buildings.

"Stroke, stroke," he ordered while shoving the rudder over.

The boat veered left and it tracked along the line of the transports. Near the end of the pier, he pushed the rudder a final time, and just before the keel hit the sandy shore Thomasious yelled, "Check. It. Down."

The rowers reversed their strokes slowing the boat so it beached softly. Harricus leaped from the boat, splashed through the deep water, and once on solid land, ran for the Legion flags. Erebus and the Legionaries jumped into the surf and hauled the boat clear of the waves. After securing the boat, they collapsed against the hull.

"Do you think we made it in time?" asked Demetrius as he inhaled deep gasps of ocean air.

"I don't see a signal fire," proclaimed Pontus while puffing and almost choking as he attempted to get a deep breath.

"You can't see anything while sitting on the beach," observed Celer who shook as his muscles tried to relax after the strain of the manic rowing.

"Someone should walk up the beach and have a look," suggested Erebus.

"That's a grand idea. Who wants to volunteer?" asked Pontus.

Demetrius rose up and the other three looked at him expectantly as though he might go see if there was a signal fire. But he lifted only enough to grab a wineskin from the boat. After snatching the container, he resettled on the beach.

"What? You thought I was going?" the Legionary asked as he drank from a long stream of watered wine. "Anybody else thirsty?"

Three arms that felt as if they were made of lead reached for the wineskin. While the oarsmen sat in exhaustion, Thomasious searched among the Legion buildings for the Century's Centurion.

"Can I help you?" a Legion Private asked.

The man had come from between two buildings. He was armored but didn't seem to be on duty.

"Where is your Centurion?" demanded Thomasious.

"He holds office time for merchants in the afternoon," advised the Private. "No appointment necessary, but you'll have to wait your turn."

His duty done as far as he knew, the young Legionary began to walk away.

"Private. I am Tribune Harricus," thundered Thomasious as he fished in a pouch for the Tribune shoulder epaulet that he'd taken from the closet. "Under direct orders from Colonel Nigellus. You will escort me to the Centurion, no matter where he is. And you will do it now. Move!"

"Sir, my apologies," the Private responded while coming to attention. "This way sir."

Thomasious' throat hurt. While he hadn't rowed, he had been calling out stroke counts for the entire trip down the Tiber. The outburst at the Private was the final punishment his voice could stand.

They walked past four buildings before arriving at a small villa behind the military structures.

"Centurion Seneca's residence, sir," the Private said as he backed away. "He usually sleeps late. By your leave sir?"

"Go and thank you," Thomasious squeaked out.

Although the words were garbled and barely understandable, the Private took the words as a dismissal, performed an about face and jogged away. Probably to avoid any more contact with the Tribune. Especially, seeing as the Tribune had pushed open the door to the Centurion's villa and let himself in unannounced.

Chapter 54 - Shifting Sands and Shifting Stances

Thomasious marched down the hallway peering into empty rooms. At the end of the hall, he stepped through an arched doorway and into the master suite of the villa. An older man lay in bed snoring.

"Centurion Seneca," he said trying to sound commanding.

Instead, his words came out in a horse whisper. Out of frustration, he kicked the bed, reached out and pulled the blanket off the sleeping form. The man sat up quickly with a dagger in his hand.

"What are you doing in my bedroom," he threatened while aiming the point at Thomasious' chest.

Knowing he didn't have the voice to communicate properly, Thomasious whispered one word.

"Nigellus," he squeezed out while extending the note.

The newly awakened Centurion shook his head. After losing the cobwebs of sleep, he studied the man holding out a piece of parchment.

"Colonel Nigellus," Thomasious whispered.

To his pleasure, he found if he spoke slowly in a whisper, while it hurt his throat, the words at least were understandable. And the Centurion got the meaning.

"I'll meet you in the study down the hall," ordered the Legion Officer.

Thomasious made hurry up motions with his hands and fingers before realizing it looked ridiculous. He stopped flexing his fingers, turned and left the bedchamber.
A short time later, the Centurion appeared. Having changed from a sleeping gown, he now wore a toga.

"You mentioned Colonel Nigellus?" inquired the Officer.

Thomasious saved his garbled words and simply handed the man the note. As the Officer read, Thomasious went to a desk and uncorked the ink container. He began writing and was still at it when the Officer finished reading.

"I am Centurion Seneca. The Colonel said to work with you," the man stated. "What can I do for you Tribune Harricus?"

For all the writing Thomasious had done over the years, he felt particularly proud of this piece for a couple of reasons. It explained the need to block the Tiber while folding in just enough of the politics to give the reason. Like any good story, it tantalized and informed without preaching. The note was so good, the Centurion read it once and announced.

"Come with me Tribune," Seneca said urgently.

He guided them out of the villa, across a lawn, and into one of the military buildings.
"Sergeant. Call out the Century," ordered the Officer. "I want three squads on the beach prepared to repel an attack from the sea. Give them extra signalmen with as many flags as they can locate. I want the Qart Hadasht navy to believe we have a Legion guarding Ostia."

"We have a squad of cavalrymen in town as well," the Sergeant informed him.

"Good. Have them mounted and walking behind the infantry as if they were commanders looking over a battlefield," suggested Seneca. "Then send three squads to the docks. We are about to commandeer the merchant ships."

"Commandeer sir? As in capture?" asked the puzzled Sergeant.

"No, Sergeant. More like borrowing them," the Centurion explained. "We have two patrol boats in port. I want them manned and ready to tow the merchants into position."

"Yes, sir," the Sergeant said before running out the door and shouting for the Century to turn out.

"Did I miss anything?" asked the Centurion.

Thomasious indicated his note. Seneca handed it over and Harricus pointed to the phrase mentioning the signal.

"Let's get the blockade done first," advised Seneca. "Once all the elements are in place, we'll go to the observation roof and take a look."

Thomasious' oarsmen were mostly recovered, yet they'd chosen to stay on the beach. Only Erebus stood. He was scanning the buildings attempting to locate Harricus. His long light colored hair was still damp and hung in wet strands down to his shoulders. The Legionaries' short cropped hair dried quickly as they dozed in the warm rising sun.

When three squads of heavy infantry marched to the top of the beach, turned and placed their shields in line, Erebus thought nothing of it. Soon, mounted cavalrymen appeared behind the squads. They all seemed to be fixated on the sea and the horizon.

The grating sounds of Legionaries shoving two patrol boats off the beach caused the northerner to look to at the far side of the beach. Turning back, Erebus located Harricus.

The Tribune and a Centurion were marching towards the dock. Following closely behind the Officers tailed three squads of infantry. Using both arms, Erebus waved to get Harricus' attention.

Harricus missed the waving arms. Unfortunately, Erebus did get the attention of the squads and the cavalry at the top of the beach. Forty pairs of eyes shifted from the horizon and locked onto the barbarian standing bare chested on the beach. Behind him, as if dead, lay three legionaries and a strange shaped boat.

When a half squad broke formation and headed down to the shore line, Erebus glanced around to see what had drawn them. He took in the three limp Legionaries and the exotic boat before panicking.

"Demetrius! Pontus! Celer," he called out. "A little help here, if you please."

Dropping to his knees, Erebus locked his elbows over his head and braced for what was coming.

"What is it?" asked Celer through closed eyes. "I was dreaming about sailing through the Straits of Messina on my own ship."

"I could use..." Erebus didn't finish.

From his knees, the northerner was hammered to the ground by an infantry shield. He lay unconscious, his breath with just enough force to roll a few grains of sand away from his nostrils.

"Is he a spy?" asked the Legionary who had reached Erebus first.

"No. He is first oarsmen for Tribune Harricus," Demetrius said as he uncurled from beside the boat and stretched to his full height. "If I were you, I'd get a medic here before the Tribune realizes you've injured his number one rower."

"Now you've done it," Pontus stated as he stood. While not as tall as Demetrius, he was also sculpted with rippling muscles. "I can't imagine what the Tribune will say or do if he wants to get back to the Capital today."

"Although Erebus does look rather peaceful laying there," Celer added as he stood and stretched. "Which one of you five is able to row at top speed for nineteen miles without a break?"

"Come on lads," Demetrius challenged. "Who's going to replace him? The Tribune will want to know."

While the half squad stammered trying to reply, a Corporal walked up.

"Report," he ordered.

"It seems we've knocked out the Tribune's first oar," one of the Legionaries replied.

"Has anybody sent for stretcher bearers?" asked the NCO as he shook his head as if to say why me. "Or, called for a medic?"

Tribune Thomasious Harricus stood beside Centurion Seneca as he bullied, pleaded, cajoled and otherwise negotiated with the three merchant captains. None wanted their vessels in the way of a Qart Hadasht warship's battering ram. Seneca explained that no one would ram their ships, as he'd place the Legion patrol boats in front to take the brunt of any attack. Eventually, each captain agreed and the towing process began.

Thomasious took a second to look at the beach where his boat was located. It looked as if four men were carrying a man on a shield. Following the bearers were his three Legionary rowers. He couldn't locate Erebus but there was a crowd of shields and armor around the stretcher so he didn't worry.

The sun was well above the horizon by the time the ships were anchored mid channel on the Tiber. Harricus and Seneca left the dock and headed for the observation roof. On the way, they passed the open door to the Post's clinic.

Erebus was stretched out in a hospital bed. Sitting around him protectively were his three Legionary rowers.

"What happened?" Harricus asked.

"Your first oar stood up when he should have shut up," Pontus replied.

"The surgeon said nothing was broken," Demetrius added. "But Erebus needs to rest for a couple of days before he can handle an oar."

"Centurion Seneca. If it's not an imposition, I'll need my rowers to billet here for a while," Harricus said. "Also, they'll require another body to get the boat back to the Capital. And I'll need a horse."

"We can handle that," Seneca replied. "Let's get to the observation roof and check out the Century's placement."

They climbed the steps to the roof. Shortly after reaching the observation platform, three runners and two signalmen joined the Officers. From the vantage point, they peered down on the squads and horsemen lining the beach. At the docks, another three squads stood vanguard on the piers. In mid-stream, the Tiber was blocked by boats and ships anchored and lashed together. Finally, they looked at the horizon.

Far out to sea, the square sails of three Qart Hadasht ships came over the horizon. Mesmerized as the sails grew until the upper decks of the ships came into view, Harricus forced himself to brake from the sight. He searched to the northwest one more time for a signal.

Thick black clouds nineteen miles away hung low over the city in an otherwise clear blue sky. Looking closely, he realized a funnel stretched from the clouds down below the landscape. He shuddered as he realized what the signal was and where it was located.

195

Chapter 55 - Ballista Love

The Qart Hadasht ships drew closer and Harricus could finally get a detailed view of them. Oars, like tentacles on a sea creature, rose and dipped propelling the large ships at high speeds.

"At that pace, they can punch through the merchant vessels and the patrol boats," said Harricus. "How many oars are they using?"

"Thirty-one on the top row, twenty-seven in the middle and twenty-seven on the bottom row," Seneca replied before turning around to the assortment of Legionaries standing behind him. "Signalman. Stand by one and two."

The man waved two flags and was mirrored by another set of flags. The reply came from a rooftop overlooking the Tiber.

"Release one and two," ordered the Centurion.

The flags dropped and there were twangs as if a lute player had struck two strings. Except, the strings would have to be as big around as your wrists to deliver the deep bass throb of these strings. Accompanying the sound was a view of two rounded rocks arching high into the sky.

The Qart Hadasht ships adjusted so they were lined up with the Tiber. As if a geyser sprouting water suddenly appeared in the sea, first one of the rocks, then the other splashed down in front of the lead ship.

"We missed," Harricus complained.

"Those were for range. And, to let make the Qart Hadasht ships understand, we know what we are doing," explained the Centurion. "Signalman. Ready three and four."

"Ready sir," the man replied after another round of flag waving.

"Release three and four," Seneca commanded.

This time the ships were closer. Before the deep twangs faded, two rocks dropped neatly onto the deck of the second ship. People began running across the deck. Harricus couldn't tell if they were running to help those injured or were scattering from the sites damaged by the rocks.

"Five and six, ship one. One and two, ship two," the Centurion ordered.

The signalman waved at two separate areas before announcing, "Ready, sir."

"Release all," Seneca commanded.

Four rocks arched through the sky and fell onto the decks of the second and first ship. Suddenly, the water churned white as one side of each ship began rowing in reverse. All three ships carved a white wake in the blue water as they turned away from the mouth of the Tiber.

"Will they come back?" Harricus asked as the Qart Hadasht ships sped away.

"I don't know," admitted Seneca. "But if they do, we'll drop the big rocks on them."

"Those weren't the big rocks?" Harricus exclaimed in surprise.

"We use smaller rocks for hits of about five hundred yards," the Centurion explained. "With the big rocks, our ballistae will only reach the mouth of the Tiber. But anyone within those two hundred fifty yards will have a really bad day."

"I'll relay your competency and your Century's readiness to Colonel Nigellus," promised Harricus. "Now, I must return to the Capital."

"Take a cavalry escort," advised Seneca. "With all that's going on, you never know what you'll run into on the road back."

Chapter 56 - The Luna Team

Alerio had already downed half a bowl of stew when Erebus and the three Legionary oarsmen carried the litters through the courtyard on their way to the Tiber. He was on the second when his meal was interrupted.

"Lance Corporal Sisera," announced a Lance Corporal with a prominent nose and piercing wide set eyes. "I'm Iacchus and this is Private Nereus. We're your team. What's the mission?"

The members of Fourth squad shifted uneasily at the mention and sight of Private Nereus. Alerio held up a finger signaling for Iacchus to wait. He took his time and savored the rest of the stew. After handing the empty bowl to the night's cook, he stood to address the squad.

"Thank you, Fourth squad," he said before looking at Iacchus. "We're going to pay a visit to Senator Ventus' villa. Hopefully, he won't be home."

"We're going to break into a Senator's villa?" asked Iacchus with tension in his voice. "Couldn't we just announce ourselves and ask permission. Come to think of it, why are we? We could get into a lot of trouble."

While Alerio and Iacchus talked about invading a Senator's home, a smile began to spread across Nereus' face. His was slightly built with a chest protruding as one would see on a gamecock. The comparison of the man and a rooster ended with his arms. Both of the arms rippled with taunt muscles, especially his right forearm. It bulged as if someone had inserted a rock under the skin. Both arms and his hands were crisscrossed with knife and gladius scars.

"We'll be searching for an amulet of Luna," Alerio responded. "If it's in Gabrielus' room, we can tie him into the murder of Senator Faunus."

"What's the problem, Lance Corporal? Afraid of sullying your reputation?" teased Nereus.

"Some of us have plans for the future," replied Iacchus. "Plans that don't include a whipping post, or a crucifixion, or dying on someone's blade."

"I haven't met the man yet, who could best me with a blade," sneered Nereus.

Sensing a confrontation developing between the Legionaries, Alerio said, "Let's get started."

He turned and Nereus caught sight of the duel gladius rig.

"What's that on your back Sisera?" challenged Nereus. "A second gladius in case you get scared and drop one?"

Alerio's hands shot to his shoulders. As he bent his knees, he pivoted and drew both gladii.

Before Nereus could react, the tip of one blade was at the Private's throat. The tip of the other blade was tucked inside the armor under Nereus' armpit.

"Would you look at that," declared Alerio as he ran his eyes along the lengths of his blades. "I was so busy eating I forgot to clean my blades. Filthy. Bad form, wouldn't you agree?"

Alerio nodded his head downward directing Nereus' attention to the blades. The steel on both gladii were streaked with dried blood. Ignoring the fact that both tips were in position to kill the Private, Alerio continued.

"You don't think it'll be a problem, do you?" asked Alerio in a conversational tone. "I'd hate to have them ground down too much. They're nicely balanced as they are."

Nereus slowly raised his eyes from the blades and peered at the Lance Corporal's face. The eyes were open and inquisitive; instead of a threatening scowl, the mouth was slightly open as if they were having a dialog; and the head was cocked to the side as if he was actually waiting for a reply.

"I don't think the blood will be a problem," ventured Nereus tentatively. "As long as you get them cleaned and oiled by the afternoon."

"You know, I really worked up an appetite when I was killing all those trolls," replied Alerio. "I neglected cleaning them. Thank you for your opinion."

Around them, Legionaries were watching intently. Nereus had prodded Sisera and they expected to see bloodshed. When Lance Corporal Sisera drew and placed his blades, everyone tensed. They lost interest as Alerio began having a conversation with Nereus instead of slitting his throat. At the mention of trolls however, their interest returned.

"Trolls. He did fight trolls," announced a Legionary from Fourth squad.

"You were fighting trolls?" asked Nereus.

"Trolls? Rowers? Who knows what was on that Qart Hadasht ship," declared Sisera while withdrawing the gladii.

As if preoccupied by the dirty blades, he backed up to examine them in the light under a lantern. Although he appeared to study the blades, he was in fact watching Nereus out of the corner of his eye. If the Private went for his gladius, there would be blood spilled.

"Don't we have a mission, Lance Corporal Sisera?" Nereus asked respectfully.

"We do have a mission," Alerio agreed.

Alerio wind-milled both blades and while they were still a blur, he raised them over his shoulders and with no hesitation slammed both into their respective sheaths. Then he looked directly at Nereus.

"Lead us out Private," directed Alerio. "Northward and stick to the alleyways. We need to avoid the City Guard."
"We'll use the alley beside the wine merchant," suggested Nereus. "I had the opportunity to, to observe it last year."

"You were casing the wine merchant's compound," stated Iacchus. "Looking for a weak spot so you could rob it. If it hadn't been for Fifth squad's Lance Corporal…"

"Iacchus. You are a spoilsport," Nereus said. "From the alley, we'll use the gate wall for cover before crossing the boulevard."

"Sounds good to me," Alerio concurred. "Were you really going to rob the wine merchant?"

"Let's just say, the Lance Corporal caught me on my second trip," Nereus chuckled as he turned and walked toward the corner of the inn.

"We shouldn't bring him," warned Iacchus. "He's going to be trouble."

"Isn't that what you said about this mission?" replied Alerio as he followed Nereus out of the courtyard.

Chapter 57 - Arrow Loops

Nereus reached out in the dark and stopped Alerio with a hand to his chest.

"I'll take a look," the Private whispered. "With all the people heading for the gate, we should be able to cross without the guard spotting us."

They were standing beside the interior defensive wall. On either side of each city gate, walls extended into the city. If an enemy breached the gate, they would be confined in a space the width of the boulevard. At the end of the interior defensive walls, the attackers would be met by the shields, javelins, and gladii of the city's defending Legionaries. Through arrow loops, holes where defenders could shoot at an advancing enemy, Alerio heard people talking. Citizens, walking or riding wagons were crowded between the defensive walls as they shuffled towards the gate on their way to the Festival of Janus.

"A patrol just passed," Nereus reported when he returned. "Now is as good a time as any to cross the road."

"Go!" ordered Alerio. He reached back and slapped Iacchus on one armored shoulder, "We're moving."

Nereus, Sisera and Iacchus walked around the end of the defensive wall. Under the lantern hanging on the wall, they stood straight, looked both ways for guardsmen and scanned the crowd.

"Make way," Nereus ordered as he picked a spot behind a wagon piled high with barrels of wine. "Make way."

The crowd parted and the three-man team marched across the boulevard unnoticed by the city guard. On the far side, they faded back into the alleyways. A few twists and turns later, they slipped into Fireguard District and relaxed. It was rare for the City Guard to patrol the district so the team felt safe staying on the main road.

For once, Alerio didn't have to worry about sneaking between the wooden buildings. As the three armored Legionaries strolled down the street, the rogues, thugs, and thieves scurried into dark alleyways.

They weaved their way down dead-end streets, through alleys and soon reached the north end of Fireguard. Alerio signaled for a stop.

"We're early," he advised Nereus and Iacchus. "We'll need to stay in the district until first light."

"We could always act like a City Guard patrol," suggested Nereus.

"And do what when we run into a real City Guard patrol?" demanded Iacchus. "Bludgeon them to the ground? Cut their throats? Just what do you propose we do?"

"I was thinking we could wave and turn down a side street," Nereus offered. "But if you're so fired up about killing and bloodletting, Lance Corporal, I'm fine with that as well."

"You two belay the argument," ordered Alerio. "At the first sign of light, we will act like a patrol and head the seven blocks to Senator Ventus' villa. Any suggestions as to how we get inside?"

Iacchus remained silent except for a snort of disgust.

"The Senator has a garden on the southeast corner of his compound," Nereus stated.

"And how would you know that?" demanded Iacchus. "Did you case his villa as well?"

"No Lance Corporal Iacchus. I was drinking with a forester who delivered pine trees and shrubs from the north to the villa," replied Nereus. "The forester was quite proud of his work at building a mini forest for Senator Ventus."

"So if we get over the wall, we'll have cover," summarized Alerio. "I think it best we not wait for first light."

Chapter 58 - A Northern Forest in the City

They marched down the center of the streets between high villa walls. At the corner of Ventus' villa, the trio crossed the intersection. Then they stepped to the side and leaned against the wall. After checking to be sure the streets were empty, Iacchus and Sisera grasped the ends of a shield. Nereus jumped up on the shield and the two Lance Corporals launched him into the air. He caught the top of the wall and pulled until he could see inside the compound.

Nereus scrambled to the top and spun around. He hung an arm down while gripping the other side of the wall with his other hand. Iacchus, aided by a lift from Alerio, jumped up and caught the arm. Once the Lance Corporal was securely on the wall, Nereus eased down the inside of the wall. He hung briefly by his fingertips before dropping to the ground.

Alerio grabbed the first shield and handed it up to Iacchus. Iacchus slid the shield over the wall and dropped it to Nereus. After the three shields were inside the compound, Alerio looked to be sure the streets were still empty. Backing up for four paces, he quickly retraced the four steps and leaped for Iacchus' outstretched arm.

While Alerio brought his lower body onto the top, Iacchus dropped inside the wall of the compound. Soon he and Nereus were joined by Alerio.

As a farmer's son, Alerio had never appreciated the aesthetics of mood lighting. Beyond the broad limbs of a pine tree, lanterns lit a gravel walkway. Each lantern had a cover to allow light to fall on the path but not on the trees. The effect was to give a person strolling among the pines in the evening a sense of being in a deep forest. The covers blocked the light so the trees and the wall behind the path were in darkness. Alerio, Iacchus, and Nereus huddled in the dark next to the wall.

Chapter 59 - Dawn at the Ventus' Compound

Only once had a house guard appeared along the path. He stopped, inhaled the pine scent, and continued on his rounds without looking into the shadows. The Luna team knew the household was awakening when the smell of breakfast cooking drifted through the pines.

As the morning brightened, Alerio crawled to the edge of the forest to get a look at the rear of the compound. Across a trimmed lawn from the main villa, a single story building crowded the northeast corner. A carriage house and stalls occupied the side of the villa closest to the pine forest. Between the villa and the carriage house a fountain bubbled happily in the early morning.

Alerio shoved back deeper under the branches on his way to report the layout to his team. On the second shove, when the branches partially hide him, the door of the single story building opened.

Gabrielus stepped out and turned. He growled to someone inside before turning back to the front. His Tribune armor looked newly polished and he had a wide smile on his face. There was something else he'd added since the last time Alerio saw him. A gold Insubri torc ringed his neck. The barbarian walked quickly to the villa and disappeared through a back door.

Alerio pushed past four pine trees to reach his team.

"Gabrielus is quartered in the building on the northeast corner," he whispered as he drew a map in the dirt. "Once the Senator leaves, we'll go have a look."

"You're going to stroll across a city block of lawn, in daylight, and expect to not be seen by the staff?" asked Iacchus. "We'd be better off knocking on the front door and announcing ourselves."

The noise of horses being harnessed and men rolling a carriage out of its shed carried around from the front. Alerio crawled back to his vantage point to observe.

Four barbarians dressed in City Guard armor came from the single story building. They marched across the lawn, by the fountain, and disappeared around the side of the villa. After some talk and the pawing of hooves, a man cracked a whip and wheels crunched gravel as they rolled, accompanied by marching boots. The sounds faded signifying that the Senator had left the villa for a busy day in the Senate.

Alerio quickly crawled back and announced, "Let's go."

"Go? Go where?" demanded Iacchus.

"Now!" Alerio replied as he and Nereus stood up.

While Iacchus climbed to his feet, the other two Legionaries secured the shields to their left forearms. They pushed through the trees and followed the path.

"The building is over there," Iacchus stated while pointing behind them.

Alerio ignored the directions. The walkway curved between the pines until it wrapped around and met a short garden wall. While the gravel path continued along the wall, the Legionaries choose to step over it.

The back of the carriage house sat ten feet away and the Luna team crossed the area swiftly.

"Are we leaving?" Iacchus asked hopefully.

"What's better than knocking at the front door and introducing yourself?" inquired Alerio.

Nereus smiled and nodded his approval.

"I don't know. What's better than introducing yourself?" replied Iacchus

"Acting as if you belong here," Alerio answered as he and Nereus stepped away from the wall of the carriage house.

They circled around the fountain as if they'd come from the front of the villa. Several of the household staff emerged to begin their day's work. None of them paid any attention as the three armored men crossed the lawn and entered the single story building.

Chapter 60 - Waking, Sleeping Barbarians

Alerio shoved open the door and stepped into a room covered in tribal decorations. He guessed Insubri based on Gabrielus' heritage. The room was long with a heavily decorated door at the far end. Barbarian shields and spears were mounted on the walls on either side of the gaudy door. Between the front door and the garish door lay ten beds with personal items scattered around the sleeping areas.

Iacchus was two steps behind and Nereus another two behind him. As Alerio focused on the decorated door, thinking it must lead to Gabrielus' room, the door to the privy opened and a barbarian strolled out.

Alerio and the barbarian locked eyes. The Legionary drew his gladius as he moved forward. The barbarian acted as well.

He cried out, reached down, and flopped a bed towards Alerio. The tumbling bed slammed into Alerio's shins. There wasn't enough force to take him off his feet, yet it did come with enough momentum to stop the Legionary's forward progress.

Four more barbarians woke at the cry. After slamming the bed into the Legionary, the first barbarian ran to the wall of weapons. He snatched a spear from the wall. The others leaped from their beds and joined him. By the time Nereus passed over the threshold, Iacchus and Alerio were crouched behind their shields. Across the room five barbarians brandished spears and held decorated shields.

A spear rocketed through the air and bounced off Nereus' shoulder. It spun him sideways. Instead of attempting to face to the front again, the Legionary let the force spin him in a complete circle. As he came around, he crouched, set his shield and ended up behind the barrier.

"The Goddess Fortuna was watching over you," Iacchus declared.

"Fortunate? I saw him cock back his arm," explained Nereus. "He was lucky. Lucky to even touch me with the spear."

"Don't discount a blessing from the Goddess, Wet One," scolded Iacchus.

"So, are we going to starve them to death?" asked Nereus. "Or go and take those pointy sticks away from those lads?"

Alerio reseated his hip gladius, unstrapped the shield from his left forearm and strapped it to his right. Then he reached up with his left hand and drew a gladius from the duel rig.

"Shields," he stated while shuffling sideways. He moved past Iacchus and tucked in beside Nereus.

The Private looked quizzically at Alerio. With the gladius gripped in his left hand and the shield secured on the right arm, the Lance Corporal's arrangement went against their training.

"Can you fight left handed?" asked Nereus.

"Yes! Shields," Alerio said sharply.

As the two Legionaries put the edges of their shields together, Iacchus' voice came loud and clear from behind them.

"Forward, march, left, stomp, left," the Lance Corporal ordered.

Alerio chanced a glance around to find Iacchus nestled in tightly behind their shields. In his hand was the misguided spear.

With eyes barely over the top of their shields, Alerio and Nereus moved almost blindly. It was Iacchus who popped up, quickly analyzing the barbarian's position before ducking to avoid a spear tip.

"Lateral right," Iacchus ordered.

As well trained Legionaries, Nereus and Alerio angled their shields and their path to the right without thought. It was, after all, Iacchus who had risked his life to get a fix on the enemy. They accepted the squad leader's direction and stomped heavily across the room. Under their feet, beds, chairs, and amphorae were splintered and crushed by the hobnailed boots and the Legion's stomp.

At first spears hit and stuck in their shields. These they ignored, as there weren't enough men in the unit to allow for falling back and dislodging the spears. When the spears stopped coming, they set their shoulders in anticipation.

"Advance!" shouted Iacchus. He stood upright and jabbed over the two Legionaries' shields with the spear.

For half a heartbeat, the barbarians smiled. One of the Legionaries stood up behind the others. They stepped forward and ran their iron tipped spears at his helmet. Unfortunately for them, they either didn't know, or had forgotten what 'Advance' meant.

Nereus and Alerio followed the preset movements. They thrust their shields forward slamming and shocking the barbarians. As the extended shields were pulled back to their chests, the Legionaries stabbed out with the gladii. In the time it took for the one-two action, both barbarians were gutted and more dead than alive as they fell.

"Lateral right. Forward!" shouted Iacchus.

Nereus and Alerio still blind to the front, stomped the bodies as they adjusted and stepped forward. Two rapid steps later Iacchus repeated the killing order.

"Advance!" he commanded.

To the three remaining barbarians, the shields were an arm's length away. They poked at the shields and over the top trying to find flesh. They found no soft targets as the Legionaries behind the barriers stayed low. Suddenly, the shields were in their faces. Blood began running from two of them with broken noses. Before they could fall back to tend their wounds, the shields withdrew.

Not a half breath later, while the barbarians were still in shock, the gladii shot forward and the nosebleeds were forgotten. Their chests lay open to their hearts. They fell to the floor.

The last barbarian raced around the falling bodies of his fellow tribesmen. Hoping to slip around the shields and reach the front door, he jumped sideways. He actually made it around the edge of Nereus' shield. With the door and safety just across the room, he focused on his goal, squared his shoulders, and took a step.

The shield came from his periphery. He didn't see Iacchus' shield until the weight smashed into his shoulder. Toppling over, the barbarian ended up sprawled on the floor.

"Private Nereus. He's yours. Afterward, guard the door," instructed Iacchus. "Sisera, you're with me. Let's check that room."

As Alerio and Iacchus reached the gaudy door, they heard a knife being drawn followed by a gurgling sound.

"I'll make sure you're not disturbed," announced Nereus.

"That's why he's nicknamed the Wet One," explained Iacchus. "Every sword fight seems to end with his opponent's throat slit. Effective, but always such a mess."

Chapter 61 - A Cubiculum Fit for an Insubri Prince

The room was large, taking up a full third of the single story building. In the center was an oversized bed with furs for bedspreads. Suspended over the bed by four posts, carved with tribal images, was an animal skin canopy.

One side of the room held a dresser and a writing desk. The Republic built furniture looked out of place. It was the other side of the room that matched the décor of the bed. Furs and quilts of animal skins were draped over a seating area and on the floor. Above the furs, more shields, spears and several long swords were mounted on the wall.

"You could take most of this room, transport it to the north, and it would look like every other room of the Insubri," proclaimed Iacchus. "Except, there would be more jewelry. I wonder where Gabrielus keeps his torcs, bracelets and arm bands?"

"I was told he stores his trophies and jewelry in a chest," said Alerio as he began pulling up furs and tossing them to the side.

Iacchus started removing furs then stopped. He slowly scanned the room. After looking intently at a section, he shook his head and shifted to another. Alerio ignored the Lance Corporal. He continued to turn over the boxes and chairs he uncovered.

"Tell me Sisera. If you were a barbarian Prince living in a hostile city, where would you keep your valuables?" inquired Iacchus.

He walked to the dresser and shoved it over. The floor beneath it was good Republic tile. Iacchus stomped on the tiles testing to be sure they were solid. The desk followed. Alerio caught the meaning and began to duplicate the testing on his side of the room. After fruitlessly hammering the floor with their boots, they met at the foot of the big bed.

The Legionaries reached down and pulled the furs off. When they attempted to lift the bed, they discovered it was constructed of massive timbers. Together with the four posts, the bed was as heavy as a block of granite.

"Maybe I was wrong," complained Iacchus.

Alerio pulled his hip gladius and using the hilt, he began tapping along the side timbers. When he shifted to the other side of the bed, the wood rang hollow in one place.

Iacchus leaned over and tested the slats. Most were solid. Three moved. He slid the three to the side and looked down at a small section of discolored wood. Using his gladius, he smashed the hidden door. It cracked revealing a passage into the timber sideboard.

"What exactly are we looking for," asked Iacchus as he reached into the opening and pulled out a handful of broaches and rings.

"It's an amulet of Luna," explained Alerio. "It was described as a gold half-moon against a blue sky of crushed sapphires with moonstones as stars. It depicts Luna driving a two-yoke chariot pulled by a team of charging bulls across the sky."

Iacchus pulled out a heavy gold bracelet and tossed it to Alerio.

"What's this?" Alerio asked as he stared down at the piece of jewelry.

"Spoils of war," Iacchus replied as he shoved another bracelet into a pouch.

"We're here to find an amulet," scolded Alerio. "Not to rob the place."

"This one's for Nereus," continued Iacchus as he pitched over a thick gold ring embedded with a precious stone.

"Are you deaf? We're here for evidence to tie Gabrielus to the death of Senator Faunus," complained Alerio. "Not to fatten our purses."

"Oh, the Prince wouldn't be needing any of this," Iacchus exclaimed as he held up the Amulet of Luna. "He'll be up on the wood by sundown for the murder of Senator Faunus."

"We should go," advised Alerio.
"We should," acknowledged Iacchus.

Chapter 62 - The Signal to the Qart Hadasht Fleet

Alerio and Nereus went out first. They separated and split the lawn, each watching their side for threats. Their mission now was to deliver the witness, Iacchus, and the Luna amulet to the Senate.

A haze hung over the compound, which wasn't there when they entered the single story building. Alerio sniffed at the aroma of burning wood, but didn't see the source in the immediate area. Ignoring the smell, they started across the lawn.

Four barbarians armored in City Guard attire appeared from the side of the villa. Their gladii drawn and shields held high, they came fast, ready for battle.

"Lance Corporal Iacchus. Don't engage," warned Alerio. "If you get the chance, go around."

"You'll need my gladius," suggested Iacchus.

Iacchus and Nereus shocked their heads in disbelief. Alerio had tossed his shield to the side, reached up, and pulled both gladii from over his shoulders.

"The Colonel needs your testimony and the amulet more," Alerio stated as he began taking long strides towards the barbarians.

Nereus aped the long, distance closing steps, although, he kept his shield. Expecting a coordinated attack, the Private gasped when Lance Corporal Sisera ratcheted up his pace from a fast march to an all-out sprint.

Thanks to Senator Ventus and the City Guard, the barbarians had trained in Legion tactics. In practice sessions with a full squad, they were adequate. A Legion unit would have created a moving front with one Legionary falling back to provide leadership. But that took full Legion training to instill the discipline and skill. These four didn't have the benefit of intense training by Sergeants of the Legion.

Alerio's weight punched one of the barbarians out of line. When another turned to chase and kill Alerio, he discovered his neck was pumping blood onto his shoulder armor. He completed the turn, and watched as the Legionary dispatched his downed partner before sinking to his knees. By the time he slumped over onto the grass, Alerio had rushed to help Nereus beat down the final two barbarians.

"Lance Corporal Iacchus. We're moving," shouted Alerio. After snatching up his shield, he ran to the corner of the villa.

With no other threats in sight, the three Legionaries marched to the front of the compound and through the front gate. There was no traffic on the usually busy thoroughfare.

The Capitol grounds were a different story. In the distance, lines of City Guardsmen and armored barbarians stretched across the lawn and disappeared as the ranks wrapped around the building. A couple of the Ambassador's Qart Hadasht guards were visible behind the rear ranks. With the Capital grounds guarded and the City Guard headquarters on the boulevard to the south, the three Legionaries turned north.

They reached the first intersection. Before crossing the thoroughfare, Alerio glanced to his right to check the street for oncoming traffic. He froze in place. Iacchus and Nereus were a step ahead before realizing Sisera had stopped.

"They've set fire to the Fireguard District," Iacchus said staring at the rolling smoke and flames pouring out of the slums. "There should be bucket brigades to prevent the flames from spreading to the rest of the city. Where is everybody?"

"At the Festival of Janus and locked outside the gates," ventured Alerio. "Let's hope Tribune Harricus was successful."

"Successful at what?" asked Nereus.

"Stopping the Qart Hadasht fleet. Burning Fireguard was the signal for the fleet to row on the Capital City," replied Alerio. "If Harricus failed, the invaders are on the way. We may be too late."

"Late or never, it doesn't matter," exclaimed Iacchus. "We have a job to do. We'll circle around the Capital building, come in from the backside, and meet up with Colonel Nigellus."

By the time their right feet hit the stone pavers, the three Legionaries were in step and powering away at a Legion jog.

Act 8

Chapter 63 - A Diamond for the Colonel

After seeing Tribune Harricus and Lance Corporal Sisera off, Corporal Gratian left the courtyard and headed back to the great room. He found Colonel Nigellus and Centurion Kellerian in a heated discussion.

"I can reach the Senate before anybody knows I'm there," insisted Nigellus.

"And without backup, you can disappear, just as anonymously," suggested Kellerian.

"Corporal. What's your opinion?" the Colonel inquired when he spied Gratian coming through the double doors.

"Sir. I was out of the room and missed the topic of conversation," admitted the Corporal.

"The Colonel is under the impression, after much thought, that he can simply ride to the Senate, meet the High Priestess, and Lance Corporal Iacchus," explained the Centurion. "Then, the three of them will waltz into the Senate and accuse a Senator of treason. We're looking for another opinion."

"Sirs. I don't know anything about politics," reported Gratian. "However, I know gambling and hedging a bet. If I had to place a wager on people who have murdered two Senators and invited war by enemies of the Republic; versus a single man, the bet would be obvious. Now, if the man had thirty-five Legion heavy infantrymen, an experienced Centurion, and a Corporal with him, I'd place all my coin on the Colonel."

Kellerian turned, shrugged, and waited for Nigellus. There are only four elements in the Republic more powerful than the Colonel of a Legion; The Major General and the General of the Legion, the sitting Consuls, and the Senate of the Republic. At this point, the arguments were over. The Centurion and the Corporal waited for the Colonel's decision.

"Corporal. Based on your superb analysis of the odds," stated Nigellus. "Have the men ready to march at first light."

"Sir. We'll put you in a diamond formation," Gratian explained. "That'll leave two guards on the Insubri Prince and another Legionary free to act as your personal bodyguard. Centurion Kellerian, and I, will command the sides of the diamond. If that meets your approval, sirs?"

"Why not a square formation?" challenged Kellerian.

"In a diamond formation, the narrow front can fold back and form a testudo to protect the Colonel," replied Gratian. "If we had five squads, I'd have suggested the square."

"A diamond straight up the boulevard to the Capital building," Nigellus stated. "That will work."

"Actually, Colonel. We're going to turn on the east-west boulevard," corrected Kellerian. "If the City Guard forms up across the north-south boulevard, we'll have to fight our way onto the Capital grounds. Then we'll be in contact as we fight our way around to the front of the building."

"You want to take a side road and approach the building head on," confirmed Nigellus.

"Yes sir. A frontal attack and a direct approach are preferable. It'll prevent us from having to maneuver laterally," advised Kellerian.

"Corporal. Ready the men," ordered Nigellus.

Chapter 64 - Maneuvers to the Capital Grounds

Thirty-two Legionaries shuffled into a diamond formation on the road in front of the Chronicles Humanum Inn. The Insubri Prince was lead out and place within the formation. Centurion Kellerian and Corporal Gratian walked the bowed lines of infantrymen and told each the mission and the route. When all the preparations were complete, Kellerian waved at the inn and Colonel Nigellus joined them.

As the Colonel took his place in the center of the formation, a tall Legionary stepped in front of him.

"I take it you're my bodyguard?" quizzed Nigellus.

"I swear by Mars," replied the Legionary. "No man, no sword, no spear will pass my guard and reach you. My shield and my life are yours."

Nigellus looked over his right shoulder and nodded his approval at Kellerian. Kellerian glanced across the diamond and held up a finger.

When the Centurion dropped the finger, Corporal Gratian shouted, "Squads One, Two, Four and Five of the Third Century, Central Legion, stand by."

The thirty-two heavy infantrymen lifted their shields and right feet. They slammed their boots into the ground, and shouted. "Ready! Corporal."

"Foreword, march," commanded Gratian. "Left, stomp, left, stomp..."

The air between the inn and the Cloth Seller's shop reverberated with the echo of boots on stone. For anyone within earshot, the sound demonstrated the power of a heavy infantry unit on the march.

At the center of the north-south boulevard, Gratian called, "Right face, march."

The Legionaries turned and began marching to the north. Without another word, each adjusted until the diamond was again pointed in the correct direction. Everyone flowed to the new position except for Colonel Nigellus. He was the center of the diamond before the turn and after the turn to the north.

The formation drew closer to the fountain with the rearing horses and the roundabout where the north-south and east-west boulevards converged.

Gratian eased across the diamond to Kellerian.

"Looks like they were alerted," he said to the Centurion.

Blocks beyond the fountain, where the City Guard headquarters' building started, were ranks of guardsmen and their barbarian auxiliary. The lines stretched across the boulevard and onto the Capital grounds.

"Pretty ranks," Kellerian replied. "I almost feel sorry about disappointing them."

As Gratian moved back to his position, he shouted, "Lead element. Follow the line."

The City Guard's mounted Centurion watched as the Legion unit moved into the roundabout. He was set to have his Sergeant ready the ranks. Just before he ordered it, the Legion unit began turning as they followed the curve around the fountain. When the front of the unit vanished behind a building, he realized his Century was out of place.

"Sergeant. They're heading west," shouted the Officer. "Move our ranks."

"Sir. Move where?" the NCO asked. "There are three main roads leading to the Capital from that direction."

"Divide your Century into thirds and cover each," ordered the Centurion.

Chapter 65 - A Guest Speaker at the Senate

Gratian glanced back to be sure the last of his Legionaries were out of sight of the City Guard.

"Double time, march," he bellowed.

The Legionaries on either side of the Insubri Prince picked him up by the arms. He started to struggle but settled down when a fist knocked the breath from his lungs. What he didn't realize was they carried him for his own good. If he tripped and fell, by accident or as a way to escape, the Legionaries jogging behind him would stomp on him as they ran by.

The formation passed the first street and didn't break stride until they neared the next major road.

"At the double, right face," Gratian announced when the unit was in the middle of the intersection.

Again they flowed into a new diamond formation after marking the sharp right turn. Now, ahead of them, they could see the greens, footpaths and trees of the Capital grounds. The Capital building towered over the tallest trees.

One block from the start of the grounds, Colonel Nigellus looked around at Gratian and said, "Let's arrive with some dignity, Corporal."

"Quick time, march," Gratian ordered and the Legionaries dropped out of the jog and into a marching step. "Left, stomp, left, stomp…"

"Colonel. Can you smell that?" Kellerian asked.

There was the acid smell of burning lumber in the air. The air was clear until they came out from between the villas' walls. To the east, flames ate at the buildings of Firebreak District. Smoke rolled off the buildings furthest away from the earthen berm and wafted down streets running westward.

"It's the signal for the Qart Hadasht fleet," observed Nigellus. "They're burning the Capital of the Republic. For what? To turn it over to a foreign Empire. It's madness."

"Shields right!" cried out Centurion Kellerian.

His view of the Capital grounds had been blocked by the walls. Now he could see all the way to the boulevard. Between the Legionaries and the thoroughfare, two squads of City Guard barbarian auxiliary were closing fast.

"Corporal. Suggestions?" the Centurion asked.

"I'm clear on this side. Let's use a squad to protect the Colonel," Gratian said. "We'll use the rest to form a second line." Seeing a bring-them-over-sign, Gratian shouted orders, "Fourth squad. Secure the Colonel. Left side. Fall in behind the right side."

There are few things in life that are truly terrifying. Watching twenty armed men running at you with murder in their eyes should be top of the list. There are some comforts to the situation. One, you know your job; there's no dispute as to your assignment. The other comfort is having a second line. If the man

222

on either side of you falls, the second rank will fill the hole. Without a second line, one breach of your line will open a floodgate and soon you'll be in a melee with no command structure.

The Legionaries from the right side of the formation hopped over. Each man upon positioning himself in the second rank, reached out and tapped a man in the first rank; letting them know they had backup.

"Draw!" commanded Kellerian.

Twenty-two gladii swished as they came out of the scabbards. With legs and shoulders braced, heads tucked protectively behind their shields, they waited for the next order.

"Advance!" shouted Kellerian.

Shields shoved forward followed by the stab of the gladii resulted in a quarter of the barbarians falling. Conversely, several of the Legionaries also suffered wounds. Automatically, men from the second rank stepped up and filled the gaps.

Kellerian strutted behind the line watching for a weak spot in the enemy's flanks. He wanted this over quickly. A battle of attrition would delay the Colonel. Plus, he worried that ships would dock at the harbor and begin spewing an army of Qart Hadasht soldiers into the Capital City.

"Right side, roll em up," he bellowed.

It started with the Legionary on the end of the line shoving his foe. He stepped forward and to his left. The next man followed and by the time four Legionaries were ahead of their line, they became a flanking unit. The barbarians found themselves fighting on two fronts.

"Break off," a mounted Centurion yelled as he galloped up. "Break off. I said to break off."

"Hold," Kellerian ordered.

The Legionaries stepped back half a step and locked shields.

"Get control of your dogs, or I'll let the lads finish them," sneered Kellerian.

"By order of the Senate, you are to remove your squads from the city," the Centurion said.

The barbarian auxiliary had ceased the attack. But they held positions close to the Legionaries. Tension between the lines was high.

"City Guard auxiliary, four steps back," he commanded.

They hesitated but finally complied with the order. Once enough distance separated the lines so no one could take a last stab, both lines relaxed.

"Remove your unit from the city," the Centurion said again.

Behind Kellerian, there was movement as Colonel Nigellus pushed aside the protective shields of Fourth squad.

"Colonel. I didn't see you," the Centurion stammered as the Colonel appeared.

"These squads are escorting me to the Senate," Nigellus explained while pointing to the Capital building and the rows of City Guards ringing the entrance. "Clear a path for me, as well as, for my personal guard."

"With all due respect Colonel, I speak with the authority of the Senate," insisted the City Guard Officer. "You, of course, may pass. The Legionaries must leave the city. I'll have guardsmen accompany you to the Senate."

"Centurion. For reasons that are beyond your rank and position, these Legionaries are my choice for personal safety,"

Nigellus growled. "I am going to speak with the Senate. These squads are coming with me. Corporal Gratian march them out."

"Fourth squad, stand by," Gratian ordered.

"Ready Corporal," they shouted back while stomping the grass.

"Colonel. At your leisure," announced Gratian.

"Centurion Kellerian. I am going to walk away with Fourth squad," Nigellus stated. "If these barbarians make any moves to stop me, kill them all, and catch up. Any questions?"

Colonel Nigellus wasn't looking at Kellerian when he spoke. His eyes were boring into the Officer of the City Guard.

"Corporal. Go," the Colonel said while stepping between the shields of Fourth squad.

"Forward, march. By your left, stomp, left, stomp," directed Gratian.

Chapter 66 - The Ladies in Blue

Alerio, Iacchus and Nereus jogged down three blocks before turning left on a street leading to the Capital grounds. Upon turning, they stopped. Gliding down the center of the street was a tall woman in a blue shimmering robe. On either side of her walked women in light blue gowns. They occupied enough of the road that the Legionaries couldn't squeeze through.

"Ladies. Good morning," Nereus said as they came up behind the women.

"Who are you?" one of the women in a blue gown asked. "And, by what right do you propose to speak with the High Priestess of Luna?"

225

"Please, accept our apologizes," Alerio said before Nereus could reply. "We are the honor guard sent by Colonel Nigellus to escort the Priestess to the Senate."

The woman looked from Alerio to Nereus and twisted her face in disgust at the sight of the blood splatter on their shields and armor.

"You! You are to escort the High Priestess of Luna?" the woman gasped.

"Oh not us ma'am. We're simple Legionaries," explained Alerio while pointing towards Iacchus. "Lance Corporal Iacchus is the NCO in charge. He's assigned to guard the Priestess."

The woman glanced at the Priestess and back to Iacchus before saying, "We find the Lance Corporal acceptable to guard our person."

"Much obligated ma'am," said Alerio as he stepped to the side while shoving Iacchus to a spot just behind the Priestess. "Stay close. She'll probably walk you right into the Senate."

Chapter 67 - Blood Splattered Honor Guard

Once through the ranks of the City Guard and the barbarian auxiliary, Fourth squad opened ranks. Now, instead of closed shields to protect Colonel Nigellus, they became a ceremonial guard. They escorted the Colonel towards the steps of the Capital building.

Standing on the landing, looking down as the squad approached, were the Ambassador's honor guard. The Qart Hadasht soldiers gave no indication they would give way for the Colonel.

"Give me two Legionaries to work with the Colonel's bodyguard," Gratian announced. "Colonel. Permission to clear away the merda."

"By all means Corporal," replied Nigellus. "Proceed."

Two men added their shields to the bodyguard's so the Colonel was again surrounded by close in protection. Relieved of guarding the principal, Gratian stepped to the side.

"Fourth squad, stand by," the Corporal shouted. His voice carried throughout the Capital grounds.

The eight Legionaries stomped their feet and replied in full voice, "Ready Corporal."

"Two ranks of four," commanded Gratian. "On my front. March."

From two files, the Legionaries stomped in unison and formed up in two ranks. Gratian looked over his parade ground straight ranks and up at the Qart Hadasht squad.

"You will move or you will die," he said. "Draw!"

Eight gladii came free. The Qart Hadasht soldiers replied by drawing their swords.

"Forward march," Gratian ordered.

Eight shields raised so only the Legionaries' eyes and helmets were visible. Their gladii gripped with the hilts held low and blade tips slightly elevated. As the first rank took the first riser, the Qart Hadasht unit shifted to a six-man front. The two additional men would allow them to close in around the Legionaries' line.

On the last step before the broad porch of the Capital building, Gratian adjusted their approach.

"Lateral right," he ordered. "Second rank shift left. Shift left."

Suddenly, the six man Qart Hadasht rank against the four Legionaries front was nullified. The end of Gratian's second rank, after two steps left would even the front while the lateral move left room for them to fight.

"Two steps and Advance," Gratian yelled.

The Legionaries placed their left foot then their right. When they stepped again, they braced and thrust their shields forward. All along the Qart Hadasht line, soldiers rocked back from the impacts. Before they could recover, the steel gladii blades replaced the shields. Men, either dead or badly injured, fell to the granite floor of the Capital building.

The Qart Hadasht unit backed up to regroup. But Gratian didn't give them time.

"Advance. Advance. Advance," he ordered again and again.

With each command the shields shot forward followed by gladii strikes. The first two met no resistance. Yet to the Qart Hadasht soldiers, the advancing line of Legionaries appeared to be a scaled, many clawed monster. It clawed the air, extended it scales and moved closer and closer. The attack was too much for the Ambassador's honor guard. They dropped their swords and dropped to their knees.

"Corporal Gratian. Hold," ordered Centurion Kellerian.

There was a little vindictiveness in giving the command to the NCO in charge. By the time Gratian relayed the order to Fourth squad, two more of the Qart Hadasht soldiers fell from deep wounds to their necks.

"Hold," shouted the Corporal. Looking around, he saw the remainder of his squads in files on either side of Colonel Nigellus and Centurion Kellerian. Behind the Officers, the Insubri Prince stood between his guards. "Orders, sir?"

"Move the Qart Hadasht scum out of the Colonel's way," replied Kellerian.

Gratian had dead, injured and living soldiers to move and he looked around the Capital grounds for a holding place. When he glanced right, he raised an arm.

Across the grounds, a line of women in blue gowns flanked a tall woman in a shimmering blue robe. On either side of the line, a Legionary was shoving guardsmen back to make room for the women. Behind the shimmering robe, another Legionary was directing the crowd clearing operation.

"Sirs. The High Priestess and Lance Corporal Sisera's team are coming," Gratian announced by pointing with the raised arm. Then he studied the blood on the granite tiles of the porch and thought about the gowns and the robe. "Give me a bucket brigade to clean the entrance."

Chapter 68 - A Gathering of Witnesses

Colonel Nigellus stood on the porch of the Capital building watching the High Priestess of Luna and her escorts. Behind him, and close enough to hear the senior Office, stood Centurion Kellerian. Off to the side, Peregrinus, the Insubri Prince, leaned against a column flanked by his two guards. Corporal Gratian walked the files, checking on the well-being his men.

"What are they doing?" Nigellus asked.

Lance Corporal Sisera and Private Nereus had raced ahead of the line of women. Each reached a different file and began pushing the Legionaries back. In essence, they were widening the space between the two lines. When they were done, one side was up against the speaker outcrop, and the other line stood at the very edge of the granite staircase.

"It seems they feel the Priestess and her followers require more space," observed Kellerian.

Once the lines were far enough apart so the Priestess and her attendees could mount the stairs without breaking their line, Private Nereus took a position at the end of one Legionary line.

"We have the Amulet of Luna, sir," Alerio reported before crossing to the end of the other line.

"That was abrupt," Nigellus complained. "I've never had a Legionary simply walk off after delivering a message."

"I believe he was playing a role, Colonel," Kellerian ventured as he watched Lance Corporal Iacchus jog around the end of the line of Priestesses.

Iacchus trotted up the stairs, performed a cross chest salute, did an about face, and, in a loud ceremonial voice announced, "Colonel Nigellus, winner of numerous awards for bravery; known as an outstanding citizen of the Republic; a man who trusts in the fates and gods, and third in command of the Central Legion, may I present the High Priestess of the Moon Goddess Luna and her handmaidens."

The line of women came majestically up the steps. As they climbed, the women on the ends stopped. On the next step, the next in line stopped. By the time the High Priestess reached Nigellus, her celebrants were evenly spread out to either side of her like a wake behind a boat.

"High Priestess. It is gracious of you to come to the rescue of a simple man," Nigellus said with a slight bow. "I trust your journey was uneventful."

"Colonel. At first we were concerned about the honor guard you dispatched," the Priestess stated to Nigellus' surprise. He hadn't sent Sisera's team as guards. He didn't even plan for them

230

to meet the Priestess. "However, after observing the efficiency of Lance Corporal Iacchus' rough men, I understand. Hard times demand hard men to protect the Republic."

"Your words convey the harsh but factual truth," replied Nigellus. "It would be my pleasure to escort you into the Senate."

The Priestess rested her hand on the cocked arm of the Colonel. As they walked towards the entrance, Nigellus indicated with his head for Iacchus to follow.

Chapter 69 - A Traitor by Any Other Name

Iacchus took half a step and stopped. He looked at Alerio, at the Legionary's blood splattered armor, which was much messier than his shield.

"Leave the shield," Iacchus instructed. Deciding he might need evidence of the struggle to procure the amulet, he said, "Come with me."

Together, the Legionaries walked through the doors and entered a wide, curved hallway. The Insubri Prince was shoved in after them. Following the Colonel and the Priestess, the Lance Corporals walked through a second door and into the Senate of the Republic.

The circular chamber rose from a central dais in progressively higher tiers. On each level, curved benches provided seating for the Senators. Sturdy arms divided each seat allowing a sitting Senator enough room to relax, turn and talk, or to pound on the arms.

A short, older man stood at the dais. Senator Ventus stood on one side of the man and the Qart Hadasht Ambassador stood on the other. None of the three were talking; unlike twenty or so Senators who were talking all at once from every tier.

On the far side of the chamber, Gabrielus leaned against the wall. Although in the shadow between lanterns, his City Guard Tribune armor gave him away.

A tall, thin man waving his arms frantically rushed up to Nigellus.

"Colonel. You can't be here," the man explained. "This is a closed session and important issues are being discussed. If you'll wait in the hall, I'll alert the President of the Senate of your arrival."

As he talked, he held out his arms and made shooing motions at the Legionnaires.

"Lance Corporal Iacchus. You have something to show the Priestess?" asked Nigellus. "Bring it to us now."

Iacchus began digging in a pouch as he crossed the distance between them. As he arrived in front of the Colonel and the Priestess, he held out the amulet.

"Can you identify this piece of jewelry?" Nigellus inquired.

The Priestess' hand shook as she reached for the amulet. She plucked it from Iacchus' palm. Tears filled her eyes as she caressed the talisman.

"Oh Lavina. May you rest gently in the Goddess' embrace," the High Priestess exclaimed with a sob. "I know this amulet. Tribune Faunus came to me and asked me to suggest a gift for his wife before he went to war. The Amulet of Luna was the gift."

"Thank you High Priestess," Nigellus said softly before spinning and shoving the tall, thin man out of his way. He strutted down the aisle between rows of benches and marched towards the dais.

As he walked, he bellowed so all the Senators could hear, "I am Colonel Nigellus of the Central Legion. And, I accuse Senator

Ventus of Treason; his henchman Gabrielus of the murder of Senator Faunus; and the Qart Hadasht Ambassador of being a spy."

"This is preposterous," exclaimed Ventus. "Sergeant at Arms. Have this man and his rubble removed from the chambers."

From the barely understandable speeches of just over twenty Senators, the chamber exploded when over a hundred began voicing opinions.

Nigellus, a man experienced in commanding men in the heat of battle, raised his voice. The voice that moved Legionaries and won battled. A voice that silenced the Senate of the Republic.

"Fireguard burns; a Qart Hadasht fleet rows up the Tiber to take our Capital; and the northern Legion is in combat with the Insubri," he thundered. "And, you squabble?"

During the silence, Senator Ventus demanded, "What proof do you have?"

Nigellus turned and held out his hand. "High Priestess of Luna. If you would bring the Amulet of Luna?" he asked inviting her to join him.

At the mention of the amulet, Gabrielus pushed off the wall and ran for a side door.

"Lance Corporal Sisera. I want the barbarian's head," commanded Nigellus. "Go!"

Chapter 70 - A Chase Through Smoke

Alerio sprinted past the Colonel, the Ambassador, the dais, and a shocked Senator Ventus. He hit the aisle and climbed the steps two at a time. At the top tier of benches, he grabbed a bench back and used it to swing in a new direction. Spying the door used by Gabrielus, he raced for it.

The hall outside the chamber was empty. On a guess, he made for the east entrance. There was no broad porch, just a simple set of clay brick steps. He leaped over the steps, landed on the pathway, and ran towards the smoke rolling in from Fireguard.

Halfway across the Capital grounds, Alerio spotted the Tribune armor in the haze. Gabrielus had slowed, figuring he'd made a clean escape.

On a street past the boulevard and the first villas, the figure disappeared.

Alerio slid to a stop at the intersection. Looking both ways, he peered into the smoke trying to separate out a shape from the rolling gray soup. Gabrielus had vanished.

"Where did you go?" Alerio asked himself as he turned from one side to the other. Then, he tried to think like a barbarian Prince in a hostile city. "I'd need a horse and the City Guard stables were only a few blocks away; with the rank of Tribune, the City Guard would open any gate; and as an Insubri Prince, I'd head north."

Alerio whirled around and jogged back to the north-south boulevard. At the thoroughfare, he set a fast pace northward toward the gate. Eight blocks later, the villas decreased in size and were soon replaced by tradesmen compounds and shops. He jogged and studied the types of businesses. A few blocks from the north gate, he saw a merchant's shop that suited his purpose.

The door was thick and locked. He bounced off the wood on his first charge. Pulling the hip gladius, Alerio shoved the steel tip into the metal lock. Steel beats iron and the rivets on the metal snapped and the front plate fell away. Using the tip of the blade, he rotated the gears and the door popped open.

Alerio rushed through the whip maker's shop and into the back room. On a wooden dowel suspended an arm's length overhead, strips of leather hung almost to the floor. He hooked an arm through the strands and ran along collecting hundreds of the thin strips.

The clop, clop, clop of a horse and rider could be heard from the smoke. Two heartbeats later, Gabrielus emerged into the hazy air. The barbarian had a lot of ground to cover once outside the city; with no apparent pursuers, he held the horse to a gentle canter.

Alerio waited for the horse to reach the far end of the compound. Then he pulled back his arm and tossed the iron plate from the lock. It whirled end over end arching up and over the awning of the whip maker's shop. When it clanged loudly to the pavers of the boulevard behind the barbarian, Gabrielus snapped his head around to investigate the noise. There was no one chasing him and he relaxed.

Alerio heaved the armload of thin leather strips. They uncoiled as they sailed through the air. Being a City Guard horse and trained to avoid crowds, wagons, carts and other city obstructions, the mount danced sideways. If it had reared up, the barbarian would have easily maintained control. But, the mare jerked to her left and Gabrielus was thrown to his right. Too busy trying to regain his balance, he failed to notice the Legionary dashing from the corner of the whip maker's compound.

Alerio sprang on his last step and wrapped his arms around Gabrielus' helmet. Already off balance and with the weight of a fully armored Legionary hanging around his neck, the barbarian came unseated. They tumbled to the clay brick pavers of the boulevard.

Chapter 71 - Battle on the Boulevard

Gabrielus landed on Alerio knocking the breath out of the Legionary's lungs. It's why the barbarian was able to gain his feet first.

"Die Republic scum," Gabrielus screamed as he drew his gladius.

It's all in the training or lack of training. The lack is what saved the Legionary. Rather than stab his enemy, Gabrielus use two hands to raise the gladius as if it were a long Insubri sword. When the blade fell, Alerio rolled away from the short blade. He rolled twice before raising to a knee.

"Gabrielus. Colonel Nigellus wants you," explained Alerio to the stooped over barbarian. "Come with me and stand trial."

"I've watched the Republic's justice for years," explained Gabrielus as he straightened up. "It always ends in a crucifixion; not me. I'm going to gut you then ride to my people. I'll be back in a few weeks with an Insubri army. Then, it'll be your Colonel Nigellus dying with a roof top view."

Alerio reached over his shoulders and as he rose from the knee, he slowly drew the gladii. Gabrielus dropped his right hand and reset his grip on the hilt with his left hand.

The last time Alerio had fought a left handed fighter, he'd been fresh off the farm and fighting under arena rules. Even if the rules were skirted by Corporal Daedalus as he attempted to kill him and collect the Cruor syndicate's bounty. This wasn't a contest with betting and Medics; this was a battle and rules didn't apply.

The two combatants circled. Gabrielus to his left, keeping the gladius low and his feet balanced. Alerio to his right acting as if he favored his right arm.

Gabrielus shuffled forward and brought his blade up trying to nick the underside of his opponent's sword arm. To protect the arm, Alerio jerked it to almost shoulder level. This left his side unprotected and Gabrielus immediately brought his blade down as he lunged to take advantage of the opening.

It's difficult to back up faster than a foe can lunge forward. Both fighters knew this and Gabrielus was confident he'd won. Except, he didn't see Alerio's left gladius. The Legionary's blade swished across body and sparks flew as the barbarian's blade was driven off the line of attack.

With his opponent's gladius out of the way, Alerio snapped his right blade downward and smashed the top of Gabrielus' helmet. The barbarian staggered back while slicing his blade through the air to prevent a follow up attack.

"Surrender Gabrielus. I don't want to carry your body back to the Senate," explained Alerio. "It'll be much easier on me if we walk."

"I'm not walking anywhere. After I kill you, I'm riding to join my people," Gabrielus replied. "Your cities and towns will burn and your people will suffer. On that, you have my word."

As Gabrielus spoke, he pulled a dagger. With his right hand and no aim, he flipped it at Alerio's face. The concept of the attack called for the thrower to charge while his opponent was occupied dodging the dagger. Gabrielus rushed forward with his blade tilted so the tip was on a line to Alerio's chin. He was dedicated to the kill and failed to notice when Alerio's left blade tapped the dagger in midflight. It tumbled harmlessly off to the side.

Alerio watched the steel tip grow as it approached his face. Inches from his chin, when the barbarian was fully committed, the Legionary raised his left blade to meet the attacking blade.

The two steel blades grated against each other. Alerio allowed for the crossed blades to slide two inches before spinning to his right.

His right gladius whirled around with his body. Just before he released the pressure with his left blade, the right gladius completed the circle and buried its sharp edge into the back of Gabrielus' neck. With the muscles and tendons detached, the barbarian's head lulled as his legs folded up.

After passing through the muscles and tendons, the blade chopped into the vertebrae severing Gabrielus' spinal cord. The Insubri Prince would never reach his warriors or extract his revenge on the Republic.

When her rider fell, the mare whinnied, turned and trotted off to the west. Presumably to complete a circuit of the Capital before returning to her stall at the City Guard stables. Alerio watched as his ride and transportation for Gabrielus' body pranced proudly away.

Chapter 72 - Emergency Measures

Corporal Gratian's boots clicked on the granite as he paced the porch of the Capital building. The blue-gowned Luna celebrants stood poised on the stairs. His men remained in their lines leaning on their shields. Centurion Kellerian had long ago been escorted into the Senate Chambers by Lance Corporal Iacchus. Throughout the grounds, the guardsmen and the auxiliary stood or sat in ranks.

The City Guard Centurion had dismounted but waited beside his horse at the foot of the stairs. Periodically, he'd cast evil glances at Gratian. The Corporal didn't take it personally. The guardsmen's Officer would naturally resent any Legionary NCO, or Officer, who ignored his orders and Gratian was handy.

Heals clicking on granite announced the arrival of several people from the building. The High Priestess of Luna, Colonel Nigellus, and Lance Corporal Iacchus came through the doorway.

"Corporal Gratian. I'll need an escort to the Chronicles Humanum Inn," the Colonel announced. "Lance Corporal Iacchus' squad will provide protection to the High Princesses and her Ladies. After seeing them safely to the temple, he's going to the harbor to set up a blocking force."

"Yes, sir," Gratian replied. "What about the rest of the squads?"

"You're to wait here for the Senate's decision," Nigellus replied. "You did a good job Corporal. I appreciate all you've done. And while I'd like to stay in the Capital and help you defend the City, the General had ordered me to join him after I spoke to the Senate."

"Thank you sir. It's been my pleasure to serve you," Gratian stated. Then turning to the lawn announced, "First squad, fall out. Reform for escort duty."

As First squad moved off the line and re-formed, Lance Corporal Iacchus descended the steps and gathered Second squad. He spoke quickly with his men and soon they were spread around the High Priestess and her blue-gowned women.

They were a study in contrasting styles; the armored and helmeted Legionaries marching across the Capital grounds with the stately blue-gowned followers of Luna.

Nigellus strolled down the stairs. Instead of going to where First squad waited, he headed for the City Guard Centurion. They exchanged salutes and the Colonel leaned in close and spoke softly to the Officer for a long time. When he leaned away, there was a horrified look on the Centurion's face.

The Colonel stepped back from the Officer, turned, and jog towards his escorts.

"First squad. I need two things," Nigellus announced as he reached them. "Get me to the inn on the double. And open the east gate. Can you do it?"

"Colonel Nigellus. Ready, sir," the squad yelled back.

"Take us out Lance Corporal," Nigellus said as he stepped between the shields.

"First squad. Double time, march," the squad leader shouted.

The squad and the Colonel trotted off leaving Gratian alone on the porch. He started to order his last two squads to relax but worried about what the guardsmen Centurion would think. Glancing down to where the Officer had been, he was surprised to see the Officer out in front of his ranks surrounded by his NCOs.

There were a few raised voices from the NCOs but hard words from the Centurion hushed them. After a long meeting, the Centurion stood scanning the ranks as the NCOs strolled back to their squads. A Sergeant and a Corporal walked to separate sides and took up positions in front of the lines. The command staff watched as all the City Guard squads gathered around their Lance Corporals.

Gratian got antsy and strolled down to the lawn. With hand signals, he called the last two of his squad leaders over.

"Something's up with the City Guard," he warned. "Pull the squads into a loose formation so we can defend ourselves if it gets ugly. Do it slowly and don't draw attention to us."

Almost casually, the Legionaries picked up their shields and wandered to a defensible place beside the speaker's outcrop of the Capital's steps. Gratian climbed to the area as if looking over his Legionaries. He was actually keeping an eye on the City Guard squads.

They were moving. The guardsmen, squad by squad, slipped between the second line, placing them to the rear of the barbarian auxiliary.

Gratian peered across the Capital grounds to where the surviving Qart Hadasht Ceremonial Guards were being held. The guardsmen there hadn't moved or responded to the movement of their fellow guardsmen.

When the City Guards pulled their gladii, Gratian snapped his head around and whispered to his Legionaries, "Stand ready."

Suddenly, the City Guards attacked the barbarian auxiliary. Outnumbered five to one, the barbarians were quickly subdued. Some lay dead, some were bleeding but most surrendered and were disarmed.

Stripped of their armor, the barbarians were marched towards the City Guard Headquarters. As the line of near naked barbarians moved away, Gratian told his Legionaries to sit down and relax. He walked to the top step and sat down to wait on the Senate's decision.

Chapter 73 - A Change of Command

From the northeast quadrant of the Capital grounds, Gratian noticed a single Legionary march onto a path. As the Legionary drew closer, Gratian could make out the helmet tucked under one arm and a basket tucked under the other. After a few more yards, he recognized Sisera.

"Lance Corporal Sisera reporting mission successful," Alerio said from the bottom of the stairs.

Gratian remained on the top step as he studied the young man.

"What mission?" he asked. "I thought you were in the Senate Chamber?"

"Gabrielus ran at the mention of the Amulet of Luna," replied Alerio. "Colonel Nigellus sent me after his head."

"And the basket?" inquired Gratian with a grin.

"Gabrielus' head," answered Alerio. "Like I said, Corporal, mission accomplished."

"Come up here and have a seat," Gratian said while patting the granite beside him. "You can tell me about it while we wait for the Senate to decide. Don't ask. I have no idea what they're deciding."

They talked about the coming battle with the soldiers from the Qart Hadasht fleet and Alerio's fight with Gabrielus.

"Where did all the City Guards and their auxiliary go?" Alerio asked as he waved his hand around indicating the mostly empty Capital grounds.

They both jumped in surprise when the answer came from directly behind them.

"The barbarian auxiliary has been arrested for the murder of Senator Faunus," Centurion Kellerian explained. "Most of the City Guard is at the harbor where we should be."

"We can get there, double time, Centurion," Gratian assured the Officer as he stood. "Just say the word."

"It's Marshal of the City. The Senate appointed me the title temporarily until they can appoint a Colonel to command the City Guard," Kellerian explained. "Corporal Gratian. You and your squads are staying here to guard the Senate. Lance Corporal Sisera. You and I are going to ride to each gate and inform the guardsmen that only Legionaries will be allowed to enter the city."

A noise from the building drew their attention. The Qart Hadasht Ambassador strolled arrogantly through the door. Closely behind, Peregrinus, the Insubri Prince, came through struggling with his two Legionaries guards.

"Ambassador. Take your Honor Guard, and your boat, and row away from my city," snarled Kellerian. Then, to the guards holding Peregrinus ordered, "Take him to the City Guard Headquarters and lock him up with the other barbarians."

"The Qart Hadasht Empire is vast and your Republic is a collection of farms surrounded by water on three sides," stated the Ambassador as he descended the steps. "Being absorbed by the Empire would give you resources to fight the tribes to your north and west. And we can protect you from invaders sailing to your shores."

"And all the Republic has to do to reap these benefits is allow Qart Hadasht to appoint a new King for us," replied Kellerian. "We threw off the yoke of a King two hundred and forty-four years ago. The Legions stand ready to defend our shores and lands. Even if we lose, we'll die as free citizens of the Republic."

There was no reply from the Ambassador. As he approached the five remaining men of his guard, they rose, and despite being herded by City Guard javelin points, they formed a ceremonial guard around the diplomat.

A roar came from the east and Kellerian, Gratian and Alerio jumped from the porch and raced to the corner of the Capital building. They all gripped their gladii expecting to see enemy troops fighting their way up the north-south boulevard. Thankfully, it wasn't an enemy force. It was a mob of citizens racing to form bucket brigades to keep Fireguard District contained.

"I guess Colonel Nigellus opened the east gate," Kellerian said while observing the mob running up the thoroughfare. "Come with me Sisera. We'll requisition horses at the City Guard stables and start our inspection at the north gate."

Chapter 74 - Riding the Gates

The air held the smell of smoke yet it was surprisingly clear. Fireguard District had burned and produced thick, spreading smoke at first. Now the fire burned with enough intensity that the smoke was swept high above the city on an updraft. To feed the blaze, oxygen from every direction was being sucked into the inferno.

As the air streamed by on its way to the fire, the Legionaries marched towards the City Guard stables. To Marshal Kellerian and Lance Corporal Sisera, it felt as if there was a natural wind blowing at their backs.

From horseback, Kellerian and Alerio saw the flames leap and erupt from Fireguard. Overhead, a boiling cloud of smoke spread out as if a thunderstorm were rolling in over the Capital. They could see housemen and slaves on the roofs of villas. Around the people guarding the homes from falling embers, were buckets of water. The Legionaries assumed other people were on the ground in the compounds with more buckets.

As they approached the north gate, one of the four City Guards called out.

"The gate is closed by order of the Senate," he announced. "None may pass."

Kellerian walked his horse close to the guardsmen before handing the reins to Alerio. Hopping to the pavers, he strolled the last few paces.

"Who can read?" he demanded while pulling a piece of parchment from a pouch.

He held the parchment out for one of them to take.

"I can, Centurion," one offered as he reached out.

His reading skills weren't classically taught. After the man had scanned the parchment three times, Kellerian proposed, "Look for these words. Marshal Kellerian, commander of the City's defenses. To make it easy for you, I am Marshal Kellerian."

The man found the words and the meaning finally sank into his brain. He snapped a salute to his chest.

"Orders Marshal?" he asked.

The other three also saluted and Kellerian returned their salutes before continuing.

"Colonel Nigellus is sending three Centuries to defend the city," explained Kellerian as he took back the parchment. "Open your gates just enough to observe the surrounding fields. If Legionaries arrived, usher them in. If a hoard of barbarians comes calling, slam the gates closed. Then one of you report it to me at the Capital building. Understand?"

"Yes, Marshal, sir," the four stammered.

Kellerian took the reins and slung himself into the saddle. He and Alerio turned their horses and headed west.

On a normal day, the streets of a city with one hundred thousand residents would be crowded with carts, wagons and people. Today the streets were empty. The Legionaries' route took them along the edge of Firebreak District. As they rode, Alerio pointed out men and women standing on the wooden roofs with buckets of water.

"If Firebreak Districts catches fire, it'll be a mess," suggested Alerio.

"If Firebreak goes up," replied Kellerian. "Forget about losing the Capital to the Qart Hadasht Empire. We'll lose it to the flames."

With that sobering thought, they continued west until Firebreak doglegged to the south. Taking the last paved road before it entered the dirt and gravel of the district, they turned south.

"Two blocks that way is the Cruor syndicate's counting house," Alerio offered while indicating a street leading into Firebreak. "I really need to have a talk with those folks."

"About the seven Republic gold on your head?" asked Kellerian. Then he suggested they had bigger worries, "Forget about it for now. We've got to get the city organized."

"Yes, Marshal," replied Alerio.

They rode to the west gate and instructed the guardsmen. At the harbor, Kellerian inspected the barricades constructed across the piers and the City Guards and Legionaries manning the obstacles. Once confident the defenders could hold off an initial attack and give reinforcements time to arrive, they rode on to the south gate.

Chapter 75 - News from Ostia

The sun was high in the sky yet only weak light filtered through the smoke. It could have been early morning or late in the evening. Meanwhile, citizens were still streaming into the city through the east gate. Kellerian and Alerio rode single file with Alerio leading and nudging pedestrians out of their way.

"In case someone decides to express an opinion about being shoved aside by a horse, and throws a hand full of merda," explained Kellerian. "I fancy it hits you, Lance Corporal Sisera, rather than me."

"Yes, Marshal Kellerian. I am your shield against spears, swords, and merda," Alerio confirmed before turning back to the front. "Make way for the Marshal. Make way for the Marshal."

They rode through the gate, circled around to the side of the crowd, and dismounted. Four city guardsmen were leaning beside the open gate.

"Who can read?" Kellerian asked as he approached them. He extended the parchment towards the guardsmen.

"I can, Centurion," replied a Corporal.

Alerio saw who it was and pulled off his helmet. He was weary to the bone and sick of hiding. Corporal Daedalus recognized him immediately. It must have come as a shock because his hand, although extended for the parchment, failed to grasp it. The warrant identifying Kellerian as Marshal of the City floated to the grass.

"Corporal do you have extraordinary distance vision?" asked Kellerian.

"Excuse me Centurion?" Daedalus asked in confusion. He was still staring at Alerio.

"The parchment Corporal. It's laying on the ground," Kellerian stated. "I assume you placed it there so you can read the words from a distance?"

"Parchment? That parchment. No sir, I dropped it by accident," Daedalus explained as he bent and picked the warrant from the ground.

Daedalus ran his eyes over it quickly, turned to the other three guardsmen, and said, "Attention."

They saluted when he did. Kellerian returned the salutes. He began explaining about the expected Centuries of Legionaries and securing the gates against barbarians. As he spoke, the sounds of four horses being ridden hard caused everyone to look down the road.

Thomasious Harricus and three cavalrymen pulled their mounts up sharply. The horses skidded to a stop and Harricus climbed stiffly from the saddle.

"Where's Colonel Nigellus?" he whispered as he limped, bowlegged, towards the Legionaries and guardsmen.

"The Colonel rejoined the General and the Legion," Kellerian stated. "He left me in charge. I'm temporarily Marshal of the City. So, Tribune Harricus, give me your report."

"He must have been desperate to leave you in charge," teased Harricus in a raspy voice. "We turned back the Qart Hadasht fleet at Ostia. There will be no attack on our Capital."

"Lance Corporal Sisera. Get to the harbor. Have one squad stay to keep an eye on the piers," ordered Kellerian. "Have the City Guard Centurion release everyone else for bucket brigade duty."

When Kellerian said Sisera, Corporal Daedalus' head snapped around. Now he had a name. A vision of him collecting the Cruor bounty danced across his mind.

Alerio noticed the greed in the Corporal's eyes but ignored it. Instead, he responded to the Marshal's order, "Yes, Marshal Kellerian. I'm on the way."

He mounted and began using his horse to create an opening in the crowd. Thankfully, no one threw anything nastier than a verbal curse as he pushed his way back into the city.

Act 9

Chapter 76 - Chronicles Humanum Inn

Alerio woke to hobnailed boots pounding down the hallway outside his room. His door flew open, an armored Legionary stuck his head in, and pulled it out after seeing, what? Alerio climbed out of bed and got dressed. Then he made his way downstairs to find out.

In the great room, Alerio saw Tribune Thomasious Harricus. Except the innkeeper didn't have the Tribune's ribbon of rank on his shoulder. He was dressed in his usually tunic and eating ham and sipping from a mug.

A Legionary Sergeant stood by the door looking serious.

"Tribune Harricus. What's with the Legionary checking my room?" asked Alerio.

"Orders from the Senate. All northern barbarians in the city are being arrested for rebellion," Harricus explained. "They're searching the city for any of them hiding out. And I've resigned, or rather been informed, I'm no longer a Tribune. I'm back to being a simple scribe and an innkeeper."

Alerio pulled out a chair, sat down, and whispered across the table, "What about Erebus?"

"As the fates would have it, he was injured at Ostia," Harricus said. "I've sent word to the boat builder to keep him there for a few days. Or at least until the crucifixions are finished."

"Who's being crucified?" inquired Alerio.

"All northern barbarians caught or living in the city," explained Harricus. "Every single one of them will see their last horizon from on high. The Legion is lining the northern road with crosses. I guess as a warning for any passing Insubri war parties. Breakfast?"

Before Alerio could reply, five Legionaries came through the double doors.

"The inn is clear of northern barbarians, Sergeant," one reported.

"Fine. Let's check the shops across the street," the NCO said as he held the door for his half squad.

"Breakfast, yes please," Alerio said once the front door closed on the half squad.

Ham, bread, olives and a mug of watered wine were placed in front of the young Legionary. He had a slice of ham on the end of his knife, half way to his mouth, when the door reopened.

Tomas Kellerian strolled in and collapsed in a chair. His armor was smeared in greasy ash and bags hung below his eyes. Alerio reached out and slid his mug of wine towards the exhausted man.

"You need this more than I do, Marshal," Alerio offered. "Is the fire out?"

"Fireguard will burn for another week," Kellerian responded after taking a deep drink. "But, we have sentries watching for embers throughout the city. Unless it gets windy, the fire is contained. As for the Marshal title? The Senate is voting on a Colonel for the city. So hopefully, by midday, I'll be back to being retired Centurion Tomas Kellerian, armorer to the gods."

They talked about the diminishing chance of an Insubri attack on the city and the resources needed to put all the barbarians up on wood. Just as Kellerian seemed to relax, Alerio rose to his feet.

"What's your rush?" Thomasious Harricus asked.

"I've got to have a conversation with the Spilled Blood," Alerio explained. "The Cruor bounty has to go, one way or another."

He went upstairs to get his duel rig and armor. When he returned to the great room, Marshal Kellerian was gone.

Chapter 77 - Unfinished Business

On the north-south boulevard, Alerio joined a steady stream of carts, horses and carriages. Unless directly affected by the fire, the citizens of the city were going about their day-to-day business. He marched northward on the shoulder to avoid the traffic.

A few blocks past the fountain, he glanced across the boulevard at the Capitol grounds. All the bodies and wounded had been removed and Corporal Gratian's squads were replaced by a full Century. As the grounds fell behind him, Alerio examined the front of the Ventus residence.

Four cavalry Officers sat indifferently on their horses watching as house slaves loaded a few belongings in a carriage. Once loaded, the slaves climbed in next to the luggage and sat waiting. Alerio was a block away when Senator Ventus appeared.

As if he were a much older man, the Senator shuffled from the gate and a manservant helped him up the steps and into the compartment. The carriage lurched forward and the cavalry kicked their mounts into motion. The carriage and riders had traveled several blocks up the boulevard before Alerio neared the villa.

Upon reaching the gate, Alerio stopped to look inside the Ventus' compound. Surprisingly, it was deserted. No cooks or cooking fires; no one on the grounds or stablemen or horses or gardeners or men at arms, it was empty.

Alerio dodged traffic as he crossed the boulevard and took a diagonal route through the city. At Firebreak District, he noted several large burned areas. Each black scar on the rough wood indicated where embers landed and fought to ignite Firebreak. Thankfully, the hotspots were extinguished before the fires could catch.

"Stata Mater, Stata Mater. Stay the flame Stata Mater. And guard us from the fire," Alerio sang as he walked between the scorched buildings.

Alerio entered the district on a main road. The last time he experienced Firebreak, he was running, bleeding, or hiding. This time, he came armored and carrying three gladii. He marched boldly down the avenue as if inviting trouble. Conversely, the thugs, waiting for easy prey, avoided eye contact with the dangerous looking Legionary.

Although Alerio wasn't familiar with the lifestyle or the ways and means of career criminals, he couldn't miss the Cruor syndicate's counting house. Two bearded, barrel-chested men in poorly maintained shoulder and chest armor stood to either side of a door. When a thin, nervous man approached, the guards made him open his robe. After vetting him for weapons, one prodded the budging pouch at the man's waist.

"Kanut isn't here yet," one of the guards stated. "If you want to wait inside, it'll cost you two coppers."

"I can't be late today. I was late with the collections yesterday," stammered the man. "Because of the fire and the City Guard closing the gates, you know."

"Two coppers to wait inside," the other guard repeated. Then he added with a smirk, "If you want us to listen to tales about your miserable life, it'll be six coppers."

Both guards were still laughing when the man dropped coins into one's palm. Alerio figured it was two coppers, as the man didn't stay to tell them more about his day. He simply passed over the threshold and disappeared into the shadowy interior of the building.

All this Alerio witnessed as he strolled down the center of the street. He also noticed two more sentries standing directly across the street watching the front of the building. Those two, plus another two on the corners, added up to six guards watching one rickety door on a low rent building in Firebreak.

"There are more guards here than in a Legion garrison," Alerio thought as he passed the building. "This is definitely the Cruor's counting house."

Chapter 78 - Drop In? Introduce Yourself?

Alerio continued down the street searching for a place where he could covertly watch the door. It wouldn't do any good attacking the building if the Cruor syndicate Lieutenant, Spurius Kanut, wasn't in residence. Unfortunately, the alleyways in daylight provided no hiding places. Especially for an armored Legionary who was obviously out of place among the poor, downtrodden, and criminal.

A man in a dirty robe, reeking of wine stumbled from around the corner of a building. Rolling from side to side, he bobbled a wineskin and, while attempting to grab the skin, tripped and fell at Alerio's feet.

"If you kick me Recruit, I'll beat you like a practice post," the drunk mumbled as he searched the ground for the wineskin. After many fruitless lunges by the drunk, Alerio bent down and picked up the wineskin and put a hand under the drunk's arm.

"Here's your drink," Alerio said as he reunited, at arm's length, the smelly drunk and his vino.

"Circle the block to your left. Go into the pottery shop," Corporal Gratian whispered as he took a drink. Then, in a loud obnoxious voice said, "How about you give me a couple of coins seeing as how you bumped into me?"

"Go about your business," warned Alerio. "Or next time, I'll boot you across the street."

He punctuated the words by shoving the drunk out of his way. From the building entrance behind him, he heard one of the guards laugh.

The pottery shop was on the next street over from the Cruor collection house. Alerio couldn't figure out how it's location helped. But, Corporal Gratian had gone through the trouble of play-acting drunk, so Alerio followed directions. He pushed aside the door beads and entered the shop.

A man working a potter's wheel glanced up briefly but went immediately back to a ball of spinning clay. One hand cupped the outside of the mound while the other clinched in a fist pressed down on the lump. As the fist bore downward, the clay parted and the excess, held in place by the cupped hand, climbed the man's arm. A vase formed. While the vase was emerging, the potter hooked a thumb under the lip and bent the upper rim outward. He ran his fingers under the newly formed flap of clay and spun the wheel faster and faster.

Then, he pulled both hands back. The potter's wheel and the vase wobbled from the centrifugal force. When it slowed, the vase at first seemed ruined. Who would want a clay vessel with a misshapen rim? But when it stopped spinning, Alerio could make out the head, body and tail of a dragon. Once trimmed, fired and painted, the mystical design would exceed in value any vase with a perfect lip.

The potter reached out, grabbed a crutch, and placed it under an arm. Next, he stood on his one remaining leg and held out a clay caked hand.

"Senior Sergeant Drumstanus, formerly First Spear of the Central Legion," the potter stated while gripping wrists with Alerio. "Corporal Gratian said to send you right up."

Alerio was shocked. A Legion's First Spear commanded all the enlisted Legionaries in a Legion. To find a former Sergeant of Drumstanus' status in Fireguard working at a potter's wheel in a small shop was confusing.

"First Sergeant Drumstanus. Pardon my ignorance but what is a former First Spear doing, well, here?" inquired Alerio. "If I'm not over stepping my place by asking?"

"Lance Corporal Sisera, right? During the war to pacify the eastern tribes, we were humping the mountains east of the city. A spear took my knee and the rot took my leg," Drumstanus said while raising the stump of his leg as if to confirm the amputation. "After my medical discharge, I took to gambling and hard drinking. Seems, I missed the rush of conflict and battle. With only one leg, I couldn't exactly go into the arena."

"So you became a potter in Firebreak?" ventured Alerio. "It's a strange choice for an artist's shop."

"Not if you burned all your friendships, and wasted your savings, and made enemies of half the Capital City," the former First Spear explained. "There was this snot nosed Private who enjoyed wagering. He found me one night after some people beat me for missing a payment, or two, or three. I can't remember. So this Private picks me up, rents a room in Firebreak, and sits with me while I dry out."

"That sounds like something Corporal Gratian would do," offered Alerio.

"He wasn't a Corporal than, but yes, it was Gratian," admitted Drumstanus. "We sat in that room talking until I came to the realization that I'd never enjoy the power and thrill of engaging an enemy again. Somewhere in the middle of one of those long nights, I expressed my desire to work with clay. Well, I had made so many people angry and owed so many more people coin, I couldn't simply walk into a pottery compound and offer to apprentice. However, the resourceful Private Gratian had a plan. He rented a carriage and drove me three days from the city. After dumping me in a strange village with a heartless, angry old potter, he disappeared for three months. When he came back, I had scars on my one leg from where the hanging buckets of wet clay or sand rubbed. See, I carried the buckets slung over my shoulder. All day I carried them to the nasty old man. And I had scars on my hands from crawling in the creek to fill the buckets. In those three months, all I'd done was haul different kinds of clay and sand for the old guy. Many times, he dumped my hard work, tossed the empty bucket at my leg and ordered me to fill it with the correct clay or sand. I was miserable, alone and no closer to becoming a potter."

"For a First Spear, it must have been rough to be treated like that," Alerio said. "So Gratian brought you back to the city?"

"Oh, no. The Private went to the old potter and asked how I was working out," Drumstanus explained. "The evil old man went to the back of his shop, pulled a cloth off of a finely crafted vase, and picked up the valuable piece. I can tell you it was a masterpiece of clay work. Well, the old guy examines the expensive vase, and then tosses it to me. Not toss as in a gentle underhanded pitch; he launched it overhead across the entire width of the shop. I pushed away my crutch, hopped once and lunged for it. I managed, just barely, to get my hands out in time to snag it out of the air. While protecting the vase, I crashed hard onto the brick pavers of the shop floor."

"What was Gratian doing while you played catch with the pottery?" inquired Alerio.

"He'd propped himself up on a workbench and sat with a stupid grin while I lay on the pavers with the rescued vase," Drumstanus reported. "Then the old potter asked me, as I lay bleeding from two scrapped elbows, what type of clay and grade of sand were used to construct the exotic vase. I was angry, and sick of his treatment. After a quick look, I told the old rascal, the exact type of clay, the grade of sand, how much water was used, and how long it needed to be baked in the kiln to create the thin but strong walls of the vase. I told him as spitefully as I could, with as much distain as I could muster, while lying on the dirty shop floor."

"I wouldn't have a clue what went into making an amphora, let alone a fine vase," admitted a surprised Alerio. "How did you know all the materials?"

"That's what Gratian asked, before the old man said I was the best apprentice he'd ever trained. Except for being slow because I only had one leg. I'd learned because the old potter used terms to describe the clay types and grades of sand while dumping my buckets," Drumstanus stated with a grin on his face. "That evening, the old man placed me at a spinning wheel and showed me how to cast clay. Four years later, I returned to the city. I was a new man, but the old me had left too many scars and ill feelings for me to start new. Gratian, a Lance Corporal by then, suggested I set up shop in Firebreak and use a front man to sell my artwork.

So this shop pays for my county villa and allows me to help a few wounded veterans. Now, enough reminiscing, Corporal Gratian wants us upstairs."

At the mention of stairs, Alerio was worried for Drumstanus. When they pushed aside the curtain separating the shop from the storage area in the back, the Lance Corporal panicked. The stairs were closer in appearance to a ladder than a gradual inclining staircase.

"Let me go first so you don't hold me up," insisted the former First Spear.

From behind the stairs, he released a thick hemp rope. Grasping the rope, former First Spear Drumstanus hauled his body up hand over hand to the second floor. When he swung his leg onto the landing, Alerio gripped the stairs and followed him.

Alerio stepped off the stairs and came face to face with Private Nereus.

"Lance Corporal Sisera, welcome to Team Spilled Blood. That's what we call ourselves," Nereus said in greeting. "Corporal Gratian just calls us Fifth squad."

"I don't understand," Alerio pleaded. "Why are you here?"

"Marshal Kellerian sent word about your suicide mission. Gratian asked for volunteers and we decided to help," explained Nereus. "What's your plan? Drop in? Introduce yourself? Die a lonely and fruitless death?"

"I just wanted to ask a Lieutenant of the Cruor syndicate for the name of a Captain further up their chain of command," Alerio said. "But Spurius Kanut isn't here yet."

"You're climbing up a frayed rope over jagged rocks," Nereus warned. "If you're going to shakedown the shakedown artists, you've got to have leverage."

"Leverage? What do you mean?" a confused Alerio asked. "I just want the name of someone high enough up to reason with."

"You don't reason with criminals, especially the Cruor," advised Nereus. "I know this because my uncles are members of the Sons of Mars. They're pirates out of Messina and they know crime on a massive scale. On the local level, I've dealt with a few fences to sell goods that fell off the back of a wagon, or two. They all work the same. If you want something from the Cruor, you'll need something to get their attention."

"I could take Kanut," ventured Alerio. "And use him as leverage."

Nereus shook his head as one would at a student who failed to understand a mathematics question.

"On the next block over they have a counting house full of ill-gotten coin," Nereus suggested. "Take their money, hold it for ransom, and they'll beg you for a meeting."

"Fine, I'll march over there, kill everyone, and take their coin," Alerio announced. Then he though more about it and added, "But that's how I got the bounty on my head in the first place; the killing, not the taking of coin."

"Fifth squad will do the killing and we'll take the coin," explained Nereus as he handed Alerio a wool scarf. "Mask up. As soon as First Sergeant Drumstanus gives us the signal, we're going in."

Alerio glanced around but couldn't locate Drumstanus. Other than the bed and dresser on the second floor, the other prominent feature was another ladder leading up and deeper into the building.

Chapter 79 Fortress Counting House

A block away from the entrance to the Cruor counting house, Corporal Gratian squatted and embraced his wineskin. When three men strutted onto the street, he perked up.

Spurius Kanut babbled at the two men flanking him. All three carried scars from street fights, and displayed long daggers to warn off anyone not smart enough to recognize the reason for the scars.

After years of surviving the alleyway battles of the Capital, the three friends had found success. Two of the thugs had been given positions as bodyguards. One had surpassed their early goals of just making it to another day and became a trusted Lieutenant of the Cruor crime syndicate. Spurius Kanut wasn't the toughest or the fastest of the three, but he was good with numbers and at negotiating. As he fought his way out of the gutter and took on more responsibilities, he pulled his two trusted friends out with him.

As the three men approached, the burley guards at the entrance straightened, smiled and acknowledged Spurius and his two bodyguards. Behind the smiles, they seethed with jealousy at the easy life of a Lieutenant and his companions.

Gratian waited for a brief time before standing and stretching. As he arched his back, he held the wineskin over his head and made small circles with it. Then, he staggered around the corner of the building. Once out from under the eyes of the counting house guards, the Corporal broke into a sprint. All signs of intoxication gone, he ran for the edge of Firebreak District.

Former First Sergeant Drumstanus couldn't see the doorway to the counting house. From his third floor perch, he barely had a view of the stoop where Corporal Gratian squatted in the dirty robe. When Gratian hoisted the wineskin, Drumstanus shoved back from the third floor window. Using his hands, and one leg, he hopped down the ladder to the floor and grabbed his crutches.

"Private Nereus. Your target has entered the kill zone," Drumstanus called down to the second floor. "Gear up Legionaries, it's time to earn your Republic coin. Let's give the citizens their coins' worth today."

"Yes, First Sergeant. We're moving," Nereus replied. Then to Alerio, he whispered, "The Fist Spear misses bossing people around. But, overall he's a good guy. Ready?"

Nereus set his helmet over the wool mask, walked to the ladder-stairs, and stepped off. With his back to the steps, he grabbed the rails behind his back and placed his feet on the rails. He slid quickly to the first floor.

"How did you do that?" asked Alerio as he turned around, backed up, and placed a foot on the first step.

"My uncles are pirates. When I was younger, I spent a summer on one of their ships," Nereus explained. "In a storm or emergency, sailors and pirates need to get from the upper deck to the main deck in a hurry. They don't have time to back up and slowly walk down, so they slide on the handrails."

The sound of hobnailed boots pounding on the gravel and dirt street came and faded. Nereus and Alerio stepped out of the potter's shop just in time to see the last Legionary of Fifth squad disappear around the corner. Alerio took two quick steps before he was hauled back by Nereus.

"Let the lads do their work," he advised.

By the time they rounded the building and arrived at the road with the Cruor counting house, Fifth squad had dropped from the run and were marching. The unit reached a spot directly in front of the Cruor door.

"Squad halt. Standby," the squad leader ordered. The guards, after a short time, grew bored watching the Legionaries stand perfectly still. When the guards relaxed, the Lance Corporal shouted, "Assignments. Break."

The two guards on either side of the door received the first hits. Four Legionaries, leading with their shields, slammed the armored guards against the rough wood of the building's exterior.

By the time the two watchers across the street realized the danger, two teams of Legionaries had sprinted to them. The watchers were driven to the ground and pummeled unconscious. Two more Legionaries came from the back of the building and scrambled the brains of the corner guards. With the six guards down, the squad leader gave a come on signal to Alerio and Nereus.

"You'll have a four-man team at your back," he announced as they ran up. "We'll get the thugs off the street and secure the door. Good luck."

Alerio looked closely at the squad. All of them were hidden behind wool masks. It made sense. None of the Legionaries wanted to be targeted by the Cruor syndicate after the operation.

Nereus pulled his gladius and Alerio reached up and drew both of his.

"After you, Lance Corporal Sisera," invited Nereus as he pointed at the doorway.

Alerio ran through the portal and directly into a kill box with murder-holes and arrow-slits.

Chapter 80 - Swift Luck and a Wizard

The door to the front was thick oak and impassible. On either side, arrow-slits allowed for archers to rake assaulters. Above the hallway, murder-holes gave access for the dropping of heavy objects on intruders. Alerio skidded to a stop.

Nereus was two steps behind Alerio. The squad leader watched Nereus charge into the building. He dropped an arm to being the four-man team forward. As the first Legionary touched the threshold, the man came flying back out. On his chest was Nereus. The two plowed into the other three and the five Legionaries rolled apart as they tumbled into the street.

The squad leader leaned his head in to see if Lance Corporal Sisera was still alive. Alerio was scrunched down between arrow-slits on one side of the hall. In the Legionary's hands were his gladii, held out as if he was aiming down the blades. Abruptly, Alerio lunged across the kill box and stabbed through two arrow-slits on the other wall.

He spun, put his back against the wall between the two slits where the sword hilts quivered, and looked towards the squad leader.

"Throw me your gladius," he hissed while pulling his hip gladius.

Without questioning the motive, the squad leader unsheathed his blade and tossed the gladius to Alerio.

As before, the Legionary crouched against the wall between slits watching and listening for movement behind the other wall.

Alerio moved. This time only one blade pierced a slit. With the other blade, he jumped back across the hallway and jammed the blade through another of the arrow-slits.

"Tortoise defense," shouted Alerio.

Nereus charged into the kill box. Behind him, the four-man backup team charged in holding their shields over their heads.

"Sisera. That's ugly. You stabbed him right through the eyeball," Nereus proclaimed as he peeked into an arrow-slit.

Alerio was studying the oak door. Not paying attention, he replied, "I'm sorry about that."

"Sorry? About skewing a Cruor archer in the face?" asked Nereus.

"No. About kicking you in the chest and forcing you back onto the street," explained Alerio. Then he squatted and rapped his knuckles on the bottom of the door and tapped up one side. "Place your palms near the top of the door and press."

"Why? What am I, a wizard now? Going to make the door disappear?" quizzed Nereus. Despite his sarcastic remarks, he placed his hands where directed and pressed.

Alerio reached to the small of his back and pulled the Golden Valley dagger. Placing the point of the dagger on the bottom seam, he kicked the pummel. The door inched up about a finger's thickness. Alerio jammed his fingers into the crack.

"We have an old style barn door at my father's farm," he stated as he began to strain and lift with the power of his legs and back. "It's so heavy, we only use pentle hinges."

"What's a pentle hinge?" asked Nereus.

"It's a pin you rest the hinge on," Alerio growled out between clinched teeth. "There are no top brackets to hold the hinges down. There's no need with a heavy door."

The oak door rose, the gap at the bottom grew higher and Alerio grunted. Nereus hands rose as well, so the Legionary pressed harder. Between the two, when the top hinge came free of the pentle, the impenetrable oak door rocked back. With the tremendous weight supported only by the bottom pentle, the pin bent and the door cantilevered inward.

"Shields," Nereus shouted as he drove back with his legs. As he attempted to back dive, he wrapped his hands around Alerio's helmet and pulled. Two crossbow bolts flew over their arched chests before the Legion shields dropped into place.

"Wet One. I didn't know you were a wizard," one of the shield holders whispered in awe. Then to the other three Legionaries announced, "You saw it didn't you? While Sisera was trying to figure it out, Nereus levitated the door."

"I saw it," another replied. "Once it was a solid oak door, then Nereus placed his hands on it and it fell as if it were made of framed goatskin. Merda, Nereus. You are a wizard."

"Alright, Wizard. Are we ready to take down this collection house?" Alerio asked from his position lying beside Nereus on the kill box floor.

Suddenly, the squad leader for Fifth squad appeared behind the shields.

"What's the enemy count?" he demanded.

"I only saw two crossbows," a Legionary reported.

"Stand by. Advance," he shouted. "Advance, advance, advance..."

The two shields slammed forward, and opened just enough for the left side Legionary to stab between the withdrawing shields. Again and again, the shields smashed and gladii stabbed as the Legionaries moved out of the kill box hallway and into a room. The other two shields linked up and the relentless killing machine of the Republic's Legion powered through the room. As they rolled forward, two stomped and butchered archers lay in their wake, as well as, two broken crossbows.

Chapter 81 – So Much Coin in One Place

The Legion line cleared the room and at a door in the rear, the squad leader pushed aside the two center shields.

"Standby. Close the gap," he said as he kicked the door and stepped back.

The door popped open. Beyond it was a short hallway leading to another room.

"Overlap, go," the Lance Corporal ordered.

The hallway wasn't wide enough for side-by-side shields, but one wouldn't cover it. The Legionaries filled the space by interlocking their edges. The room at the end of the hall was empty. However, four doorways in the room led to other parts of the building.

"Four doors, seven Legionaries," explained the squad leader. "Who is sailing solo?"

"I am," volunteered Alerio.

He handed the squad leader the borrowed gladius and walked to the far right door.

"Stand by your doors," directed the squad leader. Once all the doors had Legionaries stacked and ready, he ordered, "Open and advance."

The doors on the right and left, nearest to the short hallway, angled back. The assault pairs moved down the narrow halls toward the arrow-slits on either side of the kill box. Those four Legionaries would find archers with lacerations and puncture wounds on their faces. Three were alive when the Legionaries found them. None were breathing when they left.

Nereus and a shield holder opened the far left door. No one obstructed their progress as they stepped smartly down the hallway. At the end was a reinforced oak door, except this one had the latch on the inside. Nereus lifted the latch, pushed the door hard, and jumped back behind the shield. No arrows or vocal challenges greeted them. He peered over the shield to find a couple of odd two wheeled carts. Instead of a single cart shaft to separate the mules, these carts had duel shafts and a bar across the end.

"Human powered," explained the Legionary with the shield. "Usually you see them with vendor racks, or stripped down to haul rubble. These are polished with high sideboards. I wonder what they're made for?"

But Nereus wasn't listening or looking at the polished carts. His focus was on the wall in front of the carts. Latching pins were placed along the wall about head height. Upon closer examination, he noticed cuts running down the sides of the wall from the latches to the floor. The cuts were separated by enough space to allow the carts to pass through.

"Escape route for the coin," declared Nereus. "If Firebreak goes up in flames, the Cruor would need a way to remove their coin."

"But where are the coins?" asked the shield holder. "Where are all the coins?"

Alerio pushed open the right door farthest from the short hallway. Without a shield, he kicked the door open and stepped behind the doorframe. After glancing around to be sure the hallway was clear, he ran to the next door. When he kicked it open, surprised and angry voices greeted him.

"What are you doing here?" demanded a male voice.

Peering in, Alerio watched as three men shoved tall piles of coins off a marble table and into sacks.

"Shut the door and get back to your guard post," the man repeated as he picked up a sack and began shoving coins into it. "Do your duty. Do it now. If you know what's good for you?"

Alerio smiled then rapped on the doorframe with a gladius.

"Spurius Kanut? I'll have a word with you," Alerio said as he stepped into the room. "My name is Alerio Sisera and we need to talk."

Two of the men looked up while the third continued to package coins.

"The farmer is worth seven Republic golds," Spurius stated looking up briefly from his task. "Does one of you want to kill him and collect a nice fee?" The men on either side of him drew long knives and stepped towards the Legionary. "Or both of you, and you can split the bounty?"

One was fast and the other strong. As a team they, along with Spurius Kanut's intelligence, had terrorized the streets for years. The two were so efficient; Spurius ignored them as he returned to counting pile after pile of the Cruor's coins.

"I really just wanted to have a word with you, Master Kanut," Alerio pleaded as if he was a small lad begging for a parent's attention.

"The bounty's dead or alive," Spurius commented to his bodyguards. "I'd prefer dead, but you two decide."

Alerio's gladii were resting along the sides of his legs. Almost as if he didn't realize the danger coming for him.

"Are these two important to you?" Alerio asked casually.

The question and tone were so far from the fear his men usually instilled in their victims, the Cruor Lieutenant stopped counting and looked up.

269

"Boyhood friends and colleagues," admitted Spurius. "But it shouldn't make any difference to you. Why do you ask?"

"Because that one on my left looks fast. He'll come in and duel with me," explained Alerio. "While I'm occupied, the one on my right will rush in and beat me down. But, if I kill them that leaves you alone in more ways than one."

"Stop. Let the lad talk," instructed Spurius. "What makes you think you can take both of my bodyguards?"

Stacks of goatskin sacks were piled beside the door. Alerio reached out with each gladius and snagged two on each blade tip. With the cloth hanging as if they were flags, he swirled the sacks until they wrapped around his blades.

"To demonstrate," he began as he swished the blades in the opposite direction. "These are…"

The sacks were almost unfurled. Flying around and blurring the actual blades' locations, the bodyguards and Spurius seemed mesmerized by the spinning and snapping cloth. They failed to notice Alerio's bent knees. Before they could react, Alerio jumped.

He landed five feet off to the right and swung the flats of his gladii into the back of one bodyguard's legs. The man collapsed and Alerio kicked him in the head. Spurius' strong bodyguard was out of the fight.

Alerio stepped over the prone form and began crossing and uncrossing and re-crossing his blades.

"Your turn," teased the Legionary. "Are you ready?"

The man set his guard and began shuffling to his left. Why would he want Alerio to rotate left? Because the maneuver would place Spurius Kanut at the Legionary's back.

The bodyguard's blade came in like the wind. Fluid and relentless, his cuts were swift and you could almost feel a breeze coming from the wake of the blade. He was skilled and fast, but he was the nervous type.

The bodyguard glanced over Alerio's shoulder for less than a heartbeat. It was enough to warn the Legionary that Spurius had decided to join the fight. Alerio took a giant step back and swung his right gladius in an arc.

Spurius stopped as the tip of Alerio's blade almost took off the tip of the Cruor Lieutenant's nose. Meanwhile, the Legionary was dueling masterfully with the bodyguard facing his left gladius.

"It's your call Master Kanut," Alerio advised. "I can kill your man at any time. All I want to do is to talk."

As Alerio spoke, his right blade moved in short back and forth movements. Almost as if it were a snake coiled and dancing before striking.

"Alright, enough. Let's talk," Spurius said after watching the tip's rhythmic movements.

Alerio whipped his left blade around the bodyguard's and the man's long knife flew across the room.

"Good choice Master Kanut," advised Alerio. "Quickly now. Get against the back wall and sit down."

"Why sit down?" demanded Spurius.

"Because there are four Legionaries about to join us and they don't want to talk," advised Alerio.

When three Legionaries and their squad leader charged down the hall and into the room, they were surprised to find Lance Corporal Sisera sitting on a marble tabletop. Around him were stacks of coins; bronze and silver but the largest stacks were gold.

"Some much coin in one place," a Legionary sighed wistfully.

"Master Kanut. What I want is the name of your Cruor Captain," Alerio stated. "In exchange, you and your bodyguards will live. If not, I'll have to find another way."

"Sure why not. Master Lebbaeus is my Captain," Spurius said with a laugh. "He's a successful merchant, a lawyer, and a really big political contributor. You'll not intimidate him with a gladius or fancy dueling moves."

"I don't plan to. I'm going to take the Cruor's coin and let him come to me," Alerio explained.

"Wait. Wait," begged Kanut. "If you take the coin and we're alive and healthy, they'll come after me and my bodyguards."

Nereus arrived and heard Spurius Kanut's words.

"No, problem," he said as he crossed the room while pulling his knife. "Not alive is my specialty."

Two Legionaries grabbed Nereus and gently held him back.

"No, Wizard. If you do it wrong, you could turn all our bones to mush," one pleaded.

"It's alright. We'll beat them for you," another offered.

One Legionary standing in the back was facing the hallway and maintaining rear security.

"What? Did Wizard turn someone's bones to mush," he asked having misunderstood the remark. "Wizard be careful with that magic stuff, please."

"This is a messed up week," another exclaimed. "First we fight trolls and now Wizard is throwing around spells like they're hog feed."

Ignoring the banter, Alerio slid off the counter top and examined the coins.

272

"How much do we need to take to get the Cruor's attention?" Alerio pondered.

"Take it all," Nereus proclaimed as he picked up a handful of gold coins and let them run through his fingers.

"That's a lot of weight for seven Legionaries to carry," Alerio said reminding him of the size of their assault team.

"Not if we use the carts," Nereus exclaimed as he began tapping on a wall. "Here. It's got to be a direct route to the carts and the exit."

With no need to stack and count, the Legionaries soon had all the coins in bags. After forming a coin-sack brigade, they passed sacks of coin from one to another along the hidden passageway. Soon, the carts were laden and Nereus began releasing latches.

Two Legionaries providing exterior security were assigned corners of the counting house. Watching for any approach of a retaliatory force from the Cruor, they had their backs to the building. When a section of the wall between them fell into the street, they turned and gasped.

Private Nereus stood poised with his arms raised and his fingers open as if he had pushed a section of the wall down with his bare hands.

"Good work, Wizard," said a Legionary standing between the cart shafts of one carts.

Outside the two exterior Legionaries only heard one thing. Their squad mate had call Private Nereus, Wizard. After witnessing the display of his magic by making a section of the wall fall, they believed it.

"Where are we taking the carts?" asked the other cart puller.

"To the stockyards," said Alerio. "If we're dealing with animals, we might as well make them comfortable."

273

Chapter 82 – Wheels of Reckoning

The Legionaries surrounded the carts as they wheeled south. Once off the gravel road of Firebreak District, they rolled onto the paved streets of the city and made good time to the stockyards.

Fifth squad's Lance Corporal left them and jogged to the offices of Master Lebbaeus. At first, the house slave denied entry to the masked Legionary. He explained to the Legionary that an appointment was required to speak with Master Lebbaeus. To counter the dismissal, the squad leader handed the slave an open sack of gold coins.

"What can I do for you Legionary," asked Lebbaeus.

They were in an office with the lawyer sitting behind an imposing desk and the squad leader standing at attention in front of it. Lebbaeus had the top of the sack opened wide enough that a small stream of gold had spilled out and flowed across the deck top.

"Sir, as a representative of the Cruor syndicate, you are witness to the Legion taking coin from their counting house," the Lance Corporal explained while indicating the sack. "If you want the rest of the coins, we have them for you or any high ranking member of the Cruor."

"I have no idea what you're insinuating," countered Lebbaeus. "I'm a simple man of business and law. A member of a crime syndicate? No, no, I know nothing about that."

"Very well, sir. I will take the gold and return it to the carts," the squad leader explained. "It's almost midday. If no representative presents himself by midafternoon, the coins will be divided between the central and northern Legions. Once they go

274

into our coffers, it would be unadvisable for the Cruor to attempt to take them back."

The squad leader reached for the sack of gold coins.

"Hold. I may know someone who knows someone associated with the Cruor," Lebbaeus said. "Leave the sack and let me send a few notes to associates."

"Very good sir," the Lance Corporal said. He stepped back, preformed a toe point about face and marched from the office.

On the road just outside the stockyard fence, two carts sat side-by-side facing eastward. Spread widely, but equally placed around the carts, were masked Legionaries standing behind their shields. Although there were only eleven Legionaries in total, their numbers could swell rapidly. Legion patrols appeared and vanished as units in every direction circled surrounding blocks. It was the nearby Legion patrols that forced the Cruor to negotiate rather than attack.

Lebbaeus rode up in an ornate chariot pulled by a team of white horses. Obviously, it was an attempt to show strength and importance. The Cruor Captain stepped down from the chariot in front of the shields.

"Who is in charge here?" Lebbaeus demanded.

"Actually sir, no one," Alerio announced as he stepped from between the carts. "Would you care to inspect the sacks?" Ignoring the invitation, Lebbaeus stated, "I am empowered by the Cruor to negotiate for the release of their coins. Now, what are the Legion's demands?"

"Again, sir. No Legion commander is present because the Legion has no demands," insisted Alerio.

"Then why did they take the coins?" a flustered Lebbaeus asked.

"So I could get a meeting with you and give you this," Alerio explained as he walked to the Cruor Captain. "Hold out you hand sir, palm up."

Lebbaeus stood with his hand open and Alerio dropped seven gold coins into his open palm.

"What is this?" asked Lebbaeus.

"My name is Alerio Sisera and that is the seven Republic golds the Cruor are offering for my head," Alerio explained. "What I want is for the Cruor to rescind the bounty, take their carts and their coins, and call off the bounty hunters."

"You mean all this is because the Cruor put a price on your head?" Lebbaeus asked in astonishment. "Do you know what you've done? The Cruor doesn't stand for being blackmailed. They…"

The clop, clop of a horse's hooves on pavers caused them to turn. A big stallion forced the Legion shields apart and Tomas Kellerian nudged the horse to the negotiators.

"What in hades is going on here?" he demanded as he stepped down from the saddle.

"Just a conversation, Marshal," replied Lebbaeus. "The Lance Corporal and I were simply talking."

"Fine, you can talk anywhere," Kellerian stated. "But these carts are blocking a major road. As Marshal of the City, I can't allow anything to impede the flow of traffic. Who owns the carts? Come to think of it. Have the taxes been paid on the cargo?"

Lebbaeus shifted his eyes from the carts, to Alerio, to Marshal Kellerian, and back to the carts. He seemed as if he were about to be ill.

If he claimed ownership and the Marshal pressed for taxes, the Republic would claim a large share of the Cruor coins.

Additionally, if Alerio Sisera declared the coins property of the Cruor syndicate, the Republic could claim it all. Even if he got most of it back, who was to say the Legion wouldn't go after it again? And all the Cruor would get was the head of a lad after paying seven gold for it.

On the other hand, if he denied ownership, the Legion would get the coins and the bounty would stay active. All this because a chapter of the Cruor had assaulted a farm boy in a grain collection town and yelled for a bounty when he escaped their revenge. Before he could finish reasoning out the best solution, Alerio interrupted his thoughts.

"Counselor Lebbaeus and I were simply discussing the destination of the carts. There was a little confusion," Alerio explained to Marshal Kellerian. Then, turning to Lebbaeus with a wicked grin, asked, "So Master Lebbaeus, do we have a deal? Or should we let the Marshal decide?"

The three men remained silent. In the background, the sounds of hobnailed boots marching on pavers carried from the surrounding neighborhoods. Behind them the penned animals chewed hay and lapped water. Finally, Lebbaeus blew out a breath through his mouth and inhaled deeply through his nose.

"Lance Corporal Alerio Sisera. You will not be troubled again. Not by my associates or agents acting in their behalf," Lebbaeus stated. "Now, can you explain to the Marshal where the carts go?"

"Marshal. The cargo is simply a transfer between one storage unit owned by Master Lebbaeus to another," explained Alerio. "He hired the Legionaries to move the carts to this location where another crew will take them to another warehouse."

277

"Fine, that's fine, but get them off the road," Kellerian advised as he pulled himself into the saddle. "Now Lance Corporal. Move those carts, now."

The Marshal and his mount moved out of the ring of Legionaries. As the shields closed, Alerio called out.

"Squad leader, if you please? Pull the carts to the side of the road and dismiss the unit," ordered Alerio. He turned and saluted the Cruor Captain. "It was nice doing business with you Master Lebbaeus. Just so we're clear. If another assassin comes after me, the next thing I take from the Cruor will be your heart."

The masked Legionaries were joined by two patrols. While they marched away, the Legionaries shuffled positions and soon, no one could pick the assault squad from the others. Walking beside the combined unit, Alerio was the only one identifiable.

They were replaced at the carts by civilians. Among them was a bruised and bloody Spurius Kanut.

"I'll make arrangements for you to have a talk with Alerio Sisera, in private," promised Kanut as he limped over to his boss.

"No. I was told he was a simple lad from the country that we could sacrifice as an example," explained Lebbaeus. "It's one thing to defend your honor; it's another thing entirely different, when the cost of defending your honor is many times higher than seven Republic golds. No, let the lad go. The bounty is lifted."

Chapter 83 – Vino to Celebrate

"When do you sail?" Thomasious Harricus asked.

"The merchant trader rows out tomorrow at first light," Alerio replied. He looked across the table at Tomas Kellerian and added, "I believe it was the authority of the Marshal that tipped the scales with Lebbaeus and the Cruor bounty. Thank you."

278

"Wouldn't Lebbaeus be surprised if he discovered I'd already been relieved as Marshal when we spoke," Kellerian wondered. "Harricus. Do not put that in a gossip scroll."

"What? Me divulge sensitive information for profit?" asked Harricus as if shocked by the thought. "Here at the Chronicles Humanum Inn, we value the privacy of our customers."

"I value the lives of my customers. At the Historia Fae, I back that up with steel and leather armor," Kellerian said. "You duel with parchment and quill. I prefer a straight forward battle."

"I don't understand what became of Senator Ventus," commented Alerio interrupting their philosophical discussion. "He left the city in his carriage with his house servants and a Legion escort."

"There was no direct evidence of Ventus' involvement in any crime," explained Kellerian. "But there was enough circumstantial evidence for the Senate to shun him, strip him of his Senatorial privileges, and exile him from the Capital."

"They should have nailed him up and stretched him on the wood," Harricus sneered. "Instead, Ventus will live out his days at his villa in the mountains. It's in the Central Legion's area so Nigellus can keep an eye on his activities."

"Look who's going all blood and guts," accused Kellerian. "What happened to subtle persuasion and the power of the written word?"

"For the good of the Republic, sometimes, you have to put down the quill and just crucify the cūlus," exclaimed Harricus.

Alerio flagged down a servicing girl and ordered another pitcher of wine. When it arrived, he topped off everyone's mug.

"To the Republic," he said holding his mug over the center of the table.

Kellerian and Harricus clicked their mugs against Alerio's and repeated, "To the Republic."

The End

Thank you for reading Spilled Blood,

J. Clifton Slater

If you enjoyed this book, please check out my other novels.

Clay Warrior Stories

Clay Legionary

Spilled Blood

Bloody Water (Fall 2017)

Galactic Council Realm

On Station

On Duty

On Guard

I like chatting with readers and I do read reviews on Amazon and Goodreads.com. If you have comments or want to reach me, I am available.

Thank you,

J. Clifton Slater

E-Mail: GalacticCouncilRealm@gmail.com

Twitter: @GalacticCRealm

FB: facebook.com/Galactic Council Realm

Made in the USA
Middletown, DE
11 November 2017